HIDDEN IN THE HILLS

FLINT RIVER SERIES - BOOK 2

JODI BURNETT

1

———

Capitalists teach their multiracial degeneracy to our children. Third world criminals flood in and take the few scraps we have left away from us. We need to prepare ourselves for war to take back our American rights.

I'VE NEVER KILLED anyone before.

Liquid heat swirled through my gut, increasing my thrill. I caressed the cold metal cylinder of the homemade explosive resting in my lap. The remote-control timer lashed to the device with black electrical tape was set for five minutes. That would give us time to get far enough away for cover. I rolled my lower lip between my teeth and wished I could watch close up—see them die.

Our white, windowless van sailed toward our target. "How much farther?"

The driver glanced at me in the rearview mirror. "Calm down. We'll get there when we get there. We got plenty of time. The robbery won't happen until the explosion is all over the news and the cops are busy."

"I wish we didn't have to hurt kids." The woman riding shotgun sighed and pulled down her sun visor. She slid the cover off the mirror and popped her dry, pink lips at the reflection. A chipped hot-pink fingernail tidied up a smudge at the corner of her mouth.

The driver glanced at her. "We've gone over this a hundred times. I hate it too, but a school explosion gets the biggest reaction. Anything involving kids will be a huge news splash. No one'll be focused on anything else."

I tightened my grip on the bomb and peered out the black-tinted, driver's side window at the buildings drifting by. We turned off the highway and were soon driving through neighborhoods of tall, stately, upper middle-class homes with perfectly trimmed lawns. I scratched at the dark stubble on my jaw and wondered what it would be like to live in something that nice. Then I chided myself. I didn't need that kind of excess. Those huge houses could fit several families but instead they sat silent and empty all day. Their evening and weekend tenants were probably dual-income families with 2.5 kids.

No, filthy capitalism was one of the evils we were fighting against. What I needed was to be free from the greedy and corrupt iron-hand of the government. I needed a nation of my own, made up of my own kind, and enough land to grow my food with no one telling me what I can or can't do. We'd all had enough of a government who passed laws set directly against our beliefs, our way of life. That's what Uncle Jed had told us the bank robbery was for—money to finance a revolution.

After our crew blew up the elementary school, a second team was all set to rob the bank and come away with millions of dollars—a good start in funding our battle. Money from Chicago's Fed-Cash Central would buy a lot of guns and ammunition for our cause. My pulse danced.

I noticed the van's speed change. "Why are we slowing down?" I growled, anticipation making my hands shake.

"I'm going the speed limit, you idiot."

The woman laughed. "You don't want him to have to pay a double fine if he gets caught speeding in a school zone, do you?"

"Shut up." I shifted my weight, resisting the urge to shove against the back of her seat. If we got pulled over, it would ruin everything. The driver cracked his window for air and I heard the distant trill of children laughing and playing at the target school less than a block away. Dozens of kids ran and chased each other on the playgrounds during recess.

Those children might get lucky. Not the kids inside though, they wouldn't know what hit them—I didn't think. I imagined the adults who were in the building—the teachers, janitors, and lunch ladies. What would they do when they first heard the explosion? What would go through their minds? Besides shrapnel, I smirked to myself.

The moment the driver signaled to turn left into the school parking lot, a siren sounded behind us.

"Shit!"

I peered through the driver's side-mirror. A cop car pulled up behind us with its blue and red lights flashing. "I thought you said you were doing the limit." I slumped down in my seat so I wouldn't be seen.

"Act natural. Remember, our story is we're just here to pick my daughter up from the nurse's office. Keep your mouths shut." The driver gripped the wheel and pulled over hard, scraping up against a tall thicket of grasses and gorse growing wild at the edge of the road.

In the back seat, my pulse ticked inside my head. I had one chance, and one chance only, to get out of there. I pulled the tail of my shirt from my jeans and wiped the bomb casing free of my fingerprints. Placing the cylinder on the floor of the van behind the driver, I clicked on the timer before I crawled low across the bench seat and opened the side door enough to slide through.

"What the hell are you doing?" the woman hissed.

"Shut up. I've got this," I answered.

I lowered myself into the scrub and eased the door closed without latching it. I rolled away from the side of the van, pushing through the thick grasses. The ground fell away and I dropped into a drainage ditch filled with denser growth and old thatch. Thistles scraped and stung my skin but I didn't move or make a sound. I counted thirty seconds before I took a breath. Silently, I peered up and parted the overgrown grasses enough to assess the situation. More sirens sounded and another cop car pulled in front of the van, blocking it in.

Two cops got out of their cruisers and walked toward the van with their weapons drawn. Neither of them looked in my direction. Thirty more seconds. I waited until I could no longer see the cops. I only had three more minutes, probably less. My body pulsed with a dynamic voltage. Adrenaline surged through my brain. I had to get out of there now!

I low-crawled through a lilac hedge into the backyard of an elegant, suburban Chicago home. Dried autumn leaves carpeted the lawn and crackled under my boots, the crisp scent reminded me briefly of my woodland home. I kept to the side of the yard praying there was no family dog to raise an alarm. Fortune smiled on me.

The blast, even at that distance, blew me forward onto my face on the stone path at the side of the house. Glass shattered from the back windows. I pushed myself up to my feet and ran, only slowing my pace when I came to the front gate.

Covered by sirens, chaos, and confusion, no one noticed me. I jogged through the neighborhood for nearly two miles, before stopping to see if I was followed. There were no people around, so I took a chance. I forced my way into the side garage door of a two-story colonial and found a Lexus LS parked inside. I was prepared to hotwire it, but when I tried the door it was unlocked, and the keys were hanging in the ignition. Stupid, entitled rich people. They'll be the first to starve when the shit hits the fan.

A golf cap hung on a hook over a bag of clubs. I snatched it and pulled it down low over my eyes before I slid into the seat. The car's engine responded with a deep delicious hum. I pressed the garage door opener and backed out, knowing I'd have to get rid of the car soon. The owner would report it stolen and the car was certain to have a GPS tracking system installed. Hopefully they wouldn't make the connection between the car theft and the screwed-up bombing mission for some time. I'd lead the cops on a goose chase by heading south, opposite of the direction I needed to go.

I found my way to the highway and flew out of the city. No one tried to stop me. No one ever questioned the wealthy. When I reached the town of Champaign, I pulled into a truck stop busy with people. After I parked the car, I searched the glove compartment and console and found $62.43 in miscellaneous bills and loose change. Perfect. Combined with what I had in my wallet, I'd have enough money for the stuff I needed.

I stepped out of the Lexus and was inundated with the combined scent of diesel fuel and French fries. My stomach gnawed; a demand to be fed. Inside the convenience store, no one paid me any particular attention. I moved up and down the aisles trying to look like I was shopping when I was really listening to hear if anyone mentioned the potential bombing of the school.

A small television behind the counter aired The Price is Right. Impotent fury engulfed me. All that work for nothing. No mention on TV—hell, it wasn't even scrolling across the bottom of the screen as breaking news. I knew then the bank robbery had never happened either. Damn—there goes the funding. Damn. Damn. Damn! How could those cops have known?

I grabbed a pack of beef jerky and a carton of baby-wipes off the shelf. I pulled a large bottle of Pepsi from the refrigerator and set it all on the counter. After selecting two pre-paid burner phones, I slid my combined funds to the clerk.

Back at the car, I opened the wipes and rubbed the car and its keys clean of my fingerprints and then locked the doors. I scanned the area to see if anyone was watching me. When I was certain no one was, I threw the car keys into a nearby sewer drain. I tore open the plastic packet and bit off a hard chunk of sweet, teriyaki-flavored jerky. Then I walked out to Interstate 7 and held my thumb out to cars headed northwest.

Hitchhiking was always entertaining. I've met some crazy people out there. I liked to freak out young women who were nice enough to pick me up with an aggressive come-on or by saying, "What are you going to do when you find out I'm a serial killer?" The memories of previous experiences and terror-infused eyes made me smirk. But, I couldn't indulge my sense of humor. This time, I needed to get back to the compound ASAP. It was the only place I would be safe.

Now that I was on the road, I had time to think more about how the cops knew to pull us over. I walked along the shoulder of the highway that led past flat, unending corn-fields. A car filled with teens honked and hollered at me as they drove by. I flipped them off.

There had to be a mole. A traitor in the compound. My mind filtered through the possibilities. I was fairly sure it was Wanda, the woman in the car with us this morning. If it was her, then she was killed because of her own stupidity, she got what she had coming. Rage coursed through me, causing sweat to bead along my hairline. It seemed like days had passed already since the botched mission, even though it was only a couple of hours ago.

I'd have to tell Uncle Jed that Wanda and Dan were dead. Worse, I'd have to admit we failed our objective. Jed would be completely furious. I kicked a small rock. Damn. It wasn't my fault. I was ready with my part. My gut twisted in nervous anticipation of having to stand in the presence of Uncle Jed's fury.

Knowing it was better to face Jed on the phone than to do it in person, I reached into my pack and pulled out one of the burner phones. I tore open the package, tossed the trash on the side of the highway, and punched in the one number I had memorized. I let the phone ring until I heard a voice say "Yep?" Then I punched in my secret code, 881488, on the keypad and waited.

"What the hell happened?" Uncle Jed's harsh voice barked through the phone.

I sucked in a deep breath. "I don't know for sure. The cops stopped us before we could complete our mission."

"I saw that on the news. Damn it!"

Guess it made the national news, after all. The side of my mouth tilted up. "I was lucky to get away. Dan and Wanda weren't."

"How did the police know?"

"I'm not sure, Uncle Jed." I swallowed hard. "But I think we have a mole." Silence roared across the line. Uncomfortable with the dead air, I asked, "Did all the guys from the robbery side check in?"

"Yeah. Once your team failed, the other team dispersed." Again, the deathly quiet. "How do I know *you're* not the mole? You're the only survivor from your team and the cops let you get away."

"Uncle Jed. You have to know that's not true. I snuck out of the car. They never saw me." I rushed on, "If I were the traitor, would I be the one to tell you we had a leak?"

"Then who do you think it is?"

"I don't know, but I sure as hell am going to find out when I get back. I should be there in three days."

"No. Things are too hot right now. Find a place to lie low. I'll let you know when it's safe to return."

"No one's following me, Uncle Jed. I'm sure of it."

"I don't want to take any chances. The news said something about the FBI getting involved. Call me in two weeks."

"Two weeks?"

"You're not arguing with me, are you, boy?"

"No sir. I'll talk to you—" The phone line went dead. No goodbye, nothing. Two weeks. My chest ached. Jed was the only man I'd ever looked on as a father. I wanted to make him proud. This wasn't the heroic return I had dreamt of. I imagined coming home with bags of money and the story of our victory all over the news channels. Laurel would want me then. She couldn't ignore me if I was a hero in the compound.

I threw the phone back into my pack and slung the bag over one shoulder. Walking north-west, I stuck out my thumb and considered what I would need to wait out the next couple of weeks. I was a survivalist and was taught to live off the land. I'd head to the mountains in western Montana and wait there until the coast was clear.

I caught rides throughout the day and was in South Dakota by midnight. I found a broken down, pay-by-the-hour motel outside of Sioux Falls where the clerk didn't ask any questions as long as I paid in cash. The bed was lumpy, but I managed to get several hours of sleep before I hit the road again. When Jed gave me the all clear, I'd drop down into northern Idaho. Until then, I'd have to find some way to entertain myself in Montana.

2

———————

Tonya rattled along up the Montana mountain pass in her yellow Volkswagen Thing. Her eyes soaked up the autumn gold, orange, and red color that stood out from the green pine-scented background. She was headed home from a shopping trip to the beauty supply outlet in Butte. She loved the loose, jerky movements of her old-style car. It was funky and suited her.

Frank Sinatra crooned through the speakers of the replacement stereo. Tonya favored all things vintage, but she drew the line when it came to electronics. She had her radio replaced with a built-in Bluetooth, in-dash receiver so she could listen to her custom big-band play lists from her phone.

The problem with Sinatra was he dripped romance from the speakers which made her think of her ex-boyfriend, Trent Stone. Her mind filled with his golden boy image—wavy dark-blond hair that curled at his neck and bright blue eyes that held an ocean of mischief. Her heart twisted with her memories and her eyes filled. Trent recently broke up with her. Again. That in itself was normal. The two of them had been breaking up and getting back together since they were in junior high.

Their cat-and-mouse game exhausted her. But this time was different. He didn't trust her anymore, not after her ploy to have him catch Joscelyn with another man. A dull pain settled in the pit of her stomach when she remembered the crush Trent had on Flint River's new librarian. But, instead of forcing a wedge between them, the consequences of her plan were deadly. Her heart pinched with regret.

Tonya's stomach balled into a knot when she relived what happened—but she couldn't have known. Joscelyn was the one who'd put everybody in danger, yet everyone forgave her. Tonya shook her head and gripped the steering wheel tighter. Try as she might, she couldn't be mad at Joscelyn, it wasn't her fault either. The Stone family had forgiven Tonya—all of them except Trent. He was unmoving.

She reached to turn up the volume when the engine of her car sputtered. Steam rose from the seams of the hood.

"Not again!" Tonya puttered to the shoulder of the road. Overheating was a constant problem when she drove on the steep mountain roads. She turned off the engine and got out to open the hood. Steam rolled out, and she waved it from her face. Tonya kept water and coolant in the back of her car but she'd have to wait till the radiator cooled down.

She sat inside the VW Thing to listen to Frank's musical seduction while she waited. Leaning her head against her seat, she hummed along.

A sharp tapping sound on her window made Tonya spring forward, her heart in her throat. A man's faced peered in at her. Tonya's nerves bit into her skin. Her pulse battered her temples.

"You need help?" The man asked, his voice muted by the glass.

Tonya lowered the glass a crack. "No, thanks. This happens all the time."

Dark-brown bangs fell across the man's forehead partly obscuring eyes of the same color. "It's no bother. I know a thing or two about cars." He went to look at the engine.

Tonya glanced behind her through her rearview mirror, but there was no car parked back there. She pressed the lock down on her door and rolled her window down an inch farther. She raised her voice. "Where did you come from? Where's your car?"

The man bent sideways to look at her from behind the hood. "I don't have a car, I'm hitch-hiking. You passed me a little way back."

"Oh, I guess I was pre-occupied."

He smiled, gave her a nod, and went back to work. She saw his hands in the crack between the car and the base of the hood. He pulled out different dip-sticks to check the fluid levels. He reached for the rag she had set on top of the water jug and used it to open the radiator cap. More steam drifted up, but it was lazy and about finished.

The man came back to her door. "Just a few more minutes and I'll add the water."

"Thank you."

"Sure." His smile was the kind that caused a woman's eyes to linger on his lips. Tonya jerked her eyes up. She took in the rest of his appearance. He was maybe six feet tall, and wore jeans, a western shirt, and cowboy boots. He had on a baseball cap and carried a small backpack. The man looked like every other cowboy she'd ever known, except he could have been on the cover of Cowboy magazine with those long-lashed eyes and chiseled cheekbones. He went back to finish with the radiator and Tonya got out to watch.

"Where are you headed?" she asked.

"Sula. I have a job interview in the morning. I'm not

exactly sure how far that is from here. You're not headed anywhere near there, are you?" He raised his eyebrows.

"Not really. I'm going to Flint River which is almost an hour away from Sula." Obligation pressed on her conscience. "I guess I could drive you to the turnoff though, if you want."

"That'd be real kind. Thanks." He wiped his hands on the rag and slammed the hood shut.

Tonya nodded, smoothed her hairstyle, and got back in her car. The man opened the passenger door and took off his hat as he slid in. He held out his hand. "I'm Levi. I really appreciate the ride."

"Tonya." She shook his hand. "Happy to return a favor." Her palm felt charged in his and she pulled away. She shifted into first gear and applied the gas, but the VW Thing hopped several feet and then stalled. "For crying out the window." She tried again with the same result. On the third try she got going only to grind the gears when she shifted.

"Is this your car?" Levi asked in his baritone voice that sent a shiver through her belly.

Tonya's cheeks flamed. "Yes. I don't know what's the matter with me. I don't usually have this trouble." She pushed in the clutch and moved the shaft to neutral, inexplicably nervous.

Levi set his hand on top of hers over the gear knob. "Here, let me help you with this, and you just worry about the clutch." Tonya's heart nearly leapt through the windshield. Should she be afraid or just shocked at his approach? Was this a come on or was he only trying to help? In the midst of her thoughts the car jumped forward and stalled. A burning smell pushed away the scent of fresh mountain pine. Levi laughed out loud.

"I'm sorry. You're making me nervous." Tonya gripped the steering wheel with both hands and furrowed her eyebrows.

"You have nothing to be nervous about."

Tonya almost giggled at that, and she bit down on her lips to keep them closed.

"Do you want me to drive?"

She glanced at him. He seemed nice enough, and she wasn't getting a creeper vibe from him. But if he was in the driver's seat, well then… he was in the driver's seat. "No, thanks. I've got it."

Tonya took a deep breath and let it out slow. The fourth time was the charm, and the VW Thing moved through the gears and chugged along as it should. As they drove, Tonya relaxed and decided to get to know this good-looking stranger.

"So, where ya from?"

"All around. I travel between ranch jobs." He turned the music volume down. "Old Blue Eyes, huh? Those are some oldies but goodies." He smiled. "You from… where did you say? Flint…"

"Flint River. Yeah, I've lived there all my life."

"I can't imagine staying in one place forever."

"It can be confining, but it's nice to belong somewhere, and to be cared about by people you've known since you were born. Everybody knows your business, though. That's the downside, for sure." Tonya chuckled and settled back in her seat.

Once they started talking, it felt like they'd known each other for years. Levi was easy to listen to. He was funny and seemed interested in Tonya's life. After a while, they fell quiet and rode in companionable silence for several miles.

As they neared his turn off, Tonya asked, "Where will you sleep if you don't make it to Sula before nighttime?"

"Oh, I can make do under a tree." Levi gave her a wink. "Wouldn't be the first time."

"That's silly. Why don't you come to Flint River with me? We can get something for dinner and then I'll let you borrow my car to get over to Sula. You can drive it back to me after your interview."

Levi looked at her out of the corner of his eye. "You don't even know me."

"That's true, but I'm a good judge of character. You don't strike me as a man who would want to be caught dead driving this yellow tin contraption for too long and so will return it as fast as he can." She grinned. "Not to mention, it's a conspicuous car—hard to steal."

Levi laughed at her logic. "All of that is true. Especially the conspicuous part." They rumbled past the turn to Sula and drove toward Flint River.

"Good. Now I won't have to stay up worrying if you got lost or fell in a ditch."

"You'd worry about me?" Levi smiled and shifted in his seat to face her.

"Don't let it go to your head. I worry about stray cats too." She quirked her mouth at him. "You can see Flint River coming up on the right."

TRENT LIFTED a dark brown bottle of Lagunitas IPA to his lips and took a long cold swallow, the bitter hops soothed his tight throat. "The thing is, I don't want to see her anymore. I can't trust her and you can't have a future with someone you don't trust." He breathed in the yeasty warm air inside the brewery and sighed.

"Haven't you ever made a mistake? Done something stupid?" Tom Dietrich set his beer down on the table and braced the bottle between the fingertips of both hands. "Never mind. Don't answer that. The list would be so long we'd have to sit here all night and I want to get home to my wife."

Trent narrowed his eyes and smirked. "Sure, I've made mistakes, but not that put people's lives in danger just because I was jealous." Trent pushed his chair back, the legs stuttered on the wood floor. "You're the Sheriff. You know what happened—how dangerous that creep Leonard Perkins was." He shuddered. The memory of the gun going off in the library echoed in his mind. Trent closed his eyes against the guilt filling his chest.

Tom gave him a long, steady look and dipped his chin. "It was bad, that's true. I never saw so much blood, but it could have been worse. I'm amazed that Cade held it together. But, the fact remains, there was no way Tonya could have known any of that was going to happen. You can't really blame her."

"I can and I do." Trent gripped his beer in a tight fist. The truth was, he blamed himself too—maybe even more than Tonya. But, if she hadn't tried to trick him, they would have discovered Perkins in time. Trent couldn't stomach anymore of Tonya's manipulating.

He held up his empty bottle with a questioning look at Tom. Tom nodded, so he went up to the bar and ordered two more. On his way back to the table he walked past the storefront windows and noticed Tonya's yellow Thing sputtering up Main Street. He squinted his eyes to get a clearer view and saw she was not alone. A man he'd never seen before was riding in her passenger seat. He stopped and watched as they parked in front of Tonya's salon. Tonya and the stranger got out and went into her shop together. Heat blossomed in his head and filtered down over his shoulders. His gut tightened.

"Who the hell is that guy?"

3

———————

Tom leaned forward to look out the bar window. "Don't know. Never seen him before." He chuckled. "Why do you care?"

Trent glared. "I don't."

"Yeah, right." Tom stood and took his second beer from Trent. He put his hand on Trent's shoulder and guided him back to their table. "You and Tonya have been in love with each other since kindergarten. For God's sake, will you two just get it together already?"

Trent sat down and closed his eyes against the sick, sticky feeling surrounding his heart. He preferred the heat of his original anger. He wished he was out riding his fences and not being laid bare in front of his childhood friend.

Tom reached forward and clinked his bottle against Trent's. "You're the one making yourself crazy. Go get her. Tell her you're sorry and kiss and make up."

Trent's indignation flashed again and he glared at Tom. "Tell her *I'm* sorry?"

Tom pointed the mouth of his beer bottle toward the

window and shook his head. "Nope, you're too late. Tonya's car just drove back down the street."

Trent glanced over his shoulder and gripped his bottle with white knuckles. "She's the one who lied. She's the one who was playing games." He chugged the rest of his beer.

"You know I'm not gonna be able to let you drive home now. I am the law around here, remember?"

"Good, let's have another then."

Tom smirked. "It's my round, and I'm getting nachos to go with it."

The friends soaked up some of the alcohol swilling in their stomachs with a large platter of cheese and jalapeño-drenched tortilla chips, and turned their conversation to fishing. An hour later, Trent scraped up the last bit of queso and sat back in his chair.

A breeze from the front door swept across the worn wooden floor of the pub, carrying with it a small, old woman. Her white hair sat piled like fleece on top of her head. She wore a thin floral, cotton dress under a faded cardigan, buttoned unevenly.

Trent smiled a mischievous grin. "Well, hello Miss Hilde. What brings you into the town's drinking establishment?" Hilde Mavers had a long-standing reputation for chasing Tom around with silly allegations she insisted he investigate. This was going to be fun.

"Trenton Stone, are you drunk?" The worn old voice accused.

"No ma'am. I haven't had anywhere near enough beer to be drunk, but the evening is young."

She shook her finger at him. "I'm going to call your grandmother as soon as I can. She'll give you a whoopin' when you get home, you better believe it."

"Yes, ma'am. I believe it." Trent turned his mirth toward

Tom. "I'll bet you're looking for the Sheriff, Miss Hilde. Don't let me distract you from your mission."

"That's right, I am." She shuffled past Trent in her thick-soled shoes and stood before Tom. "Sheriff, I would like to report a chicken robbery."

Laughter swam in Tom's eyes and his brows shot up. "A chicken robbery?"

"That's right. A few minutes ago, I went out to my pen and I have a missing chicken," Hilde took hold of Tom's large hand with both her gnarled ones. "And I know she was stolen."

"Now, Miss Hilde, chickens go missing all the time. Most often they're taken by a coyote or a fox. Even a skunk could have run off with it."

"Don't be ridiculous, Sheriff." She shook her head at him like he was a schoolboy. "My chicken pen is coyote, fox, and skunk proof."

Trent laughed silently with exaggerated drama behind Hilde's back. Tom narrowed his eyes and then a sly smirk spread across his face.

"You know, Miss Hilde, Trent could come over to your house right now, and take a look at your chicken pen. I know he'd be happy to fix any little spot where predators might be getting in. How would you like that?"

Trent shook his head. "You should have Wayne go. He's your deputy. He's the one with all the special training."

Tom tried unsuccessfully to hide his laughter. "I would, but he's cleaning the jail right now. Besides, you're the best one for the job."

"I suppose you'll have to do, Trenton, but I will drive. You are in no shape to get behind the wheel. Come along." Before Trent could come up with an excuse, Miss Hilde took him by the hand and led him to the door.

"See you later, Trent." Tom laughed over the last sip of his beer. "I'm headed home for the night. You can bring me your report tomorrow."

"Paybacks, Tom. Paybacks." Trent glowered at his friend but smiled at Hilde when he opened the door for her. He settled his cowboy hat on his head as she walked through.

Tom's laughter followed them out. "Stop whining. This will get your mind off Tonya and her new man."

Miss Hilde herded Trent to her old Subaru Outback.

When Hilde pulled up in front of her tidy little house at the far edge of town, Trent got out and went around to open her car door for her. He offered her a hand, but she batted it away, preferring to finagle her own exit. It took several minutes for Hilde to organize her old bones into a standing position, but once she was up, she tromped through her side yard. Trent followed her out back to the chicken pen.

Her lot rested amid great pines that swayed in the breeze. Trent heard the chickens warbling before he saw the pen and smelled decaying pine needles mixed with the pungent scent of poultry manure. He made a mental note to bring out a couple of bags of cedar chips to lie down after he cleaned out Hilde's hen-house.

"Here it is." Hilde swept her arthritic arm wide. "As you see, no predator can get in here. The burglar went through the gate."

Trent considered the haphazard construction and wondered how anyone could tell if someone or something broke in or not. It was more probable that a four-legged predator would get trapped in the tangle of chicken wire that surrounded Hilde's hens than it was for one to successfully sneak in and steal a chicken dinner. But, at least the crooked gate had a latch.

"Well, Miss Hilde, from the look of things, the culprit was most likely a hawk or an owl. They can swoop down inside the fenced area and snatch up a hen without even so much as a howdy-do."

Hilde pursed her lips. "That's never happened before." She scanned the fence with clouded blue eyes. "Are you sure it wasn't a burglar?"

Trent rested a reassuring hand on the woman's frail shoulder. "I'm almost certain. The problem is, if a hawk has had a fine dinner once, he's likely to try again. I'd be happy to help fix up your pen for you, if you'd like."

"I'd thank you for it. In fact, since you're being so helpful, I won't call your grandma Mary to tell on you for drinking. You seem to be sobering up, anyway."

"That's too kind." Trent chuckled. He looked up at the sky. "I think there's enough daylight left to get this old stuff taken down." He reached for the Leatherman tool he carried on his belt. and wished he had his work gloves. "We'll need to run to the hardware store. It'll be best to start with a new roll of chicken wire." It took Trent over an hour to tear the ramshackle pen down and bind the ornery bundle of chicken-mesh tight enough to fit into the hatch of Hilde's car.

When he was done, he knocked on Hilde's door. "I'll have to come back in the morning to finish the job, but I bet I can get this pen into good shape by dinnertime tomorrow. I'll hang some bird netting to cover the top to keep the birds of prey out too."

"That's real nice of you, Trenton. I'll drive you back to town and we can get the supplies."

"Let me tuck the girls into their hen-house for now."

On their way back to town, Trent did his best to ignore the slow speed in which Hilde drove. He resisted the urge to tap his fingers on the armrest and instead, enjoyed the ride.

"I have another issue I want to discuss with you, young man." The little lady pointed her crooked finger at him.

He could only imagine what was coming, probably an ancient indiscretion from his youth. "Yes, ma'am?"

"You need to call that sweet girl of yours and fix the mess you two are in. You've been wasting years playing with her feelings and it is time that stops."

Trent opened his mouth to defend himself but no words came. These were the moments he hated living in a town where your personal business belonged to everyone. He gaped at the old woman.

"Close your mouth before you catch flies in it."

He pressed his lips together and blinked.

Hilde continued, "You're too old to be gallivanting around the way you do, flirting and carrying on, and I don't mind being the one to tell you it's time you grew up."

Trent swallowed hard, his Adam's apple bobbed painfully. He stared at the knobby knuckles that clutched the steering wheel. All he could think to say was, "Yes, ma'am."

Unaware of her speed, whether fast or slow, Hilde gradually increased it to almost 45mph and then didn't bother to brake when she turned the corner onto Main Street. Trent braced himself between the dash and the door. *I'd have been safer driving drunk.*

Tom stood talking to Bob Tillman in front of the hardware store.

"Pull over here, Miss Hilde. We can tell the Sheriff we think the chicken thief was a hawk, and he doesn't need to start an official investigation." She whipped the car to the right and skidded to a stop right before the men. Tom hopped back. Bob shook his head and crooked his mouth as Trent hopped out of the car.

"She's a menace," Trent whispered to Tom before Hilde pulled herself out of the driver's seat. "You might consider rescinding her driver's license."

Huffing from exertion, Hilde said, "There you are, Sheriff.

Trenton and I have just inspected my chicken pen and found it in need of some minor repair."

Tom looked from Miss Hilde to Trent and hiding his mirth, raised his eyebrows. "That so, Trent?"

Trent lifted his cowboy hat and combed his fingers back through his dark blond hair. He replaced the hat. "If you call a total rebuild *minor*. I have some time tomorrow and I promised Miss Hilde I'd take care of it. When I get done, nothing will get in or out unless they have opposable thumbs and can unlatch the gate."

Hilde moved forward and wagged her knobby finger at Tom. "Sheriff, I'm not completely convinced a burglar didn't break in and steal my hen. Just in case, what are you going to do about it?"

"About the only thing we can do at this point is write a report." Tom flashed an irritated glance at Trent who returned it with a Cheshire grin. Paybacks were a bitch.

Tom pulled his report pad out of his chest pocket and clicked his pen.

Trent snickered. "Bob, while these two are taking care of important police business, why don't you and I go inside and get the chicken pen supplies."

Bob clapped Trent on the back with a beefy hand and they went into the hardware store leaving Tom to deal with Hilde. They gathered all the items on the list. Trent paid the bill and told Bob he'd be back in a minute with his truck. He pushed open the glass door and chuckled at the sight of Miss Hilde bent over Tom's shoulder, supervising as he sat on the bench writing out her lengthy burglary report.

Trent's green Ram 3500 dually sat in front of the pub where he left it. He stepped off the curb to cross the street, but stopped at the sound of Tonya's rickety old car clattering like a rough-running sewing machine. It turned onto Main Street and headed up toward the beauty salon. Trent acted nonchalant as he watched her from under the brim of his hat. His head snapped up when he realized Tonya wasn't in the car at all. Instead, looking like he owned the Thing, the strange man he saw Tonya with earlier was driving.

"Is that Tonya's new boyfriend?" Tom needled, and earned a vicious glare from Trent.

Bob leaned forward and squinted. "I've never seen him around here before. Anybody met him yet? Where's he from?"

Trent's eyes followed the car's progression. The man parked the VW Thing and walked inside the salon. "He's not her boyfriend." With no other comment, Trent strode up the street toward his truck.

He walked past the truck and marched into Tonya's shop. The little bells almost fell off the door from the force he used to open it.

"Trent." Tonya stood from the reception chair and smoothed her dress.

Trent stared straight into the dark eyes of the stranger. "Tonya," he replied without looking at her. "Just stopping in to see if everything's all right."

"Yes." Tonya swallowed. "Why wouldn't it be?"

The man pulled convenience-store snacks and a six pack out of a plastic bag and held Trent's stare. Their eyes clashed.

"I saw a stranger driving your car and wondered if something was wrong."

Tonya crossed her arms. "So, if I make a new friend you think something is wrong?" Her sharp tone caused Trent to lose the stare-down.

"No. It's just that no one has ever seen..." Trent pointed with his chin, "this guy, around here before."

Levi drew himself up to his full height, which was several inches shorter than Trent's, and held out his hand. "Levi Barrett."

Trent narrowed his eyes. The skin on the back of his neck contracted and his gut tightened with a prickly warning. "Trent Stone." He shook the man's hand with a Hulk-ish grip. "So, how'd you two meet?"

"Funny thing. I was hitch-hiking on my way to a ranch near here, when I come upon this beautiful woman pulled over in her funky broken-down car. I helped her fill her radiator, and she offered me a ride." Levi smiled at Tonya. "I thought I was getting a lift with Marilyn Monroe."

"Tonya." Alarm rang through Trent's body. "You can't just go picking up hitch-hikers."

Tonya shrugged. "Fortunately, Levi is a good guy. Anyway, it took me a couple of tries to get the clutch right until Levi helped me." She and Levi shared a smile. "But once we got going, we had a nice drive and here we are. So, you see? Levi's completely safe—a perfect gentleman."

A tic tugged at the corner of Trent's eye. "After what happened this past summer, I can't believe you think this guy is safe just because he filled your radiator and shifted your gears."

A sharp gleam flashed in her eyes. "It's really none of your business who shifts my gears anymore, Trent."

Her pink lips turned down in such a way that made Trent want to take hold of her face and kiss her hard. He shook his head to clear the temptation and turned back to Levi.

"You'd better treat her well if you know what's good for you."

Levi cocked one side of his mouth back. "Oh, I plan to treat her real well."

At his insinuating tone, a red veil dropped over Trent's vision. It took all his concentration to nod civilly and leave before he punched Barrett's smart mouth.

4

———————

"Who was that? Your big brother?" Levi chuckled.

"No. Don't pay any attention to him." Tonya touched cool fingertips to her hot cheeks. "Are you hungry?" she asked, changing the subject. "I thought instead of snacks, maybe we could go down to Alice's Diner for a quick bite to eat. You probably want to get on your way."

"Sure, but I'm in no hurry. The interview isn't until tomorrow morning."

"Right." Out of the corner of her eye, Tonya watched Trent's truck back out of his parking spot at the brewery. She continued to watch until she saw him signal left, out of town. "Alice is known for her meatloaf," she said distantly, her mind down the street.

ALICE APPROACHED their table carrying two glasses of water with straws. "Hey, Tonya," she drawled as she glowered at Levi.

"Hi, Alice." Tonya wondered at the woman's cool tone. "This is Levi."

Alice nodded at him and shifted her gaze back to Tonya. "Where's Trent?"

The lining of Tonya's stomach burned. She wondered if Trent got this same kind of cold reception whenever he showed up around town with another woman. She doubted it. Everyone was just fine with Trent, no matter what he did.

"I don't know," Tonya retorted. "I didn't realize it was my turn to watch him."

"Just used to seeing you with him is all. No need to get huffy." Alice took out her order pad. "What can I get you?"

Both Tonya and Levi ordered the meatloaf special. When their meal came, Levi dipped a bite of beef into the rich gravy. "So, are you and Trent an item?" he asked.

"Not anymore."

Levi nodded, considering her answer. "He said something happened this past summer? Was that why you two broke up?"

Tonya's eyes dropped to her plate. "A murderer showed up in Flint River."

"Well, I guess that explains why he's so protective."

"I suppose." Tonya wished Trent's reaction was due to more than simply fear for her safety.

"You can tell me it's none of my business if you want, but why did you two break up?"

"Well," Tonya wiped her mouth on her napkin and set it back across her lap. "Trent says it's because I didn't tell anyone that I saw the guy sneaking around town. He thinks I could have prevented the whole thing if I had said something."

"That doesn't seem like a reason to break up with someone, though."

Tonya hesitated. There was a lot more to it than that, but

not that she wanted to share with someone she only met a few hours ago.

"He says he doesn't trust me anymore."

Levi dipped a chunk of bread in the remaining gravy on his plate and swirled it around. "Whatever. Sounds like an excuse to me."

AFTER DINNER, Tonya walked with Levi back up Main Street to her shop. They stopped outside in front of Tonya's car.

"I like this old barbershop pole. It's a nice touch." Levi ran his hand down the smooth red and white stripes of the old-fashioned barber's symbol that hung from the brick façade of Tonya's building.

"It came with the space. This building has housed a barbershop and now a beauty shop since the late eighteen-hundreds." Tonya unclasped her small, pink Chanel purse, and reached in. "Here you go. Take care of her." She handed Levi her key chain complete with a bedazzled, fuzzy pink-pompom attached.

He wrinkled his brow. "Can I just have the car key, or is this another theft prevention tactic?" He held the bundle up by the tip of a single key.

"Don't you like my fuzz ball?"

"Um..." Levi chuckled. "Seriously though, thanks. I'll bring your car back as soon as I can." Levi opened the door and leaned on the roof. "You have no idea how much I appreciate this, Tonya. I'll see you soon."

Tonya waved at Levi as he pulled away from the curb. *Seems like a nice guy.* She pressed her palm against a slight tingling in her belly. *Who knows...*

She went inside and walked through her shop to the backroom kitchen. Before she climbed the steep staircase to her bedroom, Tonya poured herself a glass of chardonnay. In her room, Trent's image gazed at her from the many framed photos she had covering her dresser and nightstand. She released a pain-filled sigh and gripped her glass with both hands.

"Well, Tonya," she said to herself. "Pining after a man who doesn't want you is plain stupid. It is past time to move on." Tonya took a large gulp of wine and then went about laying all the photos face down so she wouldn't have to look at Trent's mischievous eyes and tantalizing crooked smile. Tomorrow, she'd pack him away both literally and figuratively.

5

———

Tonya reached for the tarnished brass handle on the door of the Kaffee Klatch. She carried a six-inch-thick notebook filled with scraps of fabric, lace, and other miscellany in one arm and wrestled the heavy door with the other. Tonya had offered to help Joscelyn plan her wedding to Trent's brother Cade, and so, as uncomfortable as it was likely to be, here she was.

Joscelyn and Cade met last spring when she first came to town. She ended up being a god-send to Cade and his daughter Sadie. They both fell in love with her, and she with them. Now they were becoming a family. Folks talked about how Cade saved Joscelyn's life, but Tonya liked to think they saved each other.

A familiar quiver of shame washed through Tonya when memories of this past summer played across her mind. It had been an "off" time between her and Trent and he was interested in Joscelyn. She wanted Joscelyn to get caught with the man she saw sneaking in and out of her place and put an end to Trent's infatuation. She didn't know the guy was a psychopath. Still, she had to admit Trent was partly right. If she hadn't been trying to manipulate the situation for her own benefit, she could have prevented what happened. Tonya shuddered.

Joscelyn waved to her as she entered the coffee shop. The woman's bright smile worked to dissipate Tonya's regret. She wondered, for the thousandth time, how Joscelyn could forgive her but Trent could not. Tonya's throat ached, and she pressed her free hand against a bruised sensation in her chest. The dark scent of coffee and warm baked cinnamon rolls comforted her emotions. She tried to wave, but almost dropped her scrapbook, and so offered a smile instead.

"Hi, Tonya." Joscelyn pushed a chair out for her with the toe of her cowboy-boot.

Tonya dumped the heavy book on the table. "Hi." She sat, tucking her peplum pencil-skirt underneath her. "Those rolls smell delicious, don't they? How are you?" she asked.

"I'm good. Eager to get this wedding underway." Joscelyn sighed. "Cade and I can't wait to make 'us' official."

"Have you picked a date? Colors?" Tonya ran a finger over the laminated lunch menu and glanced at the sandwich choices. "How many people are you going to invite?" When Joscelyn said nothing, Tonya lifted her gaze to the woman's bewildered face. "What's wrong?"

"Well, I wasn't planning on a big fuss. Cade and I just want something simple." Joscelyn sipped her coffee. "We were thinking early October. The aspen should be beautiful by then so we don't need particular colors, and we were only going to invite the family."

Tonya stared at Joscelyn. "So, I won't get to come?" She swallowed hard. "What about Bob and Anita?" She hated the shrillness in her voice and she lowered her tone. "Or Margaret?"

"Of course, you're coming." Joscelyn drew her brows together. "You are family. Other than that though, we thought we'd send announcements with a photo, or something."

Tonya sighed. "I don't think Trent will want me there if it's only family, but it's kind of you and Cade to think of me."

"I don't care what Trent wants. It isn't his wedding." Joscelyn smiled and reached a comforting hand to Tonya's arm. "Is he still being stubborn about what happened this past summer?"

"Yeah."

"You know, the whole thing terrified him. He's not used to being afraid or helpless. I think he blames you as a way to relieve himself from the weight of his own sense of guilt and his heavy emotions."

"I agree, but I suppose it doesn't really matter why he blames me. He'll never forgive me. It's truly over between us this time." Tonya's throat thickened and she cleared it. "What about Jack? Is he coming to the wedding?"

"Cade tried to call him, but he hasn't been able to get ahold of him yet."

"Jack hasn't been back to Flint River since he left for West Point almost ten years ago." Tonya wondered if holding a grudge was a Stone brothers' trait.

"Why not?"

"There was some rift between him and Trent, but I don't think it had to do with Cade." Tonya opened her massive scrapbook and pushed it toward her friend. "Joscelyn, before you decide on an ultra-simple ceremony, let me show you some photos of wedding ideas I think you'd really like."

The waitress brought her coffee and Tonya took a bitter sip. They ordered lunch and then bent their heads over the lace and ribbon covered wedding-planner. Flipping through the pages, Tonya pointed out what she loved about each example.

"These are all beautiful, Tonya. They're just not me. Cade and I aren't fancy."

The bell on the door chimed. Tonya and Joscelyn glanced up to see Levi come in. He stood awkwardly, searching the faces until he spotted her. He smiled and lifted his hand in half a wave. "Hey, Tonya. We got done early today, so I brought your car back."

Tonya sat up, tugged at her blouse to straighten it, and touched the side of her platinum hair. "How'd it go?"

"I got the job. I've moved into the bunkhouse already, which was easy since I only have a backpack." He nodded to Joscelyn. "Hi." He thrust out a hand. "I'm Levi."

"Nice to meet you." Joscelyn raised an eyebrow at Tonya, barely covering her questioning smile as she shook his hand.

"Levi borrowed my car and is just returning it," Tonya explained. Joscelyn's smile broadened and she nodded. Heat crept up Tonya's neck, and she hoped Levi didn't notice Joscelyn's grinning insinuation.

Levi rested his hands on the back of one of the empty chairs at their table. "Yeah, thanks again for letting me use it. I parked it in front of your shop. Some lady walking up the sidewalk told me you were over here."

"You're welcome. Do you want me to drive you back out to the ranch this afternoon?"

"No, I've got it covered, thanks." Levi swallowed and his cheeks took on a deeper hue. "I'd like to take you out for dinner tonight though. If you're free. You know—to thank you for lending me your car, and all."

Tonya warmed. It'd been a long time since a man was bashful to ask her out. "I'd love—" She stopped mid-sentence. The growl of a diesel engine rattled the window and Trent's green truck pulled up in front of the coffee shop.

"Oh, for crying out the window." With frantic eyes she silently pleaded with Joscelyn who responded with a nod.

"Come with me, Levi. Let's go to my salon and we can make plans for our dinner date." Tonya took Levi's hand, but before they left, she turned to her friend. "Joscelyn, look through the notebook before you decide. And thanks for… this." Joscelyn winked at her before Tonya snuck Levi out the side door to the café's patio.

"What about your sandwich?" Levi asked as he followed Tonya with his brows drawn in confusion.

"I'm not hungry anymore. Come on." Tonya's stomach knotted. She pulled Levi through the door, past the patio, and out the rear gate. Her heart clattered when she peered around the street corner to be certain Trent was inside the coffee shop before she rushed Levi out in the open. Instead of crossing kitty-corner toward her place, Tonya directed him straight across the street. She hurried beyond the store fronts and turned down the alley that led to the back of her row of shops.

"Where are we running to?" Levi laughed at Tonya's antics. "I thought we were going to your salon?"

She uttered a breathless laugh, to cover her nerves. "I'm giving you the penny tour through the alley entrance. I have a small kitchen in the back where we can sit and have something to drink." Levi shrugged and followed her willingly.

6

———

Tonya opened the back gate behind her shop and led Levi through the door into her kitchenette.

"Here we are." She pulled out one of the two chairs from the dinette and motioned for Levi to sit. Winded from their fast escape, her words came in a rush. "I'm glad to hear your interview went well. Did you get everything done you needed to?"

Levi sat down on a pink vinyl, diner-style chair. Before he could answer her, the front door to the salon swung open, the bells above it jangled manically.

Tonya held up her hand. "Hold on a sec. Let me see who that is. I'll be right back." Tonya pulled back the curtain that separated her shop from the kitchen and peeked out.

Trent stood at the counter, filling the space. "Hey," he said, his eyes searching hers.

Her heart catapulted into her throat and she reached her fingers up to soothe the pulse in her neck. As always, her blood raced when she saw Trent, and it saddened her because she knew it always would. His sky-blue eyes were bright in his darkened face. "Trent, what's wrong?"

"Why'd you leave the coffee shop in such a hurry?"

Tonya drew in a sharp breath. She'd hoped he hadn't seen her. "What do you mean?" She blinked.

"Weren't you supposed to help Joscelyn plan her and Cade's wedding today?"

Tonya reached up to tidy her victory-roll hairdo. "I did."

Trent's lips curled, but there was a suspicious glint in his eyes. "You did? Tell me about it?"

"Trent—what do you want?" Tonya pinched her brows together.

"Just wondering why you ran away with your… friend, that's all. I saw you two sneaking into the back alley from the coffee shop window."

That did it. A flush of heat coursed through her and her face went pink. "It's not any of your business what I'm doing or who I'm doing it with. So, if you don't mind, I have company."

Levi stepped through the curtain and at the same time, Joscelyn rushed through the front door. Joscelyn drew up short when she saw everyone and made an apologetic face at Tonya. "I uh… brought your sandwich and your wedding idea album. You left them…"

"Oh…" Tonya stepped forward and took her things. She gave Joscelyn a meaningful wide-eyed look.

The door bells rang again and all four pairs of eyes turned. Deputy Wayne Brown sauntered in, his head bobbling with self-importance. "Everything all right in here, Tonya?" he asked as he narrowed his eyes at Trent.

"Mind your own business, Wayne." Trent's jaw stiffened and he rubbed the back of his neck. "This has nothing to do with you."

"It is my business, Stone. It's my job to keep the people of this town safe."

"And what makes you think someone isn't safe?" Trent glared at the deputy.

"I noticed you all rushing over here from the coffee shop and wondered what was going on." His eyes rested on Levi. "You're new around here."

Tonya took a step forward. "Yes, Wayne, this is my friend, Levi."

The deputy looked Levi up and down considering him before he nodded and turned his bulging eyes back to Trent. "I just stopped by to make sure you aren't causing any trouble."

Trent shook his head and narrowed his eyes at Wayne. The atmosphere grew heavy and Tonya stepped between the two men. Wayne had it in for Trent ever since they were in high school. One of several reasons for the animosity between he and Trent was the fact that, all those years ago, Trent broke Wayne's arm during football practice. It had been an accident, but Wayne never got over it.

"It's okay, Wayne, everything's just fine. We're all friends here." She said in an airy tone. "Thanks for checking on me though." Tonya took the deputy's arm and turned him toward the entrance. "Especially when I'm sure you have much more important matters to attend to." She opened the door for him.

"Yes, well, you know I'm only a shout away if you need me."

"Thank you, Wayne. I appreciate that." Tonya closed the door behind him and rolled her eyes to herself before she turned back to her guests. The room buzzed in miserable silence.

Trent broke the tension. "Tonya, what are you doing with this guy?" He tossed his chin in Levi's direction but his eyes never left hers.

A slow burn simmered in Tonya's chest. She pasted on a

saccharine-sweet smile and gave her voice a soft lilt. "Levi and I are friends." Tonya moved toward Levi, slid her hand into the crook of his elbow, and leaned toward him. Joscelyn turned her head to hide her smirk. Levi caught on fast enough and set his other hand on top of Tonya's.

Trent furrowed his brow. "Where are you from, Barrett?"

"All around. Just got a job over in Sula."

Tonya pulled Levi over to the row of pink vinyl chairs lined up against the wall. "Have a seat, Levi. Can I get you something to drink? Iced tea?" She pushed him down into a chair that had a chrome hairdryer dome attached to the back. He looked up at the device with a skeptical eye.

"Sure… Thanks," he answered. Tonya let her hot-pink fingernails trail down his arm. He smiled and held onto her hand for a second before Tonya stepped away to get the tea. She noted the smug look Levi shot at Trent. She hoped Levi was just playing along and not thinking she was normally so forward. "Joscelyn?" She glanced at her friend, including her in the drink offer.

"No, thanks," Joscelyn answered. Tonya turned her back on Trent as she walked toward the kitchen.

"Thanks," Trent called to her back, "I'd love a glass too." Tonya pretended not to hear him.

She filled a glass with ice and slammed it down on the counter. A deep breath cooled the fire of her irritation and she poured the tea. She brought the cold drink out to Levi.

"Here you go." To Tonya's great satisfaction, Trent's jaw muscles bulged, but he didn't ask again about his glass. While he scowled at Levi, Tonya chanced a glance at Joscelyn, who grimaced.

Joscelyn moved forward and placed a hand on the back of Trent's shoulder. "Trent, come on. Let's go."

He swung his head around to her and propped his hands

on his hips. "What do you think about Tonya picking up a hitch-hiker, Josce?"

Joscelyn smiled at Levi. "He seems like a nice guy to me."

Levi returned her smile and inclined his head in her direction.

Trent furrowed his brow. "Of all people, I would think you'd be the most cautious."

Tonya stepped toward him. "Maybe if you took five minutes to get to know him, you'd realize what the rest of us see."

Joscelyn tucked her hand around Trent's arm. "I understand your concern, but not everyone is a monster. Tonya's a grown woman. She's heard your concern, but who she chooses to be friends with is up to her."

Sharon Cline, owner of the quilt shop across the street, chose that moment to enter the salon for her cut and color appointment. She was an hour early but Tonya forced her voice to sound welcoming. "Hi, Sharon. Take a seat in my chair. I'll be right with you."

Sharon nodded. "Hello Trent… Joscelyn." Her eyes moved around the room, taking in the scene before she picked up a magazine. Sharon sat in the swivel barber chair. She nodded to Levi and pretended to read.

Tonya figured whatever happened next would be on the gossip hot-line by suppertime. Joscelyn said hello to Sharon, but Trent didn't respond. His searching eyes remained focused on Tonya.

She moved closer to Trent and lowered her voice so only he could hear. "How dare you come in here like some kind of tomcat protecting his territory? You gave up *this* territory. You can't break up with me and then act jealous of someone else." Tonya pressed her hands together. "Trent, I honestly don't think you have anything to say about what I do anymore."

Trent shook his head with disbelief. "You're right—Fine. Just try not to get killed proving it to me." He shot a final glare at Levi and with long angry strides he stormed out of the salon.

Joscelyn hurried to follow him, but turned back to mouth a quick, "Sorry."

Levi downed his tea and handed the glass to Tonya. "You said he broke up with you?"

Tonya set the glass on the reception desk and nodded.

"He sure doesn't act like it."

"Well, he did, but it doesn't matter either way. I'm not waiting around for him any longer." Tonya gestured for Sharon to move to the wash sink. "Thanks for playing along, Levi." She choked on the phrase when it left her mouth. Trent was right. She did play games all the time. Her little pretense to make Trent jealous proved it. The fact that it worked wasn't any consolation. Tonya closed her eyes against a wave of self-abasement.

Levi touched her elbow. "Thanks again for loaning me your car. I'll be back in a couple hours to pick you up for dinner. Will that work?"

"That'll be fine." Tonya smiled and nodded though her heart was heavy. Trent said he didn't want her anymore, and it was time she believed him.

Levi left and Tonya snapped a plastic cape around Sharon's neck. She bent over the wash-sink, spraying Sharon's hair with warm water and added shampoo.

When the suds were thick and fragrant, Sharon asked, "When is Trent Stone ever going to realize he is completely in love with you?"

Tonya shook her head. "When the pigs that fly come home to roost."

7

———————

Trent stepped off the curb to cross Main Street on the way to his truck, but jerked back. He held his arm out, preventing Joscelyn from walking in front of the careening Subaru that rounded the corner.

Joscelyn gripped his forearm. "Whoa—was that Hilde Mavers?"

"Yeah. Tom really needs to take her license. I think she's forgotten where the brake is." Trent shook his head. "I wonder what the crisis is this time."

"I'll leave you to find that out." Joscelyn waved. "See you later." He touched the brim of his hat and gave her a nod before he followed the old woman's car to find out what the problem was. He might get some much-needed comic relief at the same time. He was only a few paces behind the elderly woman when he entered the Sheriff's Office.

"I'm positive, this time, Sheriff. You need to come out and see for yourself. We have a chicken thief on our hands, for sure and for certain." The little lady stood with her patent-leather purse clutched to her chest and trembled with indignation.

41

"Miss Hilde," Tom reasoned. "We just went through this. No one around here needs to steal chickens. We all have our own. I'm sure that whatever ate your first missing hen has returned for another free supper. That's all."

"Thomas Dietrich, you are elected to this office by the people you are supposed to protect and defend. That means you work for me. Now, get off your duff and come to the scene of the crime. I want to press charges."

"Against who? A hawk?"

"Don't sass me, boy."

Trent stepped in. "Miss Hilde, are you sure the gate wasn't left open?"

Hilde teetered her body around and peered up at his face. "Trenton Stone, you rebuilt that chicken coop yourself. You know that no varmint can get in there and neither could any birds with the netting you strung across the top. I did not leave the gate open and three of my chickens are gone."

Trent gave his friend a shrug. "Miss Hilde is right. Nothing is getting in or out of that pen without help."

Tom sighed and sat on the edge of his desk. "Okay. I'll come out this afternoon and take a report. You can't press charges unless we have a suspect though."

"Far be it from me to tell you how to do your job, Sheriff." Hilde shuffled her way to the door and Trent pulled it open for her. "I'll see you soon." She lifted a hand in farewell.

Tom stood and moved around to the chair behind his desk. He sighed at the papers scattered across his work surface. "What's up, Trent?"

Trent sat in one of the visitors' chairs and propped his mud-caked boots on the corner of Tom's desk. "I came to see what the new legal crisis was—and maybe get a good laugh."

A scream sounded from outside and sprinted up the back of Trent's spine. He and Tom jumped to their feet at the same time and rushed to the door. Tom pushed through the exit with Trent on his heels. They found Hilde with her hands holding her face.

Tom ran to her. "What is it, Miss Hilde? What's happened?" He bent down. "Are you okay?"

Trent held the woman's arm to steady her. "It's all right, Miss Hilde. We're here."

"My car!" She held out a gnarled finger, pointing to an empty parking space. "My car has been stolen!"

Tom's body sagged with relief. "Now, Miss Hilde—" He narrowed his eyes and cocked his head. "Are you sure?" He craned his neck to look down the street and rubbed his chin. "Maybe you parked down the block and only thought it was in front of my office." He patted her shoulder. "Remember last time? You thought someone stole your car, and I found it two blocks from your house?"

"I'm old, Sheriff, not senile. I parked my car right here."

"It's true, Tom." Trent interrupted. "Her car is gone. I saw her park right there, myself. She flew around the corner right into this spot." Trent let half a smile creep up. "In fact, I wasn't sure she'd stop before she was inside the building."

"Don't be a smart-Alec, Trenton. Your driving isn't any better than mine."

Trent's grin bloomed in full.

Tom studied them. "So you two are telling me that someone stole a vehicle from right in front of the Sheriff's Office? Here in Flint River? In broad daylight?"

"Looks that way." Trent shrugged.

"But who on earth would do that?"

Trent glanced across the street at the beauty shop. "I could make an educated guess," he said under his breath. He took the old woman's arm. "Let me help you back inside, Miss Hilde. Looks like Tom is going to actually have to do his job today."

"Ha, ha." Tom followed them in and booted up his

computer to take the information. "Did you leave your keys in the car?"

Hilde adjusted her position in the wooden chair and pulled herself as tall and straight as her aged spine would allow. "Of course I did. Just like everyone else in town. Done it all my life and been fine—until today."

Tom finished the report. "I'll call out to the surrounding counties and ask the other departments to keep a look out for your car. I'll let you know if I hear anything."

Trent stood and helped Hilde to her feet. "I'd be happy to give you a ride home, Miss Hilde. Is there anything you need in town before I take you?"

"Now that you mention it…"

Trent winked at Tom over the top of Hilde's head. "I'll get her home safe and sound. You find the car thief."

8

———

Tonya finished with her last client, and Levi returned to the salon. Her stomach fluttered when he walked through the door.

"Hey, good timing. I'm all through for the day."

"Good. I hoped I wasn't too early."

It was a couple of hours before dinner-time, so Tonya decided to show Levi around Flint River. They strolled in and out of shops on Main Street and Tonya introduced Levi to some of the town's people.

She walked with her hand hooked on Levi's elbow. "What do you think of Flint River?"

Levi frowned, "Folks aren't overly friendly."

Tonya sighed. "Give them time." She knew the town's people didn't want to betray their friendship with Trent by welcoming Levi. "What did you do with yourself this afternoon?"

Levi mulled over the question, taking his time to answer. "I took a walk."

"Oh? Where'd you go?"

"Just up past the courthouse, that's all." Levi crossed his

45

arms over his chest, dislodging Tonya's hand from his elbow. "I followed a path through the woods. Why? Does it matter?"

Wondering at his defensive response, she smiled and cocked her head to the side. "Must have been quite the hike. You were gone for over two hours."

Levi shrugged.

Tonya studied his face to see if she could detect a reason for his reticence, but found none and decided she was being too sensitive. They turned toward the entrance of the Sapphire Emporium.

"Hi, Matthew," she called to the man behind the glass counter.

The old man looked up and leveled ebony eyes at her, his dark face creasing into a broad smile. His warmth cooled slightly when he moved his gaze to Levi.

His eyes flickered back to Tonya. "Hello, Tonya. What brings you in to my gallery today?"

"I'm showing my friend, Levi, around and we couldn't skip your place." Tonya gave him a pleading smile.

"Levi, is it?"

"Yeah, that's right."

"I'm Matthew Jefferson." Matthew offered his hand.

Levi hesitated for a second, staring at Matthew's hand before he briefly shook it. "Nice to meet you." He glanced around the shop. "Have you lived here a long time?" He wiped his hand down his pants leg.

Tonya noticed the move and glanced at Matthew to see if he was offended.

Matthew narrowed his eyes a fraction as he nodded his head, steel-colored hair curled tight to his scalp. "Yep. Been here over forty years. It's a good place to live." He appraised Levi for a moment longer before he turned his attention back to Tonya. "Things still up in the air between you and Trent?"

Tonya's skin itched at the uncomfortable exchange and her cheeks warmed. "No, in fact they aren't. Trent and I are no longer seeing each other." She took Levi's arm and turned him toward the door. "Come on, Levi, let's go."

"Now hold on a minute, young lady. Don't go off in a hissy." Matthew came out from behind the jewelry counter. "You and Trent have been circling each other since you were children. You can't expect folks to see things different overnight."

"It's been well over a month now, Matthew." Tonya spun around. "Trent and I are over and everyone needs to get used to it."

"All right, all right." Matthew raised his hands in surrender. "Don't get upset with an old man. It's hard to change so fast at my age." His kind eyes rested their warmth on Tonya.

Tonya sighed and her shoulders drooped with the release of air. She gave Matthew an exasperated look.

A gentle light flickered in the old man's expression. "You're right, of course." He turned his gaze to Levi. "Welcome to Flint River, Levi. I hope we see more of you." He smiled, revealing a prominent gold crown and several empty spaces where teeth used to be. "The cold front will blow over soon. Hang in there." He chuckled.

Levi met the man's eyes. "Thanks."

"Are you two headed out for supper?"

"I was going to take Levi to the Silver Spur Chop House, but with the way everyone's behaving, I think we should drive up to Missoula."

"Don't let folks chase you away or they'll never change. You hold your chin high and give 'em hell, like you did me. Everyone will accept your new young man, eventually."

Tonya's eyes grew wide. "He isn't 'my new young man'. We're just friends." Tonya wished she could dissolve into the air and blow away.

Levi slid his arm around her waist. "Don't worry, Tonya. I don't mind being thought of as your new man, and I kinda like being the cause of public unrest." He gave her a wink. "Let's have dinner right in the middle of town and give 'em something to talk about."

Matthew waved to them as they left.

LEVI HELD the heavy wooden door of the Silver Spur open for Tonya as they went inside.

"Hey, Tonya," a young waitress greeted. "Who's this?" She smiled at Levi.

"Hi, Pam. This is my friend, Levi."

"Hi, Levi." Turning back to Tonya she asked, "You guys here for dinner or just going to the bar?"

"Dinner."

Pam nodded and lifted two menus from the stack on the hostess desk. "This way."

Tonya flashed Levi a smile and followed her to the table. They slid into a quiet booth with high-back bench seats designed to offer a cozy ambiance and privacy.

"So, are you two on a date?" Pam asked. Tonya glared at her and the waitress shrugged. "Just asking. Does this mean Trent's back on the market?"

"On the market? Did you seriously just ask that?" Tonya shook her head and scoffed. She regretted bringing Levi to dinner in town. They would never have the space to get to know each other while swimming in the fish bowl that was Flint River.

Pam held her arms akimbo. "What? I was just wondering."

Tonya's jaw tightened. "I'll have a glass of merlot." She looked to Levi. "What would you like?"

Levi ordered a beer, and Pam jotted notes on a pad. She looked up with a broad smile. "I can't wait to tell Mindy."

Under her breath, Tonya uttered, "For crying out the window." Tonya stared into Pam's face. "Trent can see whomever he likes, but it will *never* be Mindy Thorpe." She took a calming breath knowing her reaction made her look jealous. Tonya bit down hard so that no more unintended words would escape.

Pam shrugged and left to get their drink order.

Levi watched Tonya with an assessing gaze. "What is it about this Trent guy?"

"What do you mean?"

"Well he's…"

"Cocky? Charming? And…" Tonya pulled in another breath as she felt the prick of tears. "He'll never commit to one woman. I don't know why I ever thought he would. I mean, why should he when he has so many waiting on his beck and call?" She gestured in the direction Pam had gone.

"No, what I mean is, he's all anyone talks to you about. Well, everyone but Joscelyn. He sounds like an ass to me."

"Well, that's because of how he's treated *you*." Tonya unrolled her silverware and spread the napkin in her lap "We're the latest hot topic. As soon as something else happens, everyone's attention will shift.

Levi leaned forward, resting his forearms on the table. "You still have feelings for him, don't you?"

She stared at Levi and then released a heavy sigh. "I've loved that stupid man for as long as I can remember. I can't change that overnight, but I'm working on it."

Levi nodded. Their drinks arrived, and he sat back to make room. After Pam left, he held up his glass. "Here's to moving on."

Tonya raised her wine glass and clinked it against his beer. "Hear, hear."

. . .

AFTER DINNER, Tonya and Levi stepped out onto Main Street under a tangerine sun that sat low on the purple mountains. Tonya watched their reflection in the plate glass storefronts they passed as they walked down the street side by side. It was strange to see herself with another man. Their hands bumped together and Levi took hers in his, another foreign sensation. His hand was narrow and slight compared to Trent's.

The lights on Main Street, fashioned after nineteenth century gas-lamps, flickered on and Levi stopped under the glow of the one outside Tonya's beauty shop.

"Thanks for today. I had fun creating a stir." His soft laugh made her smile. "It's good for folks in these dusty little towns to get shaken up once in a while." He shifted his weight from one foot to the other. "I'd better get going, though. I've got to get out to the ranch. Morning will come early." He pulled her hand to his lips and brushed a kiss across her knuckles.

Tonya observed the act as though she were in a play. She moved through the scene but her feelings were remote. She leaned her head to the side. "Are you sure you don't need a ride? It's no problem for me to drive you."

"No, I'm good. Don't worry about me. People are good about lending a ride around here." Levi stepped toward her and cupped her cheek in his hand. He bent down and claimed a kiss. Tonya's heart stuttered. For years now, Trent's lips were the only ones she wanted. Levi pressed deeper, his tongue testing her acceptance.

Tonya wanted to feel something, a rush of excitement, or perhaps shame, but neither emotion manifested inside of her. Instead, she shrugged mentally and put her arms around Levi's neck. She returned his kiss with forced fervor, knowing full well they stood under the streetlight, right in the middle of Main Street.

As their kiss lingered, her heart stopped waffling, and its

pulse grew strong with intent. Her body awakened, even if her emotions were reluctant.

Levi pulled back and grinned. "Wow. That jackass ex-boyfriend of yours doesn't know what he's losing." He kissed her again and the first sparkles of wonder glowed in Tonya's core. "I'll call you." Levi kissed the tip of her nose. "I won't get back here till next weekend though. Will you be around?"

"Yes. In fact, next Saturday is the Flint River Harvest Festival. Would you like to come?" Tonya held her breath waiting for his answer.

"Sure—sounds fun." Levi ran his fingers across her cheek and smiled. "I'll call."

Tonya swayed slightly, smiling while she watched him turn and walk down the street. She wondered for a second how he planned to get to a ranch fifty miles away, but her mind resolutely swam back to the feelings Levi's kiss stirred in her. A whispering thought of making Trent jealous brushed through her mind, but at the moment she was more interested in the champagne tingles zipping throughout her nervous system.

9

The sun had long since set and Grandma Mary had called him at least three times for dinner already. Trent kept working on the old, broken hay-bailer. The repair wasn't urgent, he didn't need the machine up and running until the first hay cutting in June of next year. But working with his hands kept his mind off his personal life. Plus, if he went inside for dinner, Gran would start in on him again.

Everybody he knew—none of whom's damn business it was—thought he should forgive Tonya for not telling anyone about seeing Perkins sneaking in and out of Joscelyn's home last July. If she'd only told Tom or Wayne. Trent fought to loosen a bolt but it wouldn't budge. He hit it several times with his small sledge hammer.

Truth be told, he was as guilty as Tonya, and he didn't forgive himself either. He should have been paying more attention. He should have seen Perkins lurking around town. If he hadn't been with Tonya, he would have been at the hospital. He might have given Joscelyn a ride home. If he had, he would have been there. Perkins would have never gotten close to Joscelyn. If Cade hadn't figured it out, she'd be dead and it would be both his and Tonya's fault.

Now Tonya put her trust in some new stranger. Didn't she learn anything? Trent gnashed his teeth together so hard his jaw hurt. Frustration forced a low growl through his lips. The screwdriver he held on the opposite side of the bolt slipped when he turned his wrench. It rammed into the tender part of his hand between his thumb and forefinger.

"Damn it!" Blood erupted from his scuffed skin and oozed together with the black grease on his hand. He pressed his injured hand onto the equally filthy leg of his jeans and jumped up. He flung his hand out as though to rid it of the pain, and knocked over an old coffee can full of nuts and bolts. They fell all over the dirt floor and were lost to him until daylight.

"Trent, what's all that racket?" Mary called from the back porch. "Are you okay?"

Trent mumbled several choice words under his breath and then hollered back. "Yes, ma'am. I'm fine."

"Sure doesn't sound like it. Come on in now. It's time you quit sulking out there and eat your dinner." Mary didn't wait for a response and let the screen door close with a slap behind her.

Trent kicked at the hardware covered in dust and threw the offending screwdriver into his toolbox which rewarded him with another loud clatter. He snatched up an old rag and pressed it against the cut.

On his way to turn out the lights in the vehicle shed, his phone buzzed. It was a text from a number he didn't recognize. When he tapped open the message, a photo filled his screen and the image of Tonya in the arms of Levi Barrett assaulted him.

"What the hell?" Red heat filled his head behind his eyes and he blinked several times. The man was kissing her, or plumbing her throat, he couldn't tell which. He read the words under the picture, "Thought you'd want to know."

Trent's thumbs pressed against the text pad on his screen, "Who is this?" He sent the text but received no answer. As he waited, he stared at the photo and a deep, dark pain in the pit of his gut sent tendrils of poisonous green smoke throughout his chest.

An ugly choking sensation lodged in Trent's throat, but he coughed it away. He wasn't the one who should feel guilty. But somehow the satisfaction of being innocent didn't alleviate the sickening malaise swirling in his gut. Trent turned his anger toward Levi and pictured punching the guy right in his sarcastic mouth. Trent turned off the light and slammed the door of the shed closed. He resolutely ignored the fact that Tonya didn't belong to him any longer.

Trent leapt up the back steps and once through the door, he slammed it shut.

"Whatever's wrong with you—don't take it out on the house," Mary hollered at him from the kitchen.

Trent kicked off his boots and strode through the mudroom to the kitchen sink.

"What happened to your hand?" When his grandma's voice softened with concern, a lump rose in Trent's throat.

He cleared it and swallowed hard. "Nothing—just a scrape." He flipped on the tap and reached for the soap.

Mary put a hand on his back and peered around his arm to see the injury. "Does it need stitches?"

Her kindness made his eyes sting. "No, Gran." He couldn't handle her compassion right now. He was already on an emotional edge. "Can't you just leave me alone?" he snapped.

Mary stepped back and stared at him. He never raised his voice to his grandmother. Shame flared hot in his cheeks and still she stared. He turned the water off and with his hands dripping, he braced his arms against the edge of the sink. He closed his eyes and lowered his chin. "I'm sorry, Gran."

Mary stood silent for several seconds. "What's got you so upset, son? Can I help?"

Trent shook his head, more to himself than in answer. He opened his eyes, but didn't meet hers. "Tonya's found another man."

Silence snaked around the room. Mary didn't say anything but she pursed her mouth closed and raised her white eyebrows. The silent accusation made Trent's ears hot. He wiped his face on his shirtsleeve and cleared his throat.

"Isn't that what you said you wanted?" She asked in a voice as soft as a breeze.

Trent shrugged and hung his head.

Mary leaned against the counter next to him and dipped her head to look him in the eye. "So, what are you going to do about it?"

10

———

s brothers we stand – related by the purity of our race – by the purity of our blood. I belong.

A SLY SMILE spread across my face. I wasn't sure what kind of luck I tripped upon, but this little town had the makings of the perfect treasure trove. Plenty of food and delightful… entertainment. The people were simple and trusting which allowed me to sneak in and out at will. The stooges even left their houses unlocked, practically inviting me to come in and take what I wanted. But today things got even better.

Today, I found myself a car. The door had been unlocked, and the keys dangled in the ignition. Hard to believe, twice in one mission, once in Chicago—where folks ought to know better—and once here. What was the matter with people? Idiots. They deserved what they got.

I knew it wasn't smart to steal the car from a nearby town but I was sick of walking. It was also becoming a real challenge to carry my loot without getting caught. If someone stopped me, how would I explain carrying a warm pie or a dead chicken down the road by its feet? A chuckle rolled up from my chest. I would have stolen a car either way, but it was impossible for me to resist the fun of taking one parked right in front of the Sheriff's Office.

The added beauty of it all was when I drove up into the mountains to find a good place to camp and hide the car, I came across an abandoned mine. It was the perfect place to hide out for a while until things cooled down, and it was far enough away from town that I could relax. For now, Flint River provided me with everything I needed.

The ceiling of the mine had a natural air vent and campfire smoke escaped through it like a chimney. This meant I could stay inside my shelter to cook. The mine made a great hiding place for any new items I might snap up for my comfort. This afternoon I lifted a couple of blankets off of someone's porch. I looked forward to sleeping on them, hidden from the bitter wind that whipped up at night.

The timeframe that Jed insisted I stay away was going to be a whole lot more comfortable than I first thought. My hide-out was warm and dry and I had plenty of food. I'd been living on roasted chicken, compliments of a little old lady who lived by herself at the edge of town. Of course, that needed to change. After all, how long could a man live on chicken alone?

The town was having a big festival on Saturday. It would be easy to blend in and enjoy the festivities, giving me a nice diversion while I waited for clearance to return to the compound. I hadn't seen or heard any news and didn't know if the cops were still investigating the bombing or not.

I smiled at the thought of Jedediah Hotchkiss. Jed wasn't my uncle by blood, but he was my personal hero. The thought of disappointing the man closed my throat. Uncle Jed was hard to please on a good day, but the mission failure was unacceptable. All the time and work we put in getting ready for the bombing and bank robbery was wasted. I was glad I wasn't home when Uncle Jed found out. There was certainly hell to pay. Now we needed to find out who the mole was, what information was leaked, and who it was leaked to.

Jed would regroup and come up with another plan before long. It was crucial to our strategy to have enough money to supply an arsenal. Jed taught me about the corrupt government and how if we didn't fight back, we were just as corrupt as they were. He taught me to be proud of my race and creed. We learned we had to take a stand or we'd lose our way of life. Uncle Jed raised an army using his fiery speeches and our regiment was ready to do everything in our power to uphold our values and maintain the purity of our race.

I shivered. It was cold out, but I saw no sense in lighting a fire tonight since it was so late. I was tired and had a full belly. The blankets called to me and I wormed my way down deep into their folds. Tomorrow, I'd call Uncle Jed and ask for updated orders, but tonight I'd close my eyes and fantasize about all the things I thirsted to do to a particularly alluring woman with soft white skin.

11

Tonya gave her attention to Kathy Ball when she stood in front of the circle of chairs. Her colorful flowing skirt reminded Tonya of a watercolor painting. Kathy's brown hair hung in a long braid down her back and showed off her handmade turquoise earrings.

"Good evening everyone. Let's quiet down and get started," Kathy trilled.

Bob, who was the chairman of the Harvest Festival Committee, hefted his heavy form out of a metal folding chair and made his way up to the front. "Thank you, Kathy."

She pinched her lips together and sniffed at Bob when he patted her on the shoulder and gestured for her to take a seat. Deflated, Kathy drifted back to her chair. He tapped a stack of papers on the table to even up the edge and peered down at the top page, adjusting his reading glasses.

"Thanks for coming out tonight, everyone. We've passed out a list of items that still need attention. Please check it over. We have addressed some of these items in the last couple of days, for example, the port-o-potty mix-up." With a silly grin on his face, Bob eyed at each person. "I'm happy to announce that as of this afternoon, the Sano-let Corporation has agreed to have twenty port-o-potties, ten at each end of the park." He chuckled. "Glad that was settled or we could have been in deep do-do."

The members of the committee groaned. Tonya smirked and sent Bob a wink.

Alice raised her hand. "How soon can the vendors set up their booths?"

Bob pointed to the map of the festival grounds hanging on a portable whiteboard. "Trucks will be allowed to enter the south entrance on Friday at noon." He ambled over and aimed a thick finger at the entrance on the map. "We've asked most vendors to park and use wagons or carts to carry their items across the grass."

Kathy waved her hand to get Bob's attention. "I can be at the park on Friday afternoon to monitor the setup. Who can help me?" She glanced pointedly around the room. Most of the committee members owned businesses in town and didn't want to spend an additional afternoon away from work. People studied their phones or fingernails until their silence prodded Tonya to raise her hand.

"My last client is at one o'clock, so I could be there by two-thirty."

"You're still planning to be at the entrance gate on Saturday morning too though, aren't you?" Kathy asked, her eyes grew wide.

Tonya let out an exasperated puff of air. "Yes. I'll be there too."

"Good, because I'm simply not a morning person." Kathy pulled her braid to the front of her shoulder.

Bob's wife, Anita, leaned over and whispered behind her hand to Tonya. "You don't always have to say yes, you know."

Tonya smiled and gave Anita's leg a gentle squeeze.

"I guess you're destined to be in the twenty percent of people who volunteer for everything."

Tonya shrugged. The annual Harvest Festival was her favorite town celebration all year, and she would do whatever it took to make sure it happened.

Kathy gathered a stack of handouts. "There's a copy of the vendor map in your packets and a list of all the rules." She passed a stapled bundle to everyone. "Please find your booth's location and make plans for transporting your wares, along with any tables and chairs you may need."

Tonya glanced through the paperwork and raised her hand. "I don't see our face-painting booth on the map, Kathy."

"Yes, it's there. Right where it is every year, next to the gazebo."

Tonya looked again, but the site they normally occupied was assigned to the Wild-life Raptor Display. She shook her head. This was the kind of thing that could make Kathy get overheated and screechy.

"I think we need to find another spot. How about squeezing into a space on the games alley?" Murmurs of agreement sounded from the group. Bob stared at the large map. He rubbed his chin and nodded his head.

"No." Kathy's eyes widened and darted from person to person. "Face painting isn't a game."

Tonya closed her eyes and breathed in a dose of patience. No matter what her suggestion was, she knew Kathy would be against it. The woman enjoyed being contrary just for the sake of it.

In a mild tone, Tonya said, "Well, I suppose we are more like a game than food or trinkets."

Kathy placed her hands on her hips. "Maybe, but face-painting is more of an arts and crafts."

Tonya studied her map for a few more minutes. "There's

no more room in the arts and crafts section. Besides, don't you think more children will be in the game area than in arts and crafts?"

Bob cleared his throat. "Let's put it to a vote. All in favor of the face-painting booth being located in the games area say 'Aye'."

Everyone except for Kathy said, 'Aye'.

"Those opposed?"

Kathy raised her hand and looked around the room for support. Finding none, she said, "Oh fine. Let's give Tonya her way—as usual." She held her arms in surrender.

Tonya willed her eyes to focus on the map in front of her rather than roll them, or worse glare at Kathy. After all, she had to spend an entire day painting little faces in the same booth with the woman. It was better to let the comment go undefended and hope she wasn't still grouchy about it on Saturday.

Bob nodded at Tonya with an encouraging smile. Everyone on the committee understood the way things were. Change happened slow-to-never in Flint River.

The other agenda items were discussed and resolved before the group enjoyed refreshments. Alice brought chocolate cookies with white chips and pecans, and Kathy provided coffee.

Through a mouthful of crumbs Bob asked, "Tonya, are you going to bring your new boyfriend to the festival?"

"He's not my boyfriend, but yes, Levi is coming."

Bob's eyebrows creased the flesh above them when they rose. "If he's not your boyfriend, why did you kiss him in the middle of the street?"

"Are you spreading gossip, Bob Tillman?" Anita came up behind him bringing him a cup of coffee.

He took the cup. "Thanks, hon." He sipped and said, "It's not gossip if people saw them."

Anita scowled. "Did you see them?"

"Well, no. But I heard it from a reliable source."

Tonya rolled her lips between her teeth and bit down to keep from laughing at Bob's logic and shook her head. "It's definitely gossip, Bob, but don't worry. It also happens to be true. I kissed Levi right there on Main Street. Satisfied?" She'd known the kiss would be fodder for gossip and Bob meant no harm. He and Anita were like family. They had kept a wing over Tonya after her mother died. She knew she wouldn't have been able to survive the loss without them. And she certainly couldn't have qualified for her business loan if Bob hadn't co-signed.

Bob, missing Tonya's point, turned to Anita. "See."

Anita grabbed her husband by the arm. "I'm sorry for him." She chuckled. "Come on Mr. Tillman, let's go home. I've a busy day tomorrow."

Bob followed his wife, but looked back over his shoulder. "I'd like to meet him," he said in his best fatherly tone.

Tonya wiggled her fingers in a goodbye wave. "I'll introduce you on Saturday. Goodnight, you two."

Kathy approached with a hopeful smile and her hands held together at her chest. "So, it's true then?"

Tonya blinked and took a quick sip of her coffee to avoid answering.

"You're finally letting Trent go?"

Unexpected tears pricked Tonya's eyes. "Oh! This coffee is hotter than I expected," she said to cover. She waved her hand as though to cool her mouth. "It's not as simple as that," she answered. "But yes. Trent and I are over."

Tonya avoided more conversation by pretending to study the event map. She thought of how Trent and she had gone to the festival together every year since... forever. They always rode the Egg Beater. He sat on the outside of the car and the centrifugal force of the ride pushed her body tight into his. She would miss that tradition and so many others, but it was time to start a few new ones with Levi.

12

September 17th. He knew she'd be here. Trent went to the cemetery with Tonya every year since she lost her mom. He'd be here for her this year too, even if he wasn't standing next to her. This ran deeper than personal differences.

Trent parked behind her car on the gravel road and looked up the hill. Tonya knelt by her mother's grave. She hadn't waited for him. He supposed she didn't expect him to come, didn't expect his support.

A call rang through the touch-screen control panel on his truck. He pushed the tab to accept. "Hey Tom, what's up?"

"You coming by later?"

"Yep. I'll be there in about an hour. I'm at the cemetery."

"Oh, yeah. It's that time of year, isn't it? Tonya asked you to go with her?"

"Some things don't need asking."

"I guess Tonya's feeling pretty fragile?"

Trent watched Tonya through his windshield. She looked so small and vulnerable crouched there all alone. A pastel splash of color on the dull overcast afternoon. A quick smile flashed across his face. In reality, he knew she was anything but vulnerable. That girl was a fighter. He thought about how she'd had to scrape and fight for everything she ever owned. Trent was proud of her grit and tenacity.

"It's always a tough day for her." Trent reached for his hat. "Hey, Tom, I gotta go. I'll be over in a bit."

"Okay, man. See ya."

Trent got out of his truck and leaned against the grille, giving Tonya her privacy. He chewed on his lower lip as his mind tiptoed through the years. After Tonya's mom died, Tonya put herself through beauty school by working at Alice's diner and setting aside every cent. By then, her sister, Brandy, had moved to Seattle. The Tillmans took to treating Tonya like the daughter they never had which had been a saving grace to all three of them.

Tom's admonishment from a week ago interrupted his thoughts. "She couldn't have known. You can't really blame her," Tom had said. Trent rubbed the back of his forearm across his face trying to rub his friend's statement away.

Tonya arranged the flowers she brought into a metal vase attached to the gravestone and pushed herself to her feet. She brushed dead leaves from her wide-legged slacks. Her hair hung down in a luscious wave. She looked like a young, blonde Katharine Hepburn.

When she turned toward the road, their eyes met for a moment. Tonya paused, pressing her lips together, before she dropped her gaze and went to him. Trent pushed up from the truck and waited for her. She walked straight into his arms and he held her, rubbing his hand up and down her back. He pressed a soft kiss on her hair and breathed in her musky perfume.

"Thanks for coming," she said into his chest.

"Always."

Tonya pulled back and without meeting his eye, went to her car, got in, and drove away.

Loss and regret hit Trent full force, center-mass, and crushed his chest. He rubbed the back of his neck as he watched her car disappear behind the trees at the bend in the road. Trent turned and braced his hands on the hood of his truck. He hung his head and waited until it no longer hurt to breathe.

Trent wandered over to the spot where the Stone family plots were and approached the two grave markers. A large one stood above the graves of both his parents who were killed in a car accident when he was two years old. He had no memory of them other than pictures and the stories he'd been told. A smaller, flat stone marked the resting place of James Stone, Trent's Pop. He was the man who Trent looked on as a father. Along with Gran, Pop raised Trent and his brothers after the death of their parents.

Trent squatted down and pulled an odd weed and several grass clumps that had grown over the granite. He swept away dirt and dried leaves. "I miss you, Pop." The words tripped in his throat.

His grandpa's voice echoed in his mind. "Days are short, son. Don't leave for tomorrow what needs to be done today. You never know if tomorrow's going to come." Trent's lip curled into a half-smile. He had garnered his work ethic from Pop, and also his fiery brand of confidence. Gran called it pride, and he supposed she was right. Gran had always been there to temper Pop's brass. She was the trowel that smoothed his rough cement before it dried hard.

Trent's thoughts floated back to Tonya. She might not use a direct approach like Gran does, but she did have a way of smoothing his ruffled feathers when something stuck in his craw. All through high school she'd run interference between him and his little brother, Jack.

Jack—another loss. Trent shook his head to clear the emotional weight and stood.

"I hope I'm making you proud, Pop," he said out loud. "Gran and I are taking good care of each other and the ranch." He scuffed the dirt with the heel of his boot. "I love you." Trent closed his eyes.

"You'd best swallow that pride of yours, son. Like your Gran always says, pride goeth before a fall." Pop's voice was as clear as if he were standing next to him.

13

———————

Saturday was the kind of autumn day Tonya wanted to drink in. The temperature was cool, but the sun warmed her skin as she walked down Main Street toward the park. Booths were already set up around the perimeter of the grassy area waiting for their vendors to occupy them. Wonderful scents greeted her when she entered the festival grounds. Hot spiced cider whispered to her, and she made her way to Alice's booth. Alice always provided spiced cider and caramel corn during the day while her secret chili recipe brewed back at her diner. She won the chili cook-off almost every year.

Artisans from as far as Butte and Missoula, as well as local craftspeople, set up their wares on long tables. Booths with caramel apples, taffy, and fudge, along with every flavor of popcorn imaginable lined the midway. One food truck prepared succulent turkey legs roasting on spits. The juices dripped down and flavored cobs of corn cooking on tines below. The greasy but intoxicating scent of deep-fried funnel cakes permeated the air. In her desire to resist that confection, Tonya rushed past a cart serving breakfast burritos and nachos, and another that offered Philly cheesesteak sandwiches. The options seemed endless. No one would go hungry today.

Tonya spoke with Levi on the phone during the week and he promised to meet her at the town park the afternoon of the Festival.

"Do you want me to drive out and get you? I'd be happy to." Tonya said as she scanned the dress options in her tiny closet.

"Didn't you say you'd be busy setting up?" Levi's voice was smooth over the phone. "It won't be hard to get a ride over. Not on a Saturday."

Tonya savored a sense of relief. As soon as the offer to drive him came out of her mouth, she realized it would be next to impossible to make the two-hour round trip and get back before time to set up. She spent months with the others on the Festival Committee planning and arranging everything for the event and didn't want to leave any of them hanging.

Tonya wound her way through the set-up to the tent that held the pumpkin carving contest. "The pumpkins sure are large this year." She smiled at Bob and Anita. Everyone in town considered Anita to be the local craft expert and she judged all the creative competitions at the festival. The Halloween costume contest and parade held at dusk were the highlight of the day.

"Yes." Anita laughed. "Hopefully, the size will force the kids to take a bit longer to carve them this year."

Tonya sipped her cider and the cinnamony steam soothed her sinuses. "Maybe. They seem to think it's more of a race than a work of art." She waggled her fingers in farewell and moved off toward her face-painting booth. Tonya and Kathy shared the task of creating magical masks on the skin of children. They painted butterflies, tigers, zombies, superheroes, flowers, or whatever the children's imagination devised.

"Good morning, Kathy. Ready for the rush?" Tonya set her cider and a tote bag filled with face-paints down on the table at the back of the tent.

"As ready as I'll ever be." Kathy twisted her braid around her wrist. "You sure took your time getting here this morning."

Tonya's neck stiffened. "I stopped by to visit Bob and Anita." She emptied her bag and arranged her paints, glitter, and paint-brushes. She pulled out several packages of baby wipes for fixing mistakes.

Kathy pinched her lips together. "And took the time to get yourself some hot cider."

"The gates don't open for another half hour." Tonya couldn't wait until lines of children kept them too busy to talk. "Have the paper towels and water containers been delivered yet?"

"No. Bob said they'd be here by a quarter-till."

"We still have plenty of time, then." Tonya worked to keep the edge out of her voice.

Tonya's heart lurched even before her eyes fully registered Trent striding down the midway. He carried a large box braced on his shoulder, and Sadie followed him, driving a Gator filled with more boxes. Tonya looked away and pretended to be busy organizing her station.

"Mornin' ladies." Trent nodded to them. "Ain't it a beautiful day for the festival?"

Kathy's limbs seemed to go all gooey. "Good mornin', Trent. Looks like they've already got you working hard." She brazenly ran a hand down Trent's bicep and giggled.

Tonya rolled her eyes to her eyebrows before she turned to greet them. "Good morning, Sadie… Trent." She bent her head back into her bag. A second later, the table shifted.

Trent dropped his heavy box on the surface and propped his elbow on it, grinning. "These are the costumes for the old-fashioned photo booth. You ladies want to dress up like saloon girls and take some pictures with me?"

Kathy kept her hand on Trent's arm and leaned into him. "You tell me when and I'll be there."

Bile swirled at the base of her throat and Tonya gagged. At both of them. Trent was over-the-top and Kathy was even worse for simpering at him.

"I'll only be in the photo if I can be a gun-slinger or Annie Oakley." Tonya answered with a tart snap in her voice.

"You can be whatever you want, darlin'." Trent's warm tone slid under her skin and simmered there.

Damn him. She wished he would go away. It was too hard to see him, let alone talk to him. Did he really think they could suddenly be casual friends? "I'll be invisible then."

Trent chuckled knowingly which infuriated her further. "Suit yourself. Guess it's just me and you, Kath."

Kathy giggled, which sounded idiotic coming from a middle-aged woman. Trent tipped his hat and picked up his box. "See you later." He left to follow Sadie's ATV tracks.

"Why are you so short with him, Tonya? He was only being friendly," Kathy chided.

"Because, we aren't on friendly terms, Kathy, and you know it." Her harsh tone had the desired effect. Kathy stopped talking and got busy with her own paint station.

HUNDREDS OF PEOPLE filled the park with chatter and laughter. Tonya painted her first little face, a lady-bug, and didn't look up from her work again until lunchtime. It was almost noon when Tonya's tummy grumbled for food. She shook out her tired hands and pulled each finger back in turn to stretch out her forearms. "I've got to take a break and get some lunch. Do you want me to bring you something, Kathy?"

"No, I'll take a break when you get back."

Tonya peeled off her paint smock and draped it over her chair. She wandered down the alley of food vendors. Tantalizing aromas drew her in every direction and she couldn't decide what to eat. She stopped to read the menu at a Celtic food truck when a pair of masculine hands slid over her eyes. She squealed with a tremor of surprise.

"Guess who?" A deep voice said in her ear.

A shiver ran down her back. "Levi!" Tonya spun around to face him. "You got here early. I'm impressed."

"It wasn't a problem. Lots of cars were headed this way." He glanced around at the crowded festival.

She nodded. "I'm so glad you're here. Have you had lunch?"

"Not yet."

Tonya glimpsed Trent heading their way, walking with Cade. She kind of liked the idea of Trent seeing her with Levi but the last thing she wanted was another run-in between the two men. She took Levi's arm and pulled him in the opposite direction. "Let's wander around and see what looks good. What type of food do you like?"

"I'm up for about anything but chicken."

"That's because you've never tried the barbeque chicken from Butte Barbeque." Tonya pointed at the line of food trucks. "I think I'm going to get a meat pie from the Culinary Celts."

"Tonya!"

Joscelyn walked toward them and waved. If they stopped to talk to her, then Cade and Trent would join them. Tonya stepped away, but Levi turned toward the voice. It was too late to escape.

She stifled a sigh. "Hi, Josce. You remember Levi?"

Joscelyn smiled at him. "Of course. How are you? Nice that you could come today."

Levi held his hand out to Joscelyn. "Yeah, looks like a good time. Lots of people."

"I'm amazed. Mary told me folks come from all over western Montana for this event, but I didn't picture this many." Joscelyn noticed Cade approaching and waved.

"Hi beautiful." Cade put an arm around Joscelyn and kissed her cheek. He whispered something in her ear that caused her cheeks to bloom. Tonya's heart constricted.

"Barrett." Trent crossed his arms over his chest. "I'm surprised to see you here." The hair on the back of Tonya's neck prickled. Tonya recognized the challenging tone in Trent's voice that accompanied the knot forming in his jaw. She slipped her arm through Levi's, ready to pull him away.

"I don't know why," Levi squared his shoulders and leaned slightly in Trent's direction. "It's still a free country."

Trent's eyes narrowed. "You sure get around a lot considering you don't own a car and work way out in Sula." He slid his hands down to his hips.

"Guess I'm a resourceful guy." Levi took a small step toward Trent and raised his chin. Tonya gripped Levi's arm, irritated at the abundance of testosterone in the air.

Cade shouldered his way in front of Trent before the posturing could go any further. "Glad you could make it." He offered Levi his hand. "Joscelyn tells me you're a friend of Tonya's. I'm Cade Stone. Nice to meet you."

Trent and Levi continued their stare-down. Tonya pulled on Levi's arm. "Levi," she said, in a brittle tone. He shrugged her hand away. Her mouth dropped open, and she closed it again, blinking in embarrassment.

Levi's eyes flickered toward Cade and he gave his head a slight shake. "Yeah, nice to meet you too. Fun times." Sarcasm laced his voice.

"They can be." Cade gripped his brother's shoulder. "Come on, little brother. You were going to buy me lunch." Cade took Joscelyn's hand, and they all walked away together. Joscelyn glanced apologetically over her shoulder at Tonya as they left.

Levi turned back to Tonya. "I don't know what you ever saw in that guy."

Indignation rooted in her chest and words formed on her tongue to defend Trent, after all, Levi wasn't blameless. But the emotion took flight. It wasn't worth the words.

"Let's just avoid Trent today and have fun." She reached for Levi's hand and pulled. "How about we go through the haunted house before lunch?"

Levi's eyes darkened and a tight smile curled his lips. "You like being scared?"

14

———————

Monday afternoon, Trent strode through the diner door and waved at Alice on his way to where Cade sat waiting for him. "Hey," he said as he took off his cowboy hat. He tossed it on the table and slid into the booth.

"Hey." Cade waited for Alice to set down two glasses of iced tea. "How's it hangin'?"

"Long and loose," Trent quipped.

"I don't know. Seems a little bent out of shape to me."

Trent picked up the menu and held it up so his brother couldn't see his face.

Cade pressed the issue. "Looks like Tonya has a new guy in her life?"

Trent swallowed hard and bit down, clenching his teeth till he thought he might crack a molar. He slapped the laminated sheet back onto the table. "He's not her new guy."

Alice spoke from two tables away. "That's not what I heard." The brothers glanced over at her. "I heard that man kissed Tonya, good and plenty, right under the streetlight on Main Street last week, in front of God and everybody."

Trent's Adam's apple bobbed up and down and he wiped his hand over his mouth. It wasn't the first public kiss he'd heard about or seen, if you count the anonymous text. He turned back to Cade. "I thought we were here to talk about taking the cattle to market? Can we stick to that?"

"We are. It's just that the chip on your shoulder is so big I can't seem to get around it."

"It's a busy time of year, as you know, and I don't have time to sit around gossiping like a couple of old biddies."

Cade cocked his head and studied Trent's face. "So you're telling me it isn't about Tonya?"

Trent met Cade's eyes and couldn't evade him. He sighed, "She's being a damn fool, and it's pissing me off."

"What do you mean?" Cade took a long sip of his iced tea and watched Trent over the top of his glass.

Trent tucked the menu behind the napkin holder on the table. He already knew what he'd order, anyway. "Did you know she picked the guy up hitch-hiking? She could have been kidnapped and hurt... even killed." The rage that rose up his throat intermingled with fear and threatened to choke him. "How can she be so naïve?"

Cade shrugged and set his glass on the paper napkin. "Okay. So it's reckless to pick up hitch-hikers, but if he was going to hurt her, he would have done it by now."

Trent glared at Cade. "You don't know that. Besides, I've got a bad feeling about him. My gut tells me he's not what he claims to be."

"Buddy, your gut is so full of jealousy, you don't know what it's telling you."

Trent picked up a fork and tapped it on the table in an agitated rhythm. "I'm not jealous. I just don't want Tonya to get hurt. I don't know how to protect her. She won't listen to me."

"Why do you think she needs protecting?"

Trent stared hard at his brother, his breath slamming in and out of his lungs. "I can't fail her like I failed Joscelyn." The words scraped low and sharp across his throat like broken glass.

Cade reached forward and gripped Trent's forearm hard. "Look man, I understand the kind of guilt you're feeling—more than you know. The same terrible images play through my mind too." His gray eyes darkened. "But *you* did not fail. If anyone screwed up that night, it was me. You didn't do anything wrong, Trent. It's only by the grace of God we all made it through." Cade released Trent and sat back against the booth.

"I can't let something horrible like that happen again. Not if I can prevent it."

"I get that. But you don't have any reason to think something bad will happen. And if you don't want Tonya in your life, then you gotta let her go. You're driving yourself and everyone else crazy."

Trent tossed the fork onto the table in a clatter.

In a slow-motion whirlwind, the diner door opened and Hilde Mavers shuffled in. She looked around the restaurant before asking, "Has anyone seen the Sheriff?" Her white, patent-leather purse hung by its strap from one arm and the other hand fluttered above her head. "He's not in his office."

Trent slid down in the booth and hid his face in his hands. He loved Hilde, but he didn't have the energy right now.

Cade stood and went to her. "What's the matter, Miss Hilde?"

"Hello, Caedon. I'm sure you heard my car was stolen," she croaked.

Cade nodded and pulled out a nearby chair for the woman and helped her sit. "I'm sorry about that. Any word?"

"No, and now my axe and maul are missing as well."

Trent couldn't resist his concern for the old woman. He scooted out of his seat and drew his phone out of his back pocket. "I'll call Tom on his cell." He crouched before Miss Hilde and punched the numbers on his screen. Trent smiled at the woman and patted her hand while he waited for the Sheriff to answer.

Sheriff Dietrich came to the diner in response to Trent's call. He walked through the door and shot an exasperated glare at Trent and then Hilde. "What's this about someone stealing from you again, Miss Hilde?"

"Don't give me any attitude, Thomas Dietrich. You didn't believe me when I told you my chickens and my car were stolen either."

Tom ran a hand over his mouth and chin. He pulled out a chair next to the old woman and straddled it backwards. "I don't mean to have an attitude, Miss Hilde. But, I am wondering if maybe you left your axe and maul somewhere and you don't remember." He leaned forward, resting his arms on the back of the chair. "That's happened before, remember?"

"You are sassing me again, and I don't like it," Hilde huffed. "I ought to wash your mouth with soap. I know my tools were in the woodshed last night. Now they're gone."

Trent stood and winked at Cade over the top of Hilde's head before he leaned down. "What were you doing with an axe and maul anyway, Miss Hilde? You shouldn't be trying to chop wood at your age." The feisty old woman turned her angry eyes to Trent. He offered a reconciliatory smile and held up his hands in surrender. "What I mean to say is, Cade and I can come over this evening after supper and chop you up some wood before the cold weather sets in."

Cade shot Trent a glare which he returned with a wicked grin.

Hilde folded her hands and rested them on top of her

purse. "If you insist, but you'll have to bring your own axe." She turned to Tom. "Because someone stole mine."

Tom adjusted his gun belt. "Miss Hilde, you've had a hard week. And I've been doing everything I can to find your car. I think you ought to get yourself a guard dog." He stood and put a hand under Hilde's elbow to help her to her feet. "Let's go up to my office and file another report." He cocked his head at Trent. "Didn't you say your ranch hand's dog had puppies a couple of weeks ago?"

Trent nodded, "That's right. Randy's got a litter of blue heeler pups."

"I don't want a dog. What I need is my car." Hilde peered up at the men.

"Tom, you ought to check out the guy Tonya brought into town. He isn't from around here and doesn't own a car even though he works an hour away. I wouldn't be at all surprised if he's the guy who stole Hilde's."

Tom said, "That's quite a leap. There are lots of people who don't own cars. Doesn't mean they'll steal one. And what would he need with an axe and maul?"

Cade smirked and shook his head. "I gotta get back to the ranch. Work to do." He waved to Alice. "Can I get that burger to go?"

Trent helped Hilde to her feet. "I'm going to go ask Tonya what she knows. Can't hurt."

"Leave her alone." Cade stared Trent in the eye.

Trent ignored his brother and left the diner. He strode up the sidewalk to the beauty salon. When he entered the shop, Tonya was sitting at the reception desk checking her appointment book.

"Hey," Trent said.

Tonya looked up and raised her eyebrows at him but said nothing. He did his best to ignore the pink-tinted curl swept up in Tonya's hairdo. An image of him pulling the pins out of her hair and combing his fingers through it until it hung long and loose flashed through his mind. He blinked his eyes to chase the tantalizing vision away.

"Someone stole Hilde's car last week and now she's missing her wood chopping tools."

"That's too bad." Tonya set her pencil down. "But, what does that have to do with me?"

"Nothin'… directly. I was just wondering where Barrett is? I saw your car parked outside." Trent shoved his hands in his jean pockets.

Tonya narrowed her eyes at him. "He's at work."

"Did you drive him over there?"

"Oh, for crying out the window, Trent. Are you accusing Levi of something?" She stood, her pencil rolled to the floor. "Get out." She pointed toward the door. "If Tom wants to ask me questions, that's one thing. You no longer have a right to do so." She came around the desk and pushed Trent toward the exit. "Go away, Trent."

He started to argue but no words formed. They had always had a rocky relationship, but Tonya never pushed him away. He had to admit to himself he didn't like it. In the past she always tried to keep him close. He was used to her chasing after him.

"But—"

"No buts, just go."

When the door closed, Trent stood on the walk outside trying to breathe through the pressure in his chest. He glanced at Tonya's car, parked in front of her shop. Tonya's car was here, and that begged the question of how Levi got himself all the way over to Sula. Trent pivoted and struck out toward the Sheriff's Office. Tom needed to investigate Levi Barrett.

15

It had been a long week getting the ranch prepped for the coming winter. After work on Friday afternoon, Trent drove into town looking forward to a cold beer with Tom. But first, he had to stop by the Sapphire Emporium. Matthew wanted to borrow his camera and Trent promised to drop it off.

"Hey, Trent." Matthew said, his full lips spreading across his face in a wide smile.

Trent nodded and held up his camera. "Bringing this in for you. How's your week been?"

"Slow." Matthew chuckled. "Thanks for lending it to me."

Trent handed him the case, and Matthew ran his thumbs over the leather. He set it on the counter and opened the latch with care.

"Do you know how to use it?" Trent reached in and pulled out the camera. "I can show you a few things, if you want."

"It isn't too difficult is it? Point and click? What I'm having a hard time learning is how to navigate all the different social media sites I want to post the pictures on. Know anything about that?"

Trent laughed. "Not me. I stay as far away from that hornet's nest as I can."

"I did too until I realized I could advertise all over the country with just a few clicks." Matthew set the camera on a black-velvet gem display pad. "I'm thinking of opening an online shop. Business can't help but get better."

"I guess."

"I'm going to hike up to the old abandoned sapphire mine and take pictures. Then I'll try to get some nice shots of the gems. Some of the most colorful sapphires in the world come from around here you know. Most folks don't even know that sapphires come in other colors than blue. It's time to inform the public." Matthew's laugh was a low rumble in his chest that ended in a cough.

"Sounds like a good plan." Trent shrugged. "Happy to help any way I can, but my camera is a little more complicated than point and click. I ought to show you a few things."

"I'm going out tomorrow morning. Want to come?"

Trent cocked his head and thought about it. "Sure, I could do that. I'm usually done feeding around seven."

"I wasn't planning to go hiking until after breakfast. Want to meet at Alice's? My treat for your letting me borrow your camera." Matthew patted the case. "When do you need it back?"

"Breakfast sounds great and you can keep the camera as long as you need to."

"Thanks. I'll take good care of it."

"I know you will." A large pink sapphire wrapped in a white gold pendant caught Trent's eye. He pointed, "That sure is pretty."

"Yes, it's a custom design." Matthew's dark eyes sparkled. "Tonya was in here admiring it just the other day."

"It looks like something she'd love." Trent mumbled before clearing his throat. "When was she in here?"

Matthew glanced up at the ceiling. "Well, let me think." He rubbed his gray five o'clock shadow. "Must have been over the weekend. That's when Levi's in town and he was in here with her too."

Trent's focus moved to Matthew. "He isn't planning on getting it for her is he?"

"Well… I don't know. They looked at it. Took it out of the case and Tonya tried it on." A ghost of a smile swirled around the older man's mouth. "He asked how much it cost."

Trent closed his eyes briefly and waited out the green wave that sloshed in his gut. "I'll take it."

Matthew didn't even try to hide his self-satisfied grin. "You will?" A chuckle escaped under his breath. "Don't you want to know the price?"

"No. Just wrap it up." Trent pulled out his wallet and tossed a credit card on the counter. *What the hell am I doing?*

Matthew unlocked the cabinet and lifted the necklace out. "You planning on giving this to Tonya?" he asked without looking up.

"Hell, I don't know." Trent took three steps away and turned and paced back. "All I know is that Barrett sure as hell isn't going to."

With a new, barely controlled expression on his face, Matthew finished up the sales transaction. "Thank you for your business and thanks for the camera. I'll see you in the morning."

"Yeah, and don't think I don't know what just happened here, Matthew."

Matthew laughed. "I think you ought to give it to her. It might help—you never know."

"Keep this to yourself, will you?"

"Of course. Discretion is my creed."

Trent pushed open the door to leave and Matthew called out, "You best fix things before it's too late."

"Mind your own business, old man." Trent looked back at his friend and winked. He almost collided with two middle-aged women walking by the shop on his way out.

Trent locked the jewelry box in the glove compartment of his truck and walked toward the Sheriff's Office. He and Tom had plans for some evening fishing. His pace slowed as he sauntered by Tonya's shop and he tried to peer in, but the glare reflected his own image. Frustrated, he crossed the street.

The bench outside the Sheriff's Office provided not only a place to wait, but a perfect view of the front of the beauty shop. He wondered if Tonya would come out. Trent wasn't used to waiting on Tonya. Usually she was the one who did the chasing. That modus operandi had worked for him for years, but now it seemed she genuinely didn't want him around. Something like heartburn ignited in his chest and he swallowed against it. She deserved better than the way he'd treated her.

Trent slid his phone out to check the time. Tom was supposed to be out there already, so Trent went inside to see what was taking him so long.

"Tom, you coming, or what?"

Tom's muffled answer came from the back room across from the jail cell.

Trent searched for his friend. "What are you doing back here?"

Tom backed out of the storage closet. "I've been cleaning out this closet. Funny, the things you find stuffed in places like this."

"Yeah, well, we're supposed to be fishing."

"I know, give me a minute. I need to lock up. There's some old rifles, ammo, and other stuff I have to keep safe. Hard to believe there's been weapons sitting back here all these years, and no one knew."

Tom locked the closet and gathered his fishing pole and tackle box. "Ready?"

"More than you know." Trent held the door open for Tom and followed him out.

Tom jutted his chin toward Trent's truck. "Let me put my gear in the back, then if you don't mind, I'd like to go see Tonya for a minute."

"What for?"

"I think you might be right about Miss Hilde's car, after all. I've searched all over town for it and haven't seen it anywhere." The men crossed the street to Trent's dually.

Trent chuckled. "I know she's forgetful, but I *saw* her park right in front of your office."

"Well, Hilde is getting on in years and she'd been going on about the ridiculous chicken robbery thing out at her place. But, I have scoured the town and I can't find her car. No one else has seen it around either." They stopped at the side of the truck. "At first, I figured you were just trying to cast suspicion on Barrett because you were jealous."

Trent unlocked the back door of his truck and helped Tom put his fishing tackle in the cab.

"Locking your truck these days?" Tom chuckled.

Trent caught the tip of Tom's rod in the rifle-rack hanging across the rear window. "Yeah, with my rifles back here and a car thief on the loose, I figure it's a good idea." He pulled the rod loose and reseated the antique rifle that had been his dad's back into its slot. He ran his hand over the brass-inlaid barrel. "So, now you think maybe Barrett's the one who stole her car?"

"I didn't say that. I just want to ask Tonya a few questions, that's all."

A thick spread of delicious self-righteousness swept through Trent. "I knew it all along. The guy is a thief." He shut the truck door and turned toward the salon. "Let's go."

"Trent, maybe you should wait here."

"Not on your life."

"Fine, but you have to keep your mouth shut." Tom hurried after him. "And take that shit-eating grin off your face."

16

―――――

Early Saturday morning, Trent pulled open the door to Alice's Diner. The place was full with the weekend crowd. Matthew waved at him from a booth by the front window. Trent breathed in the buttery scent of pancakes, bacon, and strong coffee. His stomach rumbled in response.

Across the room, Alice held up her coffee pot and Trent smiled at her and nodded.

She winked. "Be right with you, hon."

Trent slid into the booth across from Matthew. "Mornin'. Looks like we have a nice day for a hike."

"Sure does." Matthew spread a paper napkin on his lap. "I'm glad you're coming. I tried to figure out that camera last night and there are far too many buttons and levers for me to make any sense of."

Trent chuckled. "You won't need to worry about most of them—not for the kind of photos you want."

"Thank the good Lord."

Alice poured Trent's coffee and topped off Matthew's cup. "Your usual?"

"Yes ma'am. Biscuits and gravy, if you please."

"Comin' right up." She turned to Matthew. "How about you? Double order of huckleberry pancakes?"

"No, thanks. I promised my daughter I'd start taking better care of myself. How about a bowl of oatmeal with some fruit?"

Alice spiked one eyebrow. "If you're sure."

Matthew's laugh was deep and slow like molasses. "You don't know my daughter."

"Okay, I'll have breakfast right out for you boys." Alice turned on her rubber-soled shoes and went behind the counter, clipping their order to the chef's wheel.

Trent sipped his coffee. "Where do you want to hike?"

"I figured we'd stay close today, just on the outskirts of town will be fine. No need to head all the way up the mountain until I know what I'm doing with this thing."

After they finished eating, Trent and Matthew walked up Main Street toward the courthouse. When they passed Tonya's shop, Trent glanced as nonchalantly as he could into the window. Three women sat waiting, while Tonya pushed and prodded the hairstyle of a woman sitting in her barber's chair. She didn't notice him, but Matthew nodded.

"You're so in love with that girl, you don't know which way is up."

Trent snapped his eyes forward. "It's over between us Matthew, you know that." Questioning her about Levi yesterday with Tom hadn't helped matters. Tonya wouldn't even look at him when they left.

"I know nothing of the sort."

Trent didn't respond at first but kept walking. "What kind of photos are you thinking of? Landscape or close-ups of gems?"

"Both. I want to get some good photos of the deserted mine up the canyon. That'll give an old-west romantic feel to my advertising. I'll want to get some gems set out in nature and some from inside the shop."

The men rounded the courthouse and walked to where the road changed from asphalt to gravel. They followed an old footpath that veered off in the field to the left, toward the line of trees.

"Maybe you'll let me photograph that pink sapphire before you give it to Tonya." Matthew pulled the lens cap off the camera.

"Come on, Matthew." Trent shook his head. "I thought we were here so I could teach you about my camera, not so you could pester me about my love life."

"We are, but it won't hurt you to hear a little friendly advice. I've been around a whole lot longer than you, and I know a few things."

Trent rolled his eyes, but his crooked grin was fast to follow. They entered the shade of the tall pine trees and sat side by side on a large rock. "Okay. Let's have it."

"The first thing I want to say to you, is although you're my friend and I think mighty highly of you, you are not the world's answer to all women." Trent's eyebrows shot up and he opened his mouth to defend himself, but Matthew raised a hand to stop him. "For as long as I can remember the women of this town have fawned and fretted over you like you were Flint River's own Prince Charming. Worse than that, you've believed it too!"

"Come on, Matthew."

"No—you need to hear me out. I suppose you're not bad to look at and if charm was worth money, you'd be a billion-aire. The problem with all that is, that instead of being happy with the woman you love, it's turned your head and made you wonder if there is greener grass somewhere else. But it doesn't work like that, son."

"I don't think that."

"Well, you sure have acted like you do."

"It's not my fault if some of the ladies 'round here like to flirt with me."

Matthew gave him a hard, skeptical stare. "It absolutely *is* your fault."

Trent got up from the rock and paced up the trail and back. "So, what's your point?"

"All that attention has made you cocky. You think you have the world at your feet. But let me ask you a question. Do you care for any of those women who throw themselves at you?"

Trent shrugged. "I've known most of them since I was a kid. It's just the way things are."

"Well, if you ever want to find true happiness, you better change the 'way things are'. You see, son, Tonya has loved you through thick and thin. She's put up with you strutting around like a peacock for long enough.

"I know you're right." Trent turned away from his friend and perched his hands on his hips. He drew in a deep breath, straining to keep emotion out of his voice. "But it doesn't matter anymore because Tonya and I are over."

"No, Trent. You're wrong." Matthew stood and tugged on Trent's sleeve, forcing him to turn and look at him. He placed an elegant old hand on Trent's arm. "What happened this past summer would have happened anyway. It's true, Tonya made a mistake, but not as big of a mistake as you're making by refusing to forgive her. And what do you think the outcome of all of this will be?"

Trent shrugged again and swallowed the irritation that wanted to bound across his tongue at the old man. "I have forgiven her, but it doesn't matter. She doesn't want me anymore."

Matthew continued. "Tonya's dating another man and

that hasn't happened before. What about you? Do you have someone else you'd like to see, maybe marry?"

"No, but—"

"No." Matthew squeezed Trent's arm, emphasizing his point. "You turned the woman you love away because of your stubborn pride. Have you told her you've forgiven her?"

"No."

"You're going to lose her for good. Is that what you want?"

Trent kicked a rock out of the path and with his hands on his hips he stared hard at the dirt. His whole body tensed.

Matthew continued. "No one's perfect. Everyone makes mistakes and we all have lessons we need to learn. But don't you think it would be better to learn them together, with someone you love?"

Trent swallowed hard. He looked up at his friend and stared him in the eye. He nodded once not trusting himself to speak.

Matthew smiled, his gold tooth glinting in the sun. "Why don't you bring that pretty pink sapphire back into the shop and I'll reset it for you in something more appropriate."

Trent laughed in spite of himself. "Why don't you let me show you how to use that camera instead of yabbering on like some old coot?"

17

Drugs are a tool that blacks and Jews use to enslave whites and keep them dumb and docile. Muds move into our neighborhoods bringing drugs and crime, and take our jobs. It makes me ask, what am I willing to sacrifice to save the white race?

MY PILE of blankets didn't soften the rocks pushing up through the dirt floor. Shifting, I leaned against the cold wall of my hideout and stared into the fire. I ripped a piece of chicken from a leg and chewed. Grease dripped down my chin and I wiped it on my sleeve before tossing the bone into the flames.

A nice stash of supplies was stacking up in the corner. I had gathered everything I needed to survive in the wild, but I longed to go home. The axe was a great find. It was getting colder in the fall evenings and I needed it for firewood. Not to mention, slaughtering chickens was a whole lot easier with the sharp edge. Everything I knew about survival, firearms, politics, and war, I learned from Uncle Jed. He took me under his wing one afternoon, fifteen years ago, when I was only thirteen.

As a runaway, I didn't have a steady place to live. I'd wandered into a cafe—out of money, out of luck, and tweaking. My hope was maybe the waitress would have pity on me and give me something to eat, even scraps off someone's plate. I sat down next to a booth with four men eating lunch. My gut still tightens with the memory of the grinding hunger the scent of their sandwiches and fries caused me that day, and my mouth waters in sympathy.

I couldn't help but stare at their full plates. One of the men growled, "Mind your own business, boy." Which was funny because I wasn't listening in. I was only coveting their food.

The older man stepped in. "Leave him be." He picked up his plate with half a burger and a handful of fries on it. "You hungry, boy?"

I don't remember answering, but the man got up and carried his food over. He sat down in a chair at my table and set his half-full plate in front of me. He waved the waitress over and ordered me a strawberry milkshake. The man was friendly, but honest and direct.

"I'm Jedediah Hotchkiss." He stared at me. "You using drugs?"

I didn't answer, but with my body jitters, I didn't need to.

"Boy, you're better than that. If you take the drugs them wet-backs ship up here, you're just falling into their plan. They're trying to dumb you down and make you weak so you can't fight against their plot to take over our country."

I didn't know what he was talking about. The guy I got my fix from wasn't Mexican, and he cooked the meth in his basement. But Jed was so certain.

"You need to clean yourself up and start being proud to be a white American."

I nodded, willing to agree with anything he said as I gulped down the milkshake.

"You live around here?"

I shrugged. "Sorta."

Jed's shrewd eyes stared at me for a long time. He made his mind up about something and he stood. "Come on, fellas. We're taking this stray back with us." He looked at me. "You got a home now." He gripped my arm and pulled me to my feet.

That was all it took to convince me—food and a little kindness and I was happy to go. I rode in the back of their truck with a scruffy dog named Sam. After miles of bumping along on winding, unpaved forest roads, we pulled up to a hidden gate guarded by men carrying automatic weapons.

The compound became my home and was where Uncle Jed offered me a bed, plenty of food, and a job to do. At first, I fed and cleaned up after the dogs who ran loose on the grounds. Gradually, he gave me more and more responsibility. For the first time in my life, someone valued me.

Uncle Jed cleaned me up and dried me out. I was drug free after three months, and I felt better than I had in forever. It didn't matter that I couldn't leave the compound or have a phone. I'd learned to trust Uncle Jed and no one else. I would do whatever he asked of me.

Now here I was, hiding out in an abandoned mine waiting for permission to go home. Jed's disappointment in me sat in my gut like thickening paste—heavy and cold. I was an exile like the Israelites in Uncle Jed's bible, waiting to be reconciled.

For several days my hideout gave me a sense of freedom, but I'd have to stay inside more often now. A group of hikers passed by early in the morning and almost found me. Luckily, they didn't see me or the old Subaru hidden in the scrub.

The axe would come in handy if anyone started snooping around but I needed a more effective weapon.

Still, my biggest challenge was having enough food. The rabbit snares I set didn't catch much and I couldn't keep stealing chickens. It would be nice if I could hunt bigger game. The problem was I needed a rifle.

After I finished my supper, I went outside to find a spot with cell coverage. I hadn't been able to reach Uncle Jed since I spoke to him on the road from Chicago. The coverage in the mountains was crap. Jed said something about the FBI being on the case. That they suspected there was a third person in the van. I scoffed. *They can search all year but they'll never find me here.*

Still, it was better to hide out for a while than leave any kind of trail to the compound. Our chance at the money from Chicago was screwed, but we'd find another way. We lost that battle, but the war was yet to be won. Dreams of a new America flitted through my mind.

I paced the clearing at the mouth of the mine and held the cheap phone high above my head. Nothing. Damn. Uncle Jed would likely order me to camp out for another couple of weeks, maybe a month, before I made my way into Idaho and back home. I wondered if Laurel ever thought of me. But hell, there would be plenty of time to think about her. Lately my fantasies involved local female options.

My phone finally connected. I stood still and pressed 881488 before Uncle Jed came on the line. When he did, the connection was poor.

"… FBI… tracking… stay in one place… hidden… might be a long… stay out of sight."

"Uncle Jed? You're breaking up. Did you say the FBI is tracking me?"

Static turned to silence.

"Jed? Can you hear me?" I peered at the screen. "Jed?"

With a groan I clicked my phone off. "Damn it!" I marched back inside the mine and slumped down on my blankets. No more daydreaming about it. If the FBI was tracking me, I needed to rig the mine to explode and I had to get a gun. I'd blow away anybody trying to catch me.

18

The bells at the front door of the salon jingled and Tonya called down the stairs, "Be right there."

"Take your time." Levi's deep voice floated up.

Tonya applied a final cloud of hairspray to her up-do, smoothed bright red lipstick over her lips, and blotted her mouth on a tissue. She assessed her red and white polka-dot halter dress with its full skirt, in the mirror. Nodding to herself, she pulled on a white trench coat. This time of year the weather could make a quick change so she added a black scarf to her ensemble and skipped down the stairs.

He gave an appreciative whistle and Tonya smiled. "You like it?" She spun around. The skirt of her dress flared.

"Sure do. You look like an old-time movie star." He held his elbow out to her. "You ready?"

"Let me get my keys and grab my pocketbook." Tonya walked back to her kitchen beyond the curtain and pushed her palm against the flutters in her stomach. *This is a date. A real date. Am I ready for this?* Nausea wrestled with the jitters. She picked up her things and turned with determination. "Do you want to drive?"

Levi let out a small chuckle. "I'd probably better."

Tonya took his arm. "If you're referring to the day we met, that was all your fault. You made me nervous, that's all. I can drive just fine."

"Don't I make you nervous anymore?" Levi turned her and pushed her against the wall next to the front door. He stared into her with eyes so dark their depth seemed unending. "How about now?" He bent his mouth to hers and his lips hovered over hers, barely touching.

Tonya's heart bounced like a pinball. He did make her nervous, only she wasn't sure if it was the fun type of nervous or the kind she should pay attention to. Levi lingered there until sharp pin pricks of yearning teased the base of her skull. Then he kissed her full and deep. His passion chased her worries away and Tonya melted into the kiss. Enjoying his desire.

He pulled back, his gaze searching hers once again. Tonya breathed, "It's not nerves so much as…" She inhaled leaving her sentence unfinished.

Levi chuckled low in his throat. "We could stay…"

"Not a chance, Mister." Tonya slid away. "You promised me a night on the town. You're not getting out of that now." She opened the door and handed Levi the keys to her VW Thing.

She walked to the passenger door and waited, but he tossed the keys into the air and caught them on his way to the driver's side. Tonya opened the door for herself and slid in. *Chivalrous manners are nice, but maybe not necessary.* An image of Trent flashed in her mind but she blinked it away. Tonya wanted this date to be easy and fun even as her heart tripped reluctantly.

On the hour-long drive to Missoula, they listened to Tonya's big-band music. They talked about movies Tonya had seen and concerts she'd been to.

"I don't go out very often." Levi told her when she asked him. "Where are we going to dinner?"

"I was thinking of a nice place I know called the Red Bird." Tonya smoothed her skirt. "It's a little expensive but since it was my idea, it'll be my treat." She held her breath for his reaction.

"Okay, then I'll pay for the movie."

Trent would never let her pay for anything. He said it was the way he was raised, which knowing Mary, was true. But mostly, it was because Trent was old-fashioned. Something they had in common.

"Sounds good," she said. "Turn right on the next street."

The Red Bird's renowned chef served locally grown food, including the meat, but the romantic Art Déco motif and ambiance was what kept Tonya coming back. A hostess led the couple to a white linen-covered table and two white armchairs padded in gold leather. Metallic gold and light-blue filigreed wallpaper reflected the candlelight. She felt like Lana Turner, her favorite old-time movie star.

"This is quite a place," Levi said as he glanced around. "It looks like you. I'm glad you chose it 'cuz I never would have picked a restaurant like this."

Was that a compliment or a derision? She unfolded her napkin, spread it on her lap, and opened the drink menu. "Shall we have wine?"

"I've never liked wine. I'll just have a beer."

The waiter approached and Tonya ordered, "I'll have a glass of pinot noir, please." The waiter nodded and turned to Levi.

"Bud Light."

Tonya bit the inside of her cheek to keep her thoughts from registering on her face. *Bud Light? In a place like this?* Trent was all cowboy, but he knew how to appreciate the finer things in life too. He would have ordered a bottle of wine to share, probably two. Tonya bit down harder. *I have got to stop comparing Levi to Trent. It isn't fair. Levi is his own man, and he deserves a chance.*

She looked the other way when he left his napkin on the table during dinner and asked the waiter to bring his second beer in the can. Instead, she focused on his sense of humor and asked him about his childhood.

"I grew up all over. My dad was a rambler. I'm not sure where my mother was. Dad told me so many different stories about her, I never knew what to believe. I just know she wasn't there." Levi chewed a large bite of steak and spoke around his food. "I was out on my own when I was fairly young."

"How did you manage?"

"Working odd jobs where I could find them."

"Where was the favorite place you lived?"

"Wyoming, I suppose." His eyes took on a faraway look, then he dropped his gaze to his plate and cut off another hunk of steak.

Tonya tasted her chicken piccata. "Where in Wyoming?"

"How about you?" He deftly changed the subject. "You've never lived anywhere else besides Flint River?"

Tonya smiled, "No. I've never even been anywhere outside of Montana, except sometimes when I visit my sister in Seattle. She moved there after high-school. She says she 'broke free', but I love small town life. I'll never leave."

After dinner Tonya checked her phone to see what movies were playing in the local theatres.

Levi patted his stomach. "I'm so full, I don't think I'm up for sitting in a theatre for two hours. How about we walk around downtown?"

"Sure, I guess there aren't really any movies I care about seeing in the theatres anyway."

Levi held her hand as they walked through Caras Park.

When it turned cold on their stroll down the river walk, he slid his arm around her and nuzzled her cheek.

"That tickles." Tonya laughed, but her laughed faded as she gazed into Levi's dark eyes. He grew serious and intense. His mouth sought hers. Sparks flared in her belly and she kissed him back with passion.

"Let's go." Without waiting for her response, Levi lead Tonya back to her car. Her sparks turned to jangled nerves bouncing throughout her system all the way home.

Levi held her hand in the car on the way to Flint River and caressed her palm with his thumb. When they got out of the car, he sat back on the hood and pulled her into his arms. He held her tight against his body and they kissed. Tonya leaned into him, her hands on either side of his face pulling him closer. Electricity sent sharp tingles through her body.

He had her keys, so he unlocked the salon door and followed her inside. Without turning on the light, he pressed her to the wall and pushed himself against her. She recognized his desire—it matched hers. Her body ginned up, spurring her on, yet her heart flagged. Tonya pushed him away and walked to the center of the room. Her heart hammered and her body hummed along to Levi's tune, even though her mind wasn't anxious to follow.

"What's wrong?" Levi sidled up behind her and put his hands on her shoulders. He took her coat off and tossed it on a chair. His arms slid around her and one hand found her breast. Tonya leaned back against him. The vibration in her center urging her on. Levi kissed her neck and pressed himself against her backside. "Let's go upstairs."

Tonya's head shifted back and forth before her thoughts solidified. Then the words came. "No. I'm sorry Levi." She turned to face him. His eyes were dark with lust and she couldn't hold his gaze. "I can't. I'm sorry. I thought I could, but I'm not ready."

"Come on, baby." Levi reached for her and slid his hand behind her head. He pulled her into another deep, fiery kiss. Her breath came fast. Her physical yearning argued with her heart and deep inside, a voice whispered to her conscience.

"No. Really, Levi. I like you, I do. I'm just not ready." She stepped back and when she did, a flash of anger bolted through his eyes. He shuttered them and took several deep breaths.

With his face down, he asked, "What do you mean, you're not ready? You seem ready to me." He chanced a glance at her.

"I know. I realize I'm giving you mixed messages. I'm mixed up myself."

"Is it Stone? Is he why you're not ready?" His tone was bitter and she couldn't blame him.

"Maybe—sort of." Tonya took a deep breath and a step back. "He's made it clear he doesn't want me and I need to move on. I want to spend more time with you, but maybe we can take things a little slower?"

Levi was silent, likely wrestling with his own emotions. He let out a rush of air. "Shit." He rubbed a hand across his mouth. He rested his hands on his hips and took a few steps toward the door before he turned back. "It's late. Any chance I can sleep on your couch? No way I'm getting back to the bunkhouse tonight."

Tonya's face flushed. She hadn't considered how Levi would get home. A blue flame ignited in her chest when she realized he had planned on sleeping here all along. "I don't have a couch and even if I did, you couldn't stay here all night. It's a small town. News of our kiss by the car is probably all around by now, as it is." Tonya opened her purse and pulled out her phone. "Let me call Tom. I'm sure he won't mind if you sleep on a cot at the jail."

"What?"

"Well, where did you expect to sleep?" Ire filled her tone.

"I didn't think we'd be back so late. I guess I…"

"You shouldn't presume."

Levi turned his back to her and dropped his head, tension rolled off his shoulders. After she got off the phone with Tom, he faced her and gave her a tight smile. "I'm sorry, Tonya. You're right. I got carried away, but I'm not going to sleep at the jail."

"Tom said for you to go on over. He's calling Wayne— Deputy Brown will be expecting you."

He sighed. "Great." He obviously wasn't pleased but Levi approached her and put his arms around her waist. "I'll go there tonight, but can we have breakfast together in the morning?" He kissed the tip of her nose. She didn't answer him, so he kissed her nose again and she couldn't help smiling. Levi lifted a hand to her face and held her jaw. He looked deep into her eyes and kissed her. He kept his eyes open and so did she. His breath quickened. "You let me know when you're ready."

19

The next day, Trent stood on the front step of the Sheriff's Office when Tonya left her salon. She carried cloth bags in one hand, so he assumed she was going to the grocery market. He'd had a revealing chat with Tom inside, and now he concentrated on his breathing so he didn't fly into a rage.

Tonya was being foolish with this Barrett guy. She hardly knew the man, yet she drove all over Montana with him. Worst of all she brought him home with her last night. Kathy Ball called Trent that morning to tell him, in vicious detail, she had seen them making out by Tonya's car before they stumbled into the salon together.

Trent closed his eyes against a seething sickness swirling around inside his gut. Tonya called Tom and asked if Levi could sleep at the jail. That didn't mean she hadn't slept with him. It only meant she was trying to protect herself from the small-town gossip.

He crossed the street and followed Tonya, staying in the shadows until she entered the market. She stopped at the door to check her list, dipping her head in that way that made him want to kiss her delicate neck. *Stop it, man. Get a grip.* Trent passed two more storefronts and stood in front of the market doors. They opened for him automatically.

"Good morning, Trent," called the clerk, a heavy brunette he'd known for over fifteen years. He nodded in greeting and glanced around the store. "She's in aisle three, if you're lookin'," she bellowed.

Trent gave the woman an exasperated glance. *Great, now everyone in the store knows I'm here following Tonya.* Oh well, no use wasting good information. He walked toward aisle three. Tonya stood in the middle of the aisle reading the label on spaghetti sauce. She raised her eyebrows first, and hardened eyes followed.

"Yes, Trent? Are you looking for me?" She placed the jar in the basket hanging on her arm.

He strode to her, embarrassment and a queasy anger two-stepping with each other inside his head. "Can we talk—quietly?" he whispered.

"Sure, but it won't do any good and you know it. The whole town is buzzing about me and Levi… and now you storm in here to," she made air quotes with her fingers, "'talk' to me about it." She scoffed, "What do you want, Trent?"

"I do want to talk to you about Levi." He crossed his arms. "I'm worried for your safety. You don't even know this guy and you bring him back to your place in the middle of the night. Anything could happen to you."

Tonya glared at him. "I can't believe you, Trent Stone. If you want to ask me what happened last night, then too damn bad. It's none of your business. It hasn't been your business what I do or who I do it with since you told me you didn't want me in your life anymore."

He swallowed hard. This was not going how he hoped. "I'm just saying I care about you being safe, and I don't think you are with Barrett."

Tonya raised her chin, cocking her head to the side. Her voice slid out low and even. "Are you asking me if we used a condom? Because that isn't any of your goddamn business either!" She turned and walked up the aisle.

Trent would have preferred she'd reached out and slapped him hard across the face. Her verbal slug found its mark deep down, in a protected place he didn't like to show. His stomach roiled and jealousy stuck like thick green phlegm in his throat. He ran a hand through his hair and kept his face down until he was sure there was no more color in his cheeks. Then he took a breath and followed in the direction Tonya went.

He found her in the produce section. "Tonya, that isn't what I meant. I'm sorry. I want to talk to you about staying safe from harm."

Tonya looked back at him and moistened her lips to say something.

He didn't hear her because the movement with her tongue across her lips sent a jolt to his groin. He swallowed. "I'm sorry. I didn't hear what you said."

Tonya's brows drew together. "I said, I'm not in any danger." She shifted her basket to her other arm. "Levi is a good guy. He's kind and funny, and we have a fun time together."

Trent drew a deep breath. "Where did you go last night?"

"Missoula, for dinner and a movie. If it's any of your business. Which it's not." She turned back to the apple bin.

"How did he expect to get home to Sula last night?"

"Trent, none of this has anything to do with you."

"I just want you to see what his game is. He fully expected to spend the night at your place, Tonya. He didn't have a way home."

"Again—none of your business." She turned and walked toward the check-out stand.

Trent reached for her arm. Her basket tipped and apples fell and rolled across the floor. The spaghetti sauce jar shattered, and sauce exploded all over their legs.

"Damn it, Trent! You broke up with me. *You* did. So leave me alone. I can't do this with you. You don't get to have a say in my life, anymore." Tonya's eyes filled with tears and she threw the empty basket on the ground at Trent's feet. She turned and ran out the automatic doors, leaving Trent to deal with the tomato sauce and broken glass.

His heart told him to go after her, but his better judgement stopped him. Instead he called out, "Clean up in produce!"

While he helped pick up the mess, Trent came up with a plan. He knew a guy from college who owned a big cattle operation near Sula. He'd call him and to see if he knew who hired Levi.

Trent was determined to find out more about this guy. There was something fishy about him. He couldn't tell Tonya who to date, but he cared enough to want her to be safe. Trent walked back up the street to his truck, climbed in, and pulled out his phone. He searched for his old school friend's name and dialed the phone number.

"Lawson Cattle Company, how can I help you?" A pleasant female voice answered on the third ring.

"My name is Trent Stone. I'm an old college buddy of Clyde Lawson, and I'm wondering how best to get ahold of him?"

"Hold on a minute, please, Mr. Stone." The woman put him on hold and the theme song from Bonanza played on over the line. Several minutes passed. "Mr. Stone, can I get your number? Mr. Lawson will have to call you back this afternoon. The vet is out just now and they've got a passel of heifer calves in the chute."

"You bet." He gave her his number and started his truck. A

knock on his window gave him a start. He turned to find Wayne Brown glaring in at him.

Trent rolled down the glass. "What is it, Wayne?"

"You're parked in two spots, Stone. I won't give you a ticket this time, but be more careful. It's selfish to take up more than one space." Wayne brushed something invisible from his sleeve.

Trent looked up and down the street. His truck was the only vehicle parked on the block. "You expecting a big rush on the Sheriff's Office in the next hour?"

"That's not the point, Stone. You don't own this town. You have to follow the same rules as everyone else." A wicked gleam entered his eye. "By the way, Tonya's new boyfriend borrowed a cot in the jail last night."

"He's not her boyfriend, Wayne, and I'm already aware." Trent flexed his back muscles and readjusted in his seat. He did not need Wayne Brown poking his sore spots today.

"He didn't come to the jail until after 2:00 a.m. I wonder what those two were doing so late?" Wayne studied his fingernails.

"You won't find any dirt under those nails, Wayne. You'd have to go outside and do some actual work for that."

Wayne sneered. "Nice guy, Levi. I think we could be friends."

Trent revved his engine. "Good. I hope you'll be happy together. I gotta go. I have a real job. See ya 'round, Deputy Dog."

Trent's phone rang as he turned into the drive to his ranch. He answered on the truck's speaker.

"How do, Trent? This sure is a blast from the past. How the hell have ya been?" Clyde's voice was familiar even though Trent hadn't talked to him in near ten years.

"Doing fine, real fine. How about yourself?"

"Fat and happy as ever. I know you didn't call to check up on my health. What's going on?"

"I'm trying to find out about a cowboy who's shown up around here. Says he works for a ranch out Sula way. Have you hired any new hands recently? Say in the last couple of weeks?"

Clyde was silent for a few seconds. "Nope. I do all my hiring in the spring. We pare down in the fall and winter, not as much work. I ain't seen anyone new poking around, but I'll ask for you, if you want."

Ranchers didn't tend to hire this time of year. It was one of the many reasons Trent was suspicious of Levi Barrett and his magic carpet. "That'd be great."

"Hey, we got a big shindig at the Grange tonight, BBQ and square dancing. You ought to come out, it'd be great to see you and catch up."

"I've a long day still ahead of me, so I doubt I'll be up to kickin' up my heels tonight. Let's have dinner sometime soon, though. It'd be great to see you."

"Okay, well, I'll ask around and give you a call tomorrow."

20

One Saturday a month, Tonya gave a full day's-worth of haircuts, styles, and manicures to anyone at the retirement home who signed up the week before. It was first-come, first-serve for the residents and Tonya donated her time and skill, so everyone who wanted to could afford it.

By 9:00 a.m. she arrived at the reception desk with her travel beauty-bag slung over her shoulder. "Good morning, Darla." Tonya greeted the high-school student who worked there on weekends.

"Hi, Miss Anderson. They've already started lining up to see you."

"Great, but I need a cup of coffee first. Full list today?"

"As always." Darla smiled before she picked up an incoming call.

Tonya waved and walked into the break room in search of caffeine. She filled her thermal coffee cup and made her way to the room they used as the beauty shop. Inside, was a swivel chair that was actually an old desk chair, but it did the trick. Someone donated a large mirror that hung on the wall.

A mismatched dresser served as a counter with space for beauty supplies in the drawers.

Tonya scanned the sign-up sheet. Three men's haircuts were scheduled during the first hour and a half. Tonya plugged her phone in and connected it to her portable bluetooth speaker. Music from the World War II era swirled through the small room. Her clients loved that she played songs they recognized.

Mr. Cleary shuffled in, leaned his walking cane on the dresser, and dropped himself into the makeshift barber chair.

"What can I do for you today, Mr. Cleary?"

"Cut and a shave, as usual, my dear."

Tonya smiled at him in the mirror. She glanced at his almost bald head. The haircut wouldn't take more than three minutes, but by a shave, he meant his face, neck and shoulders down past his shirt collar. It seemed like his hair slid off his head and grew roots on the back of his neck.

Tonya covered him with a drape. "Anything new?"

Mr. Cleary shook his head.

"Has your daughter been to visit?" As soon as she asked, Tonya wished she could swipe the words out of the air.

Mr. Cleary's eyes grew dull and his jowls drooped. "I haven't seen or heard from her since the last time you were here."

"I'm sorry to hear that. I imagine she's very busy with her family." A weight settled on Tonya's chest. So many of the residents never saw their families.

"I look forward to your visits though. Many of us have come to think of you as family."

Tonya bit her lip. "That is so sweet. Thank you. I like to think of you all as my family too." Her throat closed over her words. She concentrated hard on the work at hand. When she finished the shave, she took out an oversized brush and dusted Mr. Cleary's shoulders.

"There you go. Handsome as ever." She rested her hands on his shoulders and he beamed at her.

"I wish you would let me pay you."

"Not on your life. It's my gift to you." Tonya slid the plastic cape off of him and shook it out. "What are your plans for the day?"

"Poker after lunch." He winked. "Then we'll all probably fall asleep watching football."

"Sounds fun." Tonya bent down and kissed him on the cheek. "I'll see you next month. Take care until then, okay?"

Mr. Cleary patted her hand before she helped him to his feet and brought him his cane.

Mrs. Nelson was scheduled for the last appointment before lunch. She was late, so Tonya tidied up her things and set up for a series of after-lunch manicures. By 11:30, when Mrs. Nelson still was not there, Tonya asked the receptionist check to on her.

"The floor supervisor says she's not in her room, but your appointment is written on her wall calendar."

"That's strange." Tonya quirked her mouth in thought. "I'll go check the cafeteria."

When she didn't find Mrs. Nelson there either, she left to get her sack lunch from her car. It was a beautiful fall day and Tonya wanted to eat outside in the courtyard with some of her clients. There was a slight chill in the air and she pulled on an ivory cardigan before she left for the parking lot.

Tonya found Mrs. Nelson sitting in the passenger seat of her VW Thing. She rushed to the car and opened the door. "Mrs. Nelson! What are you doing out here?" She squatted down so the old woman wouldn't have to crane her neck up to see her face.

Mrs. Nelson's arms jerked in short, frantic motions and her mouth gaped. Her cloudy gray-blue eyes stared wide at

Tonya and she gasped, "Oh, you startled me. I've been wondering where you wandered off to."

"We had a hair appointment at eleven. I missed you."

"I've been right here, waiting for you to drive me to the beauty parlor."

Tonya drew her brows together. "But, we don't go to the beauty parlor. I come here to you."

"Now Celia, you're not making any sense. Please, take me to the salon. I don't want to be late."

Tonya blinked her eyes several times. "I'm Tonya, Mrs. Nelson."

Mrs. Nelson held her hands together in her lap as though to anchor the jittery motion of her arms. "No more nonsense, Celia. I need you to drive me to town. I don't want to be late."

"But, Mrs. Nelson, my name is Tonya and we don't have to go to town. I do your hair right here."

The older woman stared at Tonya and her head shook back and forth, slow at first but then with increasing agitation. "No. Stop saying that, Celia. I know you've been angry with me, but don't tease me. Don't pretend you don't know me." Her arms broke free from her hand's grasp and flailed about in the air.

"Don't get upset, Mrs. Nelson. It's all right." Tonya's heart squeezed. "Everything will be all right." She stood and looked toward the facility hoping she could catch someone coming or going.

"Celia, don't leave me here." Mrs. Nelson panicked. She held one veined hand over her mouth and reached out to Tonya with the other.

"No, I won't leave. Don't worry," Tonya said. A kitchen worker wandered outside for a smoke break, she called to him and waved. "Can you help me?"

The young man jogged over. "What's the problem?"

"Will you please let someone know I found Mrs. Nelson in the parking lot and she's very confused. I need help to take her to her room."

"Celia, who is that? You shouldn't talk to strangers."

Tonya turned back to the dear, frightened woman. "You're right." She knelt back down and held Mrs. Nelson's hand. "We'll get this all sorted out."

"Why haven't you been to visit me, Celia? I've missed you terribly."

Before long, two staff members rushed out, one pushed a wheelchair. "Mrs. Nelson, you can't wonder off without telling us where you are going. We were worried."

Mrs. Nelson's eyebrows drew down. "Who are you?"

"I'm Sally, now come on. Let's get you back inside." The aides tried to pull Mrs. Nelson out of the car but the woman became frantic. She flailed her arms, her eyes bulged wide and filled with tears.

"Celia! Celia!" Mrs. Nelson tossed her head from side to side.

"There's no one here named Celia," Sally said.

The old woman shrieked, "Celia!"

Tonya ran to her. "I'm here. Sh-sh, don't worry. I'm here." The poor woman calmed and held onto Tonya's hand as tight as her arthritic joints would let her.

"Don't leave me. I need you."

"It will be okay. I'm not going anywhere." Tonya soothed her.

The nurse shook her head. "You really shouldn't encourage their delusions."

"I just don't want her to be in distress."

"It doesn't help."

Tonya fumed. "I don't see how it can hurt. She's scared." Tonya held Mrs. Nelson's hand all the way to her room and waited with her until the nurse arrived and gave her a sedative.

Just as she drifted off to sleep, Mrs. Nelson blinked at Tonya. "Did I have a hair appointment with you today?"

Tonya, filled with relief, smiled. "Yes, but we'll reschedule. I can come back tomorrow."

Mrs. Nelson smiled, her eyelids heavy and winning the sleep battle. "That's kind, Tonya. I'll see you then." She drifted off to a peaceful place. Tonya sat with her, holding her hand for another half hour before she rode the elevator back downstairs for her afternoon manicures.

21

———————

On Sunday, Tonya took Levi on what she hoped would be a romantic picnic. She planned the food with care—cold sliced tenderloin, Havarti cheese, and fresh French bread for the main dish. She packed Italian marinated vegetables for a side and baked individual apple tarts for dessert. A bottle of cabernet and a six-pack of Bud Light completed the meal. Tonya placed everything in a large basket and covered the goods with a heavy wool blanket to sit on.

Levi said he would meet her at her shop around noon. When he got there, he brought Tonya a single red rose. It looked like the kind of thing that came from a gas station, but Tonya was pleased he thought of her. "Thank you." She smiled and kissed his cheek. "Let me put this in some water."

Levi carried the picnic to her car, and they got in. She said, "There is a pretty lake up the canyon road. It takes a while to get there, but it's a nice drive. How does that sound?"

"I'm all yours." Levi's gaze slid over her and his lips curled suggestively. Tonya waited for the spark of excitement such a look should elicit, but it didn't come.

"If we're lucky, we'll see some bald eagles today." She changed the direction of the conversation as she reversed out of her parking spot, no longer nervous to drive with Levi in the car. "They nest up near the lake."

"You'll have to remind me to look. It'll be hard to take my eyes off you. You are gorgeous in that dress."

Tonya glanced down at the pale pink and white checked dress she wore under her white cardigan and wondered why his comment didn't draw a smile from her. But they were just words. Corny words, in fact. "Thank you," was all she said in reply.

The drive was quiet. Levi rested his hand on Tonya's and wound his fingers through hers until she needed to shift again. The Sleepless in Seattle soundtrack played in the background. Two hours later, just as Jimmy Durante sang *As Time Goes By* for the third time, Tonya pulled into a gravel parking area next to a breathtaking mountain lake.

They got out of the car and stretched. Tonya pointed to the left. "If we take that trail, it'll lead us to a nice picnic spot with a terrific view."

Levi followed her with the basket and they made their way to a small clearing. Birch trees framed their view of the Pintler Range peaks guarding the far side of the shimmery, silver-blue lake. They spread their blanket out on the drying grass and sat, taking in the scene. Autumn reds, oranges, and golds tipped the leaves of the trees. A flock of bald eagles fished in the waters and perched in branches across the lake. Levi poured her a glass of wine and popped the tab on a beer.

"Wine on an empty stomach?" Tonya fluttered her lashes. "I'm not sure that's a good idea." She let out a soft laugh and touched his fingers when he gave her the glass. *Fake it 'til you make it.*

Levi tapped his can on her glass. "Here's to getting tipsy." He grinned at her with obvious intention.

They sipped their drinks and stretched out in the warm sun, the ground was cool beneath them. Tonya slipped off her shoes and unpacked the lunch, spreading it out on the blanket.

Levi edged closer until their legs touched. They shared food and laughed together. After dessert, a bit of apple pie filling smeared the side of Levi's mouth and Tonya reached to wipe it away with her finger. He caught her wrist, drawing her finger into his mouth to suck the sweetness from it. Tonya smiled but was disconcerted by the recurring sense she watched herself from far away instead of being present in the moment.

When they finished with the picnic, they laid back on the blanket and gazed up at the sky peeking through the leaves above them. Levi propped himself up on his elbow and stared down at Tonya. His eyes darkened. He stroked her cheek with his fingertips and bent down to kiss her. She returned his kiss and put her arms around his neck, opening her mouth to his. His hand trailed down her throat to her breast.

Tonya wanted to feel drawn to him. She longed for the thrill she enjoyed in Trent's arms. Try as she might, Tonya could not manufacture feelings for Levi she didn't have. Frustrated, she sat up and pushed away.

"What's wrong?" Levi's voice was gruff, and he narrowed his eyes.

"I'm sorry. I don't know what's the matter with me."

Levi reached for her and pulled her into his arms. He kissed her hard. When she tried to push away, his grip tightened. Tonya's nerve endings sharpened into blades of panic and she shoved against him.

"Come on, Tonya. You brought me all the way out here, to

this secluded area. This was your idea." He pressed her back to the ground and rolled on top of her, wedging his knee between her legs.

"Stop it, Levi. I'm not ready to move this fast." She pushed against his shoulders.

"Relax, baby." He covered her mouth with his and ran a hand down her leg to the hem of her dress. "If we go any slower, we'll be going backwards."

"Levi!" Tonya turned hard to the side to escape him.

Angrily, he shoved away from her. "What the hell, Tonya? One minute you act like you want this and then the next minute you go cold."

Tonya drew her knees underneath her and sat up. She pulled her cardigan closed over her chest and smoothed her hair. "Look, Levi, I want this to work between us, but when you rush me, I realize I'm not ready. I'm asking for a little understanding."

"Oh—I understand. You've got it bad for that Stone asshole, though I can't see why." He yanked down on the leg of his jeans, readjusting himself.

"No, I don't. That's over." Heat filled her chest and flared up her neck.

"Then you need to get back on the horse, baby."

Tonya crossed her arms in front of her chest. "I want us to know each other better first, that's all. And stop calling me baby." Tonya's face burned.

Levi let out a heavy breath. He lifted his fourth beer and finished it off in one gulp. He gave her a surly look. "What is it you want to know about me?"

Anger warmed Tonya's rib cage. "You have no reason to be angry."

"I don't like being jerked around."

"I'm not jerking you around. I just don't want to become intimate as fast as you do." Tonya stuffed the left-over food back into the basket. "I like you, Levi, but that doesn't mean I'm ready to jump into bed with you."

"But you—"

"But I—nothing. I invited you on a picnic. That is all I invited you to. We were having fun, and you assumed the rest." Tonya pushed the cork back into the wine bottle. "I can understand, but you are crossing the line by being angry because I don't want to sleep with you yet."

Levi hung his head and was quiet. "You're right. I'm sorry." He peered up at her from under his dark bangs. "I'm just frustrated, you know?" He reached for her hand. "I really like you, Tonya. I want to be with you."

"If that's true, then you should be willing to wait." Tonya stood and lifted the basket. "Right now, I want to go home."

22

———————

Tonya hoped having Mary join Joscelyn and her for lunch would help spur the wedding plans forward. Perhaps Mary could convince Josce to have an actual ceremony, with bridesmaids, flowers, and most of all —a wedding gown. Tonya sighed as she walked down the street.

Joscelyn and Mary waited for her in front of the diner. Over burgers and Cokes, Joscelyn shared, "Cade and I think the perfect wedding would be on a beautiful fall day at Wolf Run. Nature will provide the decorations and we'll have the family we love around us. That's all we need."

"What do you think, Mary?" Tonya asked. "Don't you want something more… more formal for your grandson's wedding?"

Mary glanced between the young women. She reached for Tonya's hand and patted it. "This is Cade's second marriage. I don't think he wants a big fuss."

"Okay, but what about Joscelyn?" Tonya heard the strain in her own voice so she took a long drink of her soda. "I mean, it doesn't have to be a big fuss, maybe just a color scheme and some flowers. And what about a cake? And food?" She peered at Joscelyn. "Don't you want to toast your wedding with champagne?"

Alice arrived at the table to refill their drinks, and Tonya waited till she left. "Don't you at least want a special dress?" A lump formed in her throat. *Why am I so invested in this?*

Joscelyn's gaze softened and a small smile curved the corners of her mouth. "Yes. I should have a nice dress. Maybe you and I could drive up to Missoula next weekend and go shopping?"

"That sounds like fun." Tonya's heart lightened.

"But you have to let me pick my own style. I'd look ridiculous is some flouncy layered number."

Mary laughed. "I bet Sadie would like to go with you, too."

"Great idea, Mary," said Tonya. "We could all go—make it a girl's day." A day at a bridal shop might inspire Joscelyn to want an actual wedding party. Sadie was sure to want a bridesmaid dress.

"Sounds like a plan," Mary wiped her mouth on a napkin. "I do agree with Tonya though, you should have a cake and champagne, but I can take care of that."

Joscelyn clasped her hands together on the table. "That sounds just right. Thank you."

Mary wrote a note to herself and tucked it in her purse. She swirled her last few French fries in a mound of catsup and ventured, "So, Tonya, how are things between you and Trent?"

The lump of emotion hovering in her throat exploded in between her vocal chords and Tonya choked on her Coke. She held a napkin over her mouth and then blotted it against her eyes. "We are over, Mary. I thought Trent made that perfectly clear." She blinked against the moisture forming on her lashes.

"How is this different from all the other times you two have broken up?" Mary patted Tonya's hand.

"It's different because Trent meant it when he said he didn't trust me and frankly, I am done with this on and off game. I tried to apologize—to explain, but he won't listen." Tonya flattened her napkin out on her lap. "Besides, I'm the one who's finished now. If Trent ever *really* wanted me, we'd already be married by now. So, I'm moving on." Tonya flushed. She hadn't meant to rant, but there it was. She pushed her chair back.

Mary gaped at Tonya and reached for her hand. "I didn't mean to upset you."

Tonya sighed. "It's not you, Mary. I've just finally had enough."

Joscelyn dipped a fry in a small cup of ranch dressing and bit into it. "Frankly, I don't blame you. He's been taking you for granted for far too long."

Mary drew her brows together. "I suppose, but it's the way you two have always been. I figured you would eventually give in to each other and get married one day." Mary looked out the window. "I can't imagine life without you at the ranch."

Tonya closed her eyes for a brief second and swallowed. "I've met someone, did you hear?"

"Trent mentioned it." Mary brought her gaze back to Tonya.

Joscelyn smiled at Tonya and turned to Mary. "His name is Levi. I've met him and he seems very nice." She nodded encouragingly at Tonya, then stirred the ice in her soda with the straw. "Of course, Trent hates him." She winked.

"That grandson of mine." Mary released a big sigh. "He doesn't want to eat his cake, but he sure doesn't want anyone else to have it either."

Tonya stood, her chair grating on the floor. "I've had

more than enough of being someone's cake." She set her napkin on top of her barely tasted burger. "If you ladies don't mind, I have clients this afternoon." She picked up her purse. "Call me about the girls shopping trip." Tonya tossed some cash on the table and rushed out the door.

23

———————

Trent pulled up to the farmhouse gate. It was dark now that the autumn sun was going to bed early again. Soon it would be time to set the clocks back. He was bone tired, but the next couple of days demanded a lot of work on the ranch. He dragged himself out of the truck and up the walk to the porch. He could smell Italian spices from outside and his stomach cinched.

"Hey, Gran," he said when he walked through the door. "Dinner sure smells great. I'm starved."

"I'll bet you are. Long day?"

"Yes, ma'am." He washed his hands in the kitchen sink and slid down into his chair. Mary brought him a plate filled with sausage lasagna. She set a tossed green salad and a basket of buttery garlic bread on the table between them. His gut tore at him.

"You know, I'll never need another woman in my life, Gran. No one could take care of me better than you do." He tried to give her his full-court charm but his face was too tired to comply.

"Don't be a fool. Cooking and cleaning is *not* what you

need a woman in your life for." Mary sat down heavily in her chair. "Trent, I hear things are truly over between you and Tonya, for good."

He swallowed a mammoth-sized mouthful of lasagna and nodded. "Yeah. It's different this time." He swirled his fork in his pasta. "She doesn't even want to talk to me anymore, Gran." He ate another bite. "Too much muddy water has gone under the bridge."

"You know she didn't purposefully put anyone in danger this past summer. Right?"

"That may be true, but she hasn't learned. She's been hanging around some guy she picked up hitch-hiking. Hitch-hiking, Gran. She's reckless." Trent reached for a slice of hot garlic bread. "And she's driving me crazy."

Mary's eyes grew tender and affection shone out from the soft folds of her face. "Trent, she drives you crazy because you love her. If you didn't, you wouldn't care." She stood from her chair and slid into the one next to him. "Child, I'm getting ready to say something you might not like, so remember, I love you."

Trent's neck tensed but he looked his grandmother in the eye.

"You revel in the light of the sun when it's shining on you. You're just like your father and your grandfather before him. You've always been the center of attention and God knows women adore you. But none of them stick around. None, except for Tonya. She's put up with more than her fair share of your nonsense, there's no doubt." Mary clasped his hand. "Now, it's true, she made a mistake. One she made trying to get you back—I might add—and you dismissed her like last week's gossip."

Trent's face was hot, and he searched Mary's eyes. There was no judgement, only love.

"I had lunch with Tonya and Joscelyn today. Honey, I

think she is finally through. You may have pushed her too far this time. She seems serious about that other man now."

A flash of anger erupted behind his eyes. Bitter gall rose in his throat. "She's not serious about him," Trent snapped.

Mary nodded. "Yes, son. I think she is." She gave his hand a squeeze and returned to her own seat. "Maybe you're feeling a bit of what you've put Tonya through these past years." His grandma sounded disappointed in him. And what was worse—she was right. Trent tried to shrug the unwanted pain away, but it stuck like pine sap.

A second after Trent took a bite of his bread, his border collie, Lucy, started barking frantically outside. He leaned back in his chair to look out through the front window, but it was too dark to see anything. The sound of shattering glass caused him to bolt upright, all senses on alert. Trent ran to the fireplace, grabbed the rifle hanging above the hearth, and dashed to the door.

"Stay here, Gran," he shouted. Trent leapt off the porch in time to see two red taillights fishtailing down the long gravel drive. He gripped the rifle with all his frustrated strength and called Lucy to his side. He checked her from head to tail. She wasn't hurt and relief cooled some of his temper until he saw the shattered back window of his truck.

"What the hell?" It was seconds before a dawning realization took over his confusion. He ran to the truck. It was gone. His dad's antique rifle, the only thing Trent had left of him, was gone. "God damnit!"

Trent felt for the keys in his jeans pocket. He meant to chase down the thief but when he opened the truck door, he noticed the bastard had slashed his front tire. Impotent rage vibrated through his arm when he slammed the door.

"What's happened, Trent? Are you all right?" Mary called from the porch.

Trent braced himself against the side of the truck and

worked to regulate his breathing. "I'm fine, Gran, but some-body broke into my truck and stole Dad's rifle." He slapped the hood and stalked toward the house. He pulled his phone out of his back pocket and dialed the Sheriff.

Tom arrived twenty-five minutes later with his deputy in tow. He nodded to Mary, "Evenin' Miss Mary."

Trent paced the length of the front porch.

"Any idea who might want to do this?" Tom asked.

"Yeah. My money's on Levi Barrett." Trent spat over the porch railing.

Tom gave his head a slight shake. "Let's take a look for evidence. Did you touch anything?"

"No. Just the front door when I was gonna chase the guy."

Deputy Brown pushed his thumbs into the waistband of his uniform trousers and narrowed his eyes. "You probably contaminated the crime scene." In a lower voice he added, "If it is a crime scene."

Trent's head snapped up. "What the hell do you mean by that, Wayne?"

"Nothin'. Just we have to look at every angle. Even I know how much that rifle is worth. Who's to say you aren't making the whole thing up to collect insurance money? That's called fraud, you know."

Tom put his hand on Trent's chest to hold him back. "Wayne, that isn't even a consideration. Keep your thoughts to yourself."

Wayne gave Trent a spiteful smirk. Trent stepped forward as though he was coming at the deputy and Wayne flinched, throwing his arms up in front of his face, and hid behind Tom.

The Sheriff stood between the men and held both hands out. "That's enough. Wayne, if you can't be professional, you can wait in the squad car." He took out a pad of paper. "Okay, Trent, do you have any reason to believe it was

Barrett who did this? Other than the fact he's seeing Tonya?"

"He's a stranger in town who doesn't have a thing to his name. Suddenly there are chickens missing, someone steals a car, an axe, and now my rifle. Also, I talked to a friend of mine in Sula and he asked around. No one out there ever heard of Levi Barrett."

Tom cocked his head to the side and pursed his lips. "There is no evidence Barrett had anything to do with any of those crimes, and your friend could be mistaken."

"Yeah, well, there's no evidence he didn't steal them, either." Trent grabbed the porch railing hard.

"It doesn't work that way and you know it," Tom said. "I'll look into the Sula connection, but you have to stay out of it." He gave Trent's shoulder a pat. "We'll dust your truck for prints. What did the guy break the window with? Is it inside the truck?" Tom nodded to Wayne who flicked on his flashlight and left to investigate.

"I'm not sure. I didn't look."

"How about the taillights?" Tom asked. "You saw them driving away?"

Trent shook his head. "I don't know what kind of car it was."

"But it was a car, not a truck?"

"Yeah." Trent realized he could tell something by the lights. "Also, the lights were the old style, not LED. So it must have been an older model." He placed his hands on his hips. "It could have been Miss Hilde's car."

"It could have been, but even if it was, we don't know who was driving."

Trent rolled his eyes and in that moment decided next time he saw Levi, he would follow him. He'd find his own proof. It wouldn't be for the next several days, though. It was vaccination and pregnancy-testing time on the ranch. He'd be stuck working out here for a while, but after they finished running through the cows he'd have plenty of time to investigate.

TRENT WAS TACKED and ready to go before dawn stretched across the horizon. His reliable ranch horse, King, finished his morning feed and was antsy to get going. Trent divided the miles of fence line between his ranch hand, Randy, and himself.

They would spend the morning looking for broken or stretched wire, and downed fence posts. Trent made a practice of checking his fences before branding, separating his cow/calf pairs for weaning, and again when he drove his herd in toward the ranch for the fall veterinary work.

Trent rode the fence on horseback, like his dad and grandad always did. Randy preferred to take the ATV to check the fence and for rounding up the cattle. By the end of the afternoon they'd have the herd corralled in the final holding pens to await their vet checks the following morning.

Mary trudged through the barn door wearing an old flannel robe and cowboy boots. Her hair stood at odd angles. "I brought you boys some food. Bagel sandwiches with egg and cheese for breakfast, and a packed lunch." She passed the food out. "Dinner'll be at half-past sundown. I know you'll be hungry."

"Thanks Gran." Trent bent to kiss Mary on the cheek. He was grateful to have her but he couldn't resist teasing. "Looks like you had a nice visit from the hair-fairy."

Mary pinched the cheek rounding on the one side of his lopsided grin. "Don't get smart with me. I'm the one who knows what goes into your food." She winked at him.

"Thank you, Ms. Stone," Randy said before he took a giant bite of his breakfast.

Mary nodded to Randy. She patted Trent's cheek where she had pinched him. "You two be careful out there," she said, before she ambled back to the farmhouse.

"Let's get going. We've got a lot of miles to ride." Trent finished his sandwich in four huge bites, buttoned his Carhartt against the morning chill, and led King outside. "Meet you at the herd 'round lunchtime," he said as he swung his leg over his saddle and loped off toward the first pasture.

Trent rode along the perimeter of his ranch for a couple of hours before the sun warmed the air and he stopped to take off his jacket. So far the fence was in good shape. He rolled his coat tight and tied it with concho strings behind the cantle of his saddle.

He pulled a canteen out of his saddlebag. When he tipped his head back to pour the cool water in his mouth, he noticed a stream of smoke filtering up through the pine trees about twenty miles away.

He twisted the cap back on the jug and considered the smoke. It wasn't enough to be a forest fire. It was a small, steady stream. Maybe a campfire. It drifted up from close to where their family hunting cabin was though. *Did Cade say something about going hunting today?*

Trent made a guttural noise and remounted his horse. He had miles to go. He'd call Cade later, if he could find phone coverage somewhere out here.

When the sun sat high overhead, Trent stopped by a stream to give his horse a drink. He'd done two fence repairs, but only needed to stretch the wire and tighten the posts. King meandered over to the water while Trent stretched out in the shade of a tall pine. He checked his phone. There were two bars, so maybe. He dialed.

"Cade?"

"Yep."

"You up at the hunting cabin?"

"Nope."

"Huh."

Cade's line crackled. "Why?"

"I saw smoke from up there this morning."

"What?"

"Can you hear me?"

"Did you say smoke?"

"Yeah. Never mind. I don't think it's smoking up there anymore. I'll check it out after I'm done fixing fence."

"What?"

"Never mind. Talk to you later." Trent hung up the phone and laughed at himself. He knew better than to try to call from out on the range. He squinted and shaded his eyes with his hand to see better. He searched the bright sky for signs of more smoke. The sky was clear. If Cade wasn't up there, who was?

With the fence in good shape, Trent rode to meet Randy at the corral. Together with Lucy's help, he and Randy finished moving the herd to the pens near the chutes by four o'clock. Since he had a couple of free hours, he would drive on up to the cabin and check it out.

During his long afternoon under the sun, Trent's imagination determined it could be Levi holing up in the empty cabin. After all, Trent didn't believe for a minute Barrett hitch-hiked back and forth between Flint River and Sula. Maybe he's the one who stole Hilde's car, or maybe he slept in the Stone's cabin. Either way, he knew something was up with that guy—knew it deep in his gut.

24

History furnishes us with innumerable instances that prove this law. It shows, with a startling clarity, that whenever Aryans have mingled their blood with that of an inferior race the result has been the downfall of the people who were the standard-bearers of a higher culture.

(Hitler, Adolf. Mein Kampf - My Struggle: Unabridged edition of Hitler's original book - Four and a Half Years of Struggle against Lies, Stupidity, and Cowardice (p. 125). Unknown. Kindle Edition.)

UNSPENT RAGE CHOKED ME. My muscles buzzed with anger, itching to go to the bar and beat my frustration out on some unsuspecting slob. Having a woman would've helped—but that obviously wasn't happening. Breaking the truck window and getting my hands on that fancy rifle gave me some relief. But sitting around, with nothing to do, had me pacing and throwing rocks at chipmunks.

I hadn't seen any wild game to hunt, though there were plenty of cattle taunting me with the idea of a juicy steak. Trespassing onto a ranch and taking a cow right out from under a local rancher's nose would be amusing. Plus, beef would make a welcome change.

I was hungry, but while I still had daylight, I should wash my shirts. They smelled rank, and I needed to blend in. I pulled my t-shirt off and together with my other two, I dunked them in a nearby stream. With the bar of soap I took the last time I was in town, I scrubbed the stink away. I spread the wet shirts across the branches of a bush to dry.

The sun took the chill out of the air and I leaned back to bake in its warmth while my clothes dried. I ran my fingers over the tattoo inked across my chest, over my heart. I'd never forget the day Uncle Jed told me I'd finally earned my place in the family.

I had the right to bear the mark of belonging which was a bald eagle with his wings spread wide ready for war, and his breast emblazoned with a red and black swastika. He clutched a sword and hammer in his talons and hovered above the Dixie flag. Underneath the flag was the name of our future country spelled out in bold: AMERIKKKA. Land of the pure and the brave. Below the words were the symbolic numbers 14/88. 14—the number of words in our creed: "We must secure the existence of our people and a future for white children." And H, the 8th letter in the alphabet. 88 stood for Heil Hitler. The tattoo proved I belonged.

I longed to go home, and waiting to hear from Jed tried my patience. In the meantime, I collected the few household items I needed to build a small bomb. If the FBI *was* on my tail, I wouldn't go down without taking a few of those brainwashed drones with me.

Jed hadn't answered his phone the last two times I called.

Whispered thoughts crept into my mind that Jed decided to cut me out or that he picked up camp and disappeared somewhere I'd never find them. I tapped my head back against the rock. Those thoughts scared the shit out of me. Who would I be if I no longer belonged?

25

———————

Trent had to pass through Flint River to get to the mountain access road leading to his family's hunting cabin. Since it was on his way—he told himself, he'd stop at the beauty shop and explain to Tonya all the new things he suspected about Barrett. He strode into the ammonia saturated salon and the luscious view of Tonya bent over a dustpan greeted him.

Warmth spread through his body. "That's a mighty nice vision to welcome customers with."

Tonya stood and turned to face him with an icy glare. "What do you want, Trent?"

He dropped his cocky grin and shoved his hands in his jeans pockets. "I stopped in to warn you one more time about Levi. I called Clyde Lawson, a rancher friend of mine in Sula. He told me he hasn't heard of anyone named Barrett working out there and he even asked around for me."

"You've got to be kidding me." Tonya glowered at him.

"It's obvious Barrett's lying about his job and I think he might be squatting in our hunting cabin."

"What are you talking about now?" Tonya swept up the

last pile of hair from the floor, this time aiming her backside away from him. "You're being ridiculous. The fact your friend hasn't heard of him doesn't mean anything."

"I think he's lying."

Tonya scowled at him. "You have no reason to think he isn't telling the truth. You don't know anything about him. Besides, I was with him all afternoon, so he wasn't at your cabin."

"Did you drop him off in Sula?"

"No, he asked me to let him off on the highway so he could hitch a ride."

"Have you ever taken him to Sula?"

Tonya raised her chin. "No, but that doesn't mean anything either. He doesn't want to take advantage of me." Tonya glanced away, her cheeks flushing warm.

Trent's awareness went into overdrive. They may not be together anymore, but he could tell when something was off with her. "If you're so sure he's telling you the truth, then come up to the cabin with me and we can find out for certain."

"Why would he be hiding out in your cabin? You're being paranoid."

Trent swept his hand toward the door. "Fine—let's go see."

"Fine." Tonya dumped the contents of the dustpan into the trash bin. She glanced at her appointment schedule before she snatched a sweater from the rack and said, "Let's go."

Trent opened the door for her and enjoyed watching her hips sway when she walked through. Her skirt swung back and forth like a bell and his hands itched to glide over her curves. He closed his eyes, swallowed, and reminded himself he was angry. He let out the breath stuck in his lungs and followed her to his truck.

Tonya climbed into the front seat and latched her seat-belt. The strap pressed down tight between her breasts. Trent bit the corner of his lower lip and looked away, pressing hard on the gas. He drove faster than was comfortable out of town and up the rugged dirt road toward the cabin, trying to outrun his feelings.

THEY DROVE by the turn leading to some cabins up north. Trent's truck bumped past the road to the old mine and finally, they turned south on the stretch that ended at the Stone's cabin.

The thin line of smoke twisting into the sky from the chimney surprised Tonya. "Could Cade be here?"

"No, I asked him already." Trent slowed the truck and parked about 100 yards away from the clearing around the cabin.

He reached across her lap to the glove compartment and took out his pistol. Tonya jumped and sucked in a breath when his arm grazed her thigh. Heat blossomed where he touched her. His eyes met hers. She expected him to tease her about her reaction, but instead he held her gaze before he cleared his throat.

"Let's go check it out. Stay behind me."

Tonya nodded. Without a noise, they walked together up the road toward the cabin. Thirty feet away, Trent slipped into the trees, pulling Tonya with him. He nudged her behind him as they approached the cabin and paused to listen. No sounds from inside.

Tonya followed Trent close on his heels and when he stopped, she bumped into him. His back stiffened, and she felt the solidness of his body in the core of hers. She wanted to slip her hands around his arm for reassurance, his strength always made her feel safe.

"Sorry," she whispered.

He shook his head and gestured for her to stay close. They inched their way up the stairs of the porch and peered through the front window. Trent shrugged and crept to the door. He tried the latch—it was unlocked. Trent's gaze flew to Tonya's, and he held his finger to his lips. He silently opened the door. They peered inside the one-room cabin.

No one was there.

They both let out their pent-up breath. A nervous laugh escape through Tonya's throat. "I'm not sure what we expected—the boogie man?"

"You never know." Trent strode through the room looking for evidence of someone living there. "Look," he pointed to the fireplace. "Someone definitely had a fire. It's still smoking, the embers are hot."

"It couldn't have been Levi though, because he's in Sula."

Trent spun to face her. Anger sharpened his features, and he breathed hard. His chest pressed against his shirt, straining the buttons. Tonya couldn't drag her gaze away.

Tonya's tongue ran over the pink of her lips and Trent's vision teetered. She was infuriating... and intoxicating. He couldn't control the feelings stirring inside and it pissed him off. He stepped toward her and grasped her shoulders. Blood pounded in his extremities. Damn. He shouldn't have touched her.

She turned her face away from him and his gaze fell to the tiny tattoo of a columbine hiding behind her ear. He wanted to kiss her there, taste her. Sudden desire swelled inside of him. Her big clear-blue eyes flashed up at him.

He held her, afraid to stir. His own breath seemed intrusive, in—out, in—out, he forced himself not to breathe too fast. He didn't want to disturb the air. It was completely still, as though there was no oxygen left in the room.

His heart slammed against his ribs. The beat bounced in his head, echoed in his core, and tapped down his legs. Trent wondered if Tonya could hear it too.

He was aware of his every breath. The tension between him and Tonya was exquisite—almost painful. Who would make the first move? Should he? Will she?

Her hand tentatively reached around his waist and her fingers brushed along his spine. A fountain of sparks shot up his back, into his brain. Trent inhaled and tasted her perfume, making him ache to taste her skin. He imagined his tongue running across its silkiness.

Trent touched her side with his fingertips and followed the line of her ribs to the flat of her back. He drew her gently near, his lips almost touching the baby-fine hairs on her forehead. God, he wanted her. He needed her. His body responded beyond his control. Damn. He didn't want to frighten her. He didn't want her to run away.

Trent shifted backward but her hips followed his. He lost it then and closed his arms tight around her. He dissolved into their embrace.

TONYA RESISTED the static snapping through her frame at Trent's touch. She could not allow herself to fall for him again, no matter how much she wanted him—wanted to lose herself in his arms.

Her mind worked hard to convince her body, but her body wouldn't listen. He pulled away and her hips followed his like a magnet. Her arms rose of their own volition, wrapping around him. Tonya wanted him. She needed him like a drug. She felt drunk and out of control. Or maybe she wanted to leave her inhibitions on the floor along with her skirt. *What am I doing? I can't do this again.*

Tonya took his hand and brought his fingers to her lips. She touched the tips with her tongue and sucked one into her mouth. Trent groaned and his eyes swam with desire. Her body responded as though called. He was irresistible and she couldn't seem to stop herself though she knew this was foolish, knew it was wrong.

His grip on her shoulder tightened and the blue of his eyes deepened as they mined the depth of hers. Tonya's mind screamed a last-ditch alarm, and she stepped back. As though cold water splashed over her body, she shrugged his hands away and slapped Trent across the face.

He was momentarily stunned and then that damn irresistible crooked smile spread across his lips. "Do you want me to stop?"

Tonya willed the word "yes" to come out of her mouth, but her head shook no and she reached for him.

Trent drew her into a consuming kiss. He plunged his tongue into her mouth like he was starving. Against her rationale, her mind completely let go and her body melded into his. She returned his kiss, pushing her fingers into his hair.

HE THOUGHT HE WOULD COMBUST. He had to have her, make her his again. He lifted her and took her with him to the pine-framed bed. He laid her down on top of the flannel quilt Gran made and he stood over her. Her chest heaved and he wanted to tear open the front of her blouse. He couldn't read her expression but she reached up for him.

He pulled off his shirt and knelt down next to her to start on her buttons. His fingers fumbled with the tiny pearl fasteners. Tonya reached for his belt and undid the buckle. Right when she popped the button of his jeans and slid the zipper down, the cabin door swung open.

"What the hell?"

Trent jumped up and spun around, blocking any view of Tonya with his body.

The two men stared at each other. There were no words.

Finally, Trent uttered, "Jack?"

Trent's younger brother, Jack stared back at him. His dark hair the same as Cade's, but the blue eyes taking him in were his own—their mother's. Jack was as tall, if not taller than Trent's 6'4" frame. He hadn't been that tall when he left, but that was a long time ago. Sometime over the passing years the boy had become a man.

"You posing for a sexy cowboy calendar?" Jack's eyes glittered but his face remained passive. He set a bag of groceries on the table.

"Shit." Trent turned to find Tonya clutching her blouse to her chest, her cheeks stained a bright red. "Ton…"

Her eyes shot sparks. "I should never have come up here with you. This was all a horrible mistake." She turned her back to the men and buttoned her front. After the last button, she slid off the bed and ran toward the door.

"Tonya!" Trent called as he buttoned his jeans and followed her. She slammed the door in his face. "Great timing, Jack," he said and reached for his shirt. He tugged it on and opened the door to follow Tonya. He got to the porch in time to see the tail end of his truck bumping down the road. "Damn it!" he shouted.

Trent's frustration surged to a head, and he spun around to face Jack. He thrust his arms out, palms up and stared at his kid brother—no longer a kid.

Jack shrugged and opened a cupboard to put his groceries in. "You shouldn't leave your keys in your truck."

"What the hell are you doing here?"

"I'm here in an official capacity." Jack reached in the bag, grabbed a six-pack and popped open a can of beer. "Want one?" Without waiting for an answer, he tossed a can at Trent.

Trent caught it one handed, popped the top and chugged it half way. He wiped his mouth with the back of his hand. "What do you mean, official capacity?" His mind spun with the shock of seeing Jack so suddenly after ten years.

Jack pulled out a chair and sat at the table. "I'm tracking a fugitive who's holed up somewhere near here."

Trent wasn't sure which direction to take his questions. *Why did Jack reappear after so many years without telling anyone? What has he been doing? Where has he been? Why hasn't he ever called me? Does he need help?* He settled for, "A fugitive?"

"Yeah. I'm with the FBI, and we're tracking the guy—hoping he leads us to his militia compound. He's a bad guy, but the group he's associated with is a band of cold-blooded Nazi terrorists."

"Here? Near Flint River?"

"We think it's Idaho, but we're letting him lead us there."

Trent let the information settle. He nodded and took another swig of beer. "Why didn't you call?"

Jack's shoulders stiffened. "I'm not here for a social visit."

"Calling Gran isn't social. She's family—the closest thing you have to a mother." Trent turned and braced one arm against the fireplace mantle, and old anger brewed in his gut. "What happened, Jack? Why didn't you ever come home after you left for college?"

"That's a lot of water under the bridge." Jack finished his can and crushed it before throwing it across the room to the trash-bin. He missed. He stood to pick up the empty can, and he asked, "You going to need a ride back to town?"

Trent couldn't resist a grin. "Looks like it."

On the way back down to Flint River, bumping down the road in Jack's black Explorer, Trent asked, "What'd the guy you're chasing do?"

"He's a neo-Nazi terrorist. Home-grown." Jack didn't expound.

"What does he look like? Would we have seen him around town?"

Jack eyed Trent and considered his answer. "White male, approximately six feet, brown hair. No vehicle. He stole a car in Illinois but he ditched it. Since then he's been on foot."

Trent's muscles tensed as a chill coursed through him. "I might know the guy you're chasing."

Jack's head snapped to face his brother, and his brow cinched together.

Trent clenched his jaw. "Hurry up. We need to get to Tonya's fast. She's been seeing a guy who's new to town and meets your description. The guy doesn't have a car." He hit the dashboard. "I knew I didn't trust him."

"Tonya's been seeing him?" Jack pressed the accelerator.

26

The loud growl of the engine startled Tonya when she turned the key. She wasn't used to driving such a huge vehicle, let alone one that responded with raw power to the slightest touch of the gas pedal. As soon as she was out of sight from the cabin, she pulled over to adjust the seat forward. She couldn't reach the pedals with the seatbelt on. Her tiny frame was no match for Trent's 6'4" length.

Once she adjusted the seat far enough forward, she took off again—faster than she should, given her experience level. The Ram truck bounced hard on the ridges of the road. Tonya glanced at the dashboard wondering if she should shift into 4-wheel drive but there was a 4W high and a 4W low. She didn't know which one was right, so unless she got stuck, she would continue careening down the road like she was until it leveled out.

With her brains scrambled and teeth rattled, Tonya finally arrived at a smoother section of the dirt road. It was only about five miles to town from there. *What was I thinking? I can't trust myself with Trent.* Tonya groaned. *I have to stay away*

146

from him. Everyone in town laughs at how I hang around waiting for him.

Now Jack. Even Jack, who's been gone for years, isn't shocked to see me panting after Trent. Tonya hit her fist against the steering wheel. She was angry, true, but she cringed at ever seeing Trent or Jack again. Tonya wished she could disappear. She didn't know why she allowed herself to be treated like this. She always ran back at Trent's whim. *Well, no more.*

Tonya stubbornly pushed away the memory of the fierce desire he stirred in her simply with his irresistible crooked smile and those eyes. Her mind was sneaky though and kept at her from all angles. Her thoughts flashed to the way he grinned after she slapped him, as though her action was only an encouragement. She did it as much to wake herself up as him. But he pulled her close and kissed her hard and she acquiesced, melting into him like she starved for him. Tonya's cheeks stung and she hit the steering wheel twice more. She wiped at angry tears with the back of her hand.

Tonya slowed down when she got to the paved road behind the courthouse and turned on to the circle drive that led to Main Street. Her driving Trent's truck into town from the mountains would start a whole new flurry of gossip. She didn't need to add speeding to the mix.

She eased into a parking space at the end of her block and opening the door, she jumped down from the side-step. Without looking to see who watched her, she held her head high, and walked into the salon. Once there, she rushed to the back kitchen, collapsed into a chair, and indulged in a good cry. She pressed a dish towel over her eyes and sobbed, choking on her shame.

When she finally settled down, Tonya went upstairs to wash her face and put on fresh make-up. No one could know how much her heart ached. Especially Trent—and she expected him any minute. He would be angry she took his truck, his prized possession. *Well, too bad!* It would be easier to stay mad at him if he yelled or stormed and raged.

Tonya brewed herself a cup of strong black tea. She stirred in sugar and a good amount of milk and waited. She sat at the reception desk and leafed through her appointment book, relieved there was no one scheduled for the rest of the day.

She heard them before she saw Jack's SUV. A strained engine whined outside before the sound of tires squealing to a stop. Jack's Explorer lurched into the spot right in front of her shop. *Well, that arrival will sure add more fuel to the blazing firestorm of rumors.*

WHEN THE TIRES found purchase on the paved road, Jack sped up. They skidded into a parking spot in front of the beauty shop. Both men leapt from the Explorer and dashed into the salon. Tonya stood behind the reception desk swinging Trent's keys on her index finger.

"Take it, and go," she snapped.

Ignoring the keys, Trent burst out, "Tonya, when is the last time you saw Levi?"

Tonya's eyes narrowed. "Why?"

"When?"

Jack stepped in front of Trent. "Hi Tonya."

"Jack. It's good to see you. I can't believe you're home after all this time. Have you seen Mary yet?"

Trent thrust his hands to his hips. "This isn't a social call, Tonya. You two can catch up another time."

Jack gave his brother a sidelong glance and answered Tonya in a calm and friendly tone. "No I haven't had a chance. I'm here on FBI business—tracking a fugitive who happened to come through Flint River. Trent thinks a friend of yours matches his description."

Tonya's gaze flew to Trent. "I can't believe you."

Her cheeks flushed a charming bright pink. She was mad at him again.

Her gaze narrowed. "Levi is not running from the FBI. You need to stop this."

Tonya turned back to Jack, she leveled her tone but the color in her cheeks remained high. She explained, "My friend's name is Levi Barrett. He recently got hired as a hand on a ranch about an hour away. I don't expect to see him again until next weekend."

"Do you have any pictures of him? Maybe on your phone?" Jack's tone was kind and soothing. Trent wondered if that was part of his training.

"No, I've never taken his picture. But I'm sure the man you're looking for is not Levi. Trent doesn't like him, but that doesn't make him a criminal." She flashed her eyes at Trent.

Jack reached for his wallet. "Here's my number. Will you call me when you hear from him again?"

"Sure." Tonya took his business card and read it. "You really are an FBI Agent?" She looked at Jack's face and then took in his whole frame. "Last time I saw you, you were just a kid."

Jack flashed her a quick, shy smile before his face returned to a neutral expression. "It's been a long time. It's good to see you, Tonya."

"How sweet," Trent grumbled at his brother. He stepped forward, braced both hands on the reception desk, and searched Tonya's face. As much as he wanted to catch the miserable son-of-a-bitch who broke into his truck and stole his rifle, he was more worried about how he and Tonya left things at the cabin. "Ton, are you okay?" He drew his brows together and pierced her eyes with his. "I'm sorry..."

Tonya's cheeks flared again, and she dropped her gaze to the counter. "I'm fine. Really, it's better Jack showed up when he did."

Jack cleared his throat and stepped toward the door. "I'll, uh, wait for you outside."

Trent ignored him. Little brothers were a pain in the ass even when they were grown. "No, it wasn't better. I'm sorry. I didn't plan for—for us…" He took a deep breath and started again. "I thought Barrett was using the cabin, and I wanted to prove it to you, so you would see you can't trust him. I didn't mean to… it just happened."

"Like it always 'just happens'. Trent, I can't be around you anymore. It's too hard." Her words punctured his heart. Even though it was his idea to break up—it didn't mean he didn't have feelings for her. In fact, his feelings had a way of growing like the bindweed in the vegetable garden.

"Maybe you're right. I'll stay out of your way from now on, but you have to be smart about Levi Barrett. I'm telling you—he's no good. You shouldn't trust him."

"So, what then, Trent? Am I supposed to spend the rest of my life alone because you don't want me, but you don't want me to be with anyone else either? Go to hell!" She turned her back to him.

"Ton, it isn't that I don't want you. Obviously, after this afternoon you have to know that isn't true."

Her face was red with fury when she spun back to face him. "That's just lust. I don't mean you don't want to have sex with me. I mean, you don't want me for anything else. You don't trust me anymore. Are you so perfect you've never made a mistake?" Tears laced with black mascara slipped down her face. "You are such a hypocrite!"

"How am I a hypocrite? I've always been honest with you, Tonya. Even when I saw other women, it was only when we were apart and I never lied."

Tonya pulled herself up and seemed taller than her 5'4" frame. Her voice grew calm and clear. "Being honest about being wrong doesn't make what you're doing right. You are right about one thing though, I did try to manipulate you. I did withhold information that ended up putting Sadie and Joscelyn in danger. I did it for what I thought were the right reasons, but I've learned I was wrong." She stepped forward and poked Trent in the chest. "When are you ever going to realize you're wrong too?"

Trent's chest ached. "I just can't stomach the manipulation, Tonya. What kind of relationship do we have if you feel you need to do that?"

"Are you going to stand there and pretend like you don't play games? You are the biggest player in town." Tonya's voice grew shrill.

He wanted to be angry at her, but it was near impossible. She was adorable when she was mad. Her pink curl escaped from her ponytail and curved deliciously under her chin. He wanted to twist the curl around his finger and kiss her jaw where it brushed against her.

"Trent, are you listening to me?"

He blinked his eyes and snapped his attention back to their argument. "Yes, how could I not? You're screaming in my face."

She swallowed, let go of a defeated sigh, and started again. "Look, it's not worth fighting over. We've both been wrong. The problem is, all you see are my faults and not your own. You have no high-horse to ride on here." She pushed his chest again. "It's time for you to leave and let me get on with my life. And will you please leave Levi alone?"

Trent's jaw hardened at the mention of Levi Barrett. He shook his head and swallowed. "Okay, if that's what you want, have a good evening, then." He turned to go, his heart wrenched like it was torn out through the slats of his ribcage.

He told everyone he was through trying to work things out with Tonya, but his heart didn't believe him anymore than anyone else did. He left to find Jack.

Jack pushed himself up from leaning on the brick wall. "Didn't sound like that went too well."

"Mind your own goddamned business."

Jack chuckled. "I was trying, but half the town could hear you two hollering."

"Let's go."

"I'm headed back up to the cabin."

"Like hell you are. You have a family and you're coming home with me. You aren't going to sneak into town without seeing Gran."

Jack let out a heavy breath. "I know."

27

————

Trent kept an eye on his rearview mirror to make sure Jack followed him all the way to their childhood home. On the road to the ranch, Trent called Cade to inform him their wayward brother had returned. Then he phoned Mary to warn her ahead of time before Jack appeared at her dinner table. When the brothers pulled into Stone Ranch, Mary stood on the porch wringing a dishcloth in her hands.

Jack approached the steps and waited at the bottom. "Hi Gran."

Mary hurried down the stairs and threw her arms around her youngest grandson. "Jackson David Stone, I wondered when I'd finally get to see you again." She looked up at him. "Welcome home."

Trent was overjoyed to see Jack after all these years, but he was angry too. And hurt. But he didn't want to think about that. "I called Cade. He, Josce, and Sadie are on their way."

Jack met his glower with questioning eyes, but then he

glanced away. Which was fine, Trent wasn't in the mood to catch him up on the family news.

"Come in, come in," Mary blustered. "I have a pot of spaghetti on the stove. It's not fancy, but I didn't know you were coming."

"It's fine, Gran, thanks." Jack's expression was stoic. The only sign he felt anything was the ruddy flush on his neck.

"What can I get you? Something to drink?" Mary kept ahold of Jack's arm on the way back into the house. "Let me take your jacket. Sit… sit." Mary's words tumbled together.

Her nervousness plucked at Trent's heart.

"I'm fine. Really." Jack turned to look out the window at the sound of an old truck.

Cade parked and got out. He ran up the porch steps but stopped in front of the weathered screen door. He stared at his little brother through the mesh for several seconds before yanking open the door and striding over to him. He reached out and clasped Jack by the back of the neck and pulled him in for a fast hug. When they released each other, both men's eyes glistened above rock hard jaws.

Joscelyn and Sadie entered and walked slowly over to stand next to Trent. He stretched his neck to each side and looked for something to do with his hands.

"Where the hell have you been?" Cade asked their youngest sibling.

"After West Point—Army Intel," Jack shoved his hands into his jean's pockets, "now the FBI."

"Afghanistan?"

"Yeah."

"Me too."

Trent watched Cade and Jack appraise each other. He was clearly the odd man out.

Cade held his hand out to Joscelyn who stepped forward. "This is my fiancée, Joscelyn Turner."

Joscelyn smiled, "Nice to meet you, Jack."

"You too." Jack nodded, then narrowed his eyes at Cade.

"Louanne and I are divorced. She took off when I was deployed." Cade answered Jack's unspoken question.

Jack pressed his lips together and then turned to Sadie. "Look at you, Sadie Lou. Last time I saw you…" He held his hand up to his thigh indicating how little Sadie was when he last saw her.

"I remember you, Uncle Jack. You used to give me rides on your shoulders." Sadie beamed at him.

Jack gave their niece a rare smile. "Now you've gone and grown into a beauty."

Sadie blushed and wrapped her arms around her middle.

Gran went to the stove to stir the sauce. "Come on to the table Joscelyn, Sadie… boys." Everyone followed, but no one spoke until dinner sat before them.

Cade cleared his throat. "So, you're an FBI agent?"

"Yeah."

Trent swallowed a mouthful of pasta. "The smoke I saw at the hunting cabin? It was Jack's."

Jack chuckled. "Yeah, Trent and Tonya were at the cabin *investigating*." An ornery glint flashed in his eyes.

Trent sent him a glare. "I wondered about the smoke and thought maybe that guy Tonya's been hanging around with lately was squatting up there."

"Why?" Joscelyn narrowed her eyes and studied him like a shrink.

"I'm not crazy, Josce. I thought Barrett might be camping in the cabin because I can't believe he hitch-hikes back and forth to Sula every couple of days. Plus, I called Clyde Lawson, who lives over there and he says no one there has ever heard of any Levi Barrett."

The room got quiet and Trent rolled his shoulders to

release the tension. Joscelyn gave him a quizzical stare he did his best to ignore.

"Trent," Joscelyn said gently, "You need to let that go. Let Tonya move on with her life."

"I am, I just don't have a good feeling about that guy."

Jack snorted. "Sure didn't look like you two were moving on to me."

Cade turned his gray eyes to Trent and gave him a long level appraisal. He shook his head one time and then turned back to Jack. "So what is the FBI doing in Flint River?"

"Tracking a domestic terrorist. Hoping he'll lead us back to their militia compound."

Cade was stunned. "In Montana?"

"Actually, we're certain it's in northern Idaho, but haven't pinpointed it."

Joscelyn set her fork on her plate. "I didn't hear anything on the news."

"Did you hear about the car bomb in Chicago a couple of weeks ago?"

All eyes stared at Jack.

Cade wiped his mouth on his napkin. "I heard about it, but not that it was a domestic terrorist attack. Weren't only four people killed?"

"Thank God." Jack pushed his chair back several inches from the table. "We believe they intended to blow up the school across the street. We got an anonymous tip, and the police were able to stop the bombers. Unfortunately, the bomb blew up anyway and killed two good officers."

Trent remembered the news report. It was hard to believe his baby brother was the special agent on the case.

Sadie whispered, "Who were the other two people that were killed."

"The bombers. Our informant said there were supposed

to be three bombers, so the FBI investigated and we believe we picked up the guy's trail."

"There hasn't been anything in the news about a third bomber." Trent leaned back in his chair.

"The Bureau is purposefully keeping it out of the press so the perp doesn't get wind we're following him. It's imperative he leads us to the location of his compound."

Sadie's eyes were the size of golf balls. "How did you pick up his trail?"

Jack smiled at his niece. "Well, first there was a car stolen from the surrounding neighborhood. Cops found it later and it seemed like the perp was heading south until we caught a lucky break." He leaned his forearms against the table and met each gaze before he continued.

"The owner of the convenience store where they found the stolen car has a son. After hearing the story, he remembered he and some friends saw a guy hitch-hiking along the highway a couple of hours before. Our agents checked it out and discovered a plastic bag from the store with an empty burner phone package inside and some other trash thrown on the side of the road."

"But what does that prove?" Mary asked before she went into the kitchen to get an apple cobbler for dessert.

"It doesn't prove anything, but we're following a hunch and it's the only lead we have." Jack's eyes went wide at the sight and scent of the warm cobbler. "Gran, I sure have missed your cooking."

Trent breathed in the tart apple-cinnamon scent that wafted across the dining table. He scanned the faces of his family and his heart eased.

Sadie bounced on her chair. "Keep telling your story, Uncle Jack."

He laughed. "Okay, so when they found the potential evidence and knew the guy was on foot, they called in the K-

9 tracking teams. They followed the suspect up into Montana. After that, we think he got a long ride with a trucker because they lost his trail."

Trent collected the dinner plates and carried them to the counter while Mary served bowls of cobbler and ice cream around the table.

Jack took a bite and closed his eyes for a second, before he continued. "They called me in because of my tracking expertise and my familiarity with the area. The FBI picked up his trail again in Butte when he used an internet cafe to email someone we hope is from the compound. I've been tracking the perp ever since but I lost him in the hills around here. I've been watching for signs of him moving toward Idaho, but I can't find his trail."

Mary sat down and frowned. "I don't like the idea of you chasing a terrorist all over the mountains."

Jack put his hand over hers. "I promise to be safe, Gran, but you have to admit we have to catch this guy."

"Yes, but we just got you back. I can't bear the thought of losing you again." Mary blinked up at Jack.

Trent cleared his throat. "So tell us, Jack. Why didn't you ever come home after college? Why do we never hear from you?"

Jack shoved a huge bite of the cobbler into his mouth.

Mary, who sat next to his younger brother, patted his forearm. "Let the boy eat his dessert before you start grilling him. He's just got home."

Jack took his time chewing and swallowing before he answered. "It's not a big deal. Cade built his own place and you were set to inherit Stone Ranch. Damned if I would work for you my whole life, so I left."

"But why didn't you ever call or come home to visit?" Trent pressed.

"I write to Gran a couple of times a year and I call at

Christmas, but I've been busy." Jack wiped his mouth with his napkin. "Cade, did you write home all the time when you were deployed?"

Cade glanced at Sadie and looked down at his plate. "Not as often as I would have liked. It's not always easy to write or call when you're in-country."

Trent wouldn't let Jack off that easy. "Yeah, but admit it Jack, you left angry and never contacted us because you were pissed. What I want to know is why were you so mad? Why couldn't you at least let us know where you were?"

Jack shoved his chair away from the table and dropped his napkin into his bowl. "The only person I didn't contact was you. Maybe you need to think back to how you acted when you first took control of the ranch, Trent. It was clear you wanted things a certain way and if I disagreed, I could suck it."

"Jackson, you are still at my dinner table and I'll thank you to watch your mouth." Mary said, but her tone lacked heat and her eyes pleaded with Trent. "That was a long time ago. You were both very young."

"I figured since Cade had his own place and Grandpa left Stone Ranch to Trent, I needed to find my own way—so I did."

Cade cocked his head. "Jack, Grandma and Grandpa planned to leave Stone Ranch to all three of us, not just Trent."

"Yeah," Trent agreed. "I bought Cade out last year. You still own a third of the ranch but obviously you don't care—Mr. FBI. Hell, you probably can't even sit a horse anymore."

Jack's eyes narrowed. "What?" He looked from Trent to Cade and then swung his gaze to Mary before returning his piercing scowl to Trent. "Trent, you told me Grandpa left the ranch to you and I could do what you said or leave. So I left for college."

Mary's eyes widened, and she stared at Trent. "Trenton?"

"You've got to be kidding." Trent pushed his chair back and stood. "You were a kid, Jack. You didn't know how to run things yet, so I took charge. I meant Grandpa left me in charge."

"You told me Grandpa left the ranch to you." Jack and Trent stared each other down.

Cade broke the silence. "Trent?"

Trent set his hands on his hips and looked at the floor. "I might have said something like that, but I was still a stupid kid myself." He looked back up and straight into Jack's eyes. "That's why you didn't come home? Why you've been gone so long without a word? Didn't you ever ask Gran?"

Jack picked up his and Mary's plates and set them on the counter by the sink. He turned back to his family. "It's why I wanted to leave, but when I was accepted to West Point, I took the opportunity to make my own way. After that, I guess it just was never my habit to call. I deployed and life took over."

Trent's heart wrenched at the lost time and the lost relationship over one stupid comment. He was partly to blame, but they had been kids. The fact the Jack blew him off for ten years was too much.

"What's your excuse for not calling when you got to town? You're staying in our hunting cabin. Were you going to just pass through without saying anything?"

Jack held his stare for a moment before he looked away. "I was going to call after we caught our guy, but I've been completely focused on the mission."

"What a dick." Trent pushed his chair in and knocked the table. He took up his bowl and tossed it in the sink. The dish broke when it landed.

"Trenton Andrew." Mary stood, trying to appear stern but her eyes were gentle.

"I can't believe you think that's okay, Gran. He wasn't even going to come and see you."

Mary's face fell in sad folds. "We all need to forgive and forget. Those were hard years after we lost your grandpa but they are long past. Let's let all the anger go and focus on the future. It's been so wonderful to have all three of my boys sitting together again."

"It was great to see you, Gran. Thanks for dinner." Jack kissed his grandmother's cheek. "Cade." He gave his oldest brother a nod. "Sadie, I can't believe how grown up you are." Jack lightly tugged her ponytail. "Joscelyn, nice to meet you."

"You're not leaving?" Mary's voice held panic.

"Clearly, I'm still not welcome by the Lord of the Manor."

Trent scoffed, "Man up, Jack. Self-pity doesn't suit you."

Jack glared at Trent. "Neither do you. I'll be in touch, Gran." He strode to the door.

Cade stood. "Jack." But Jack walked out and seconds later they heard his SUV speed away.

Mary dabbed at her eyes with a dish towel. Cade shook his head and let out a puff of air. "I'll go see him day after tomorrow, on Thursday, after we finish with the first half of the cows." He stacked his bowl on Joscelyn's, picked them up, and gave Trent a pointed look. "And you're going with me."

28

And so I believe to-day that my conduct is in accordance with the will of the Almighty Creator. In standing guard against the Jew [Muds]. I am defending the handiwork of the Lord.

(Hitler, Adolf. Mein Kampf - My Struggle: Unabridged edition of Hitlers original book - Four and a Half Years of Struggle against Lies, Stupidity, and Cowardice (p. 38). Unknown. Kindle Edition.)

FOOTSTEPS SOUNDED outside the entrance of my hide-out. I held my breath and listened intently over the pulse pounding in my ears. Without making a noise, I reached for the rifle propped up next to me against the dirt wall, the brass plating cold in my hand. The steps grew louder. I searched for something to hide behind and considered sneaking further down the shaft, but there was no way I could cover the fact I'd been camping there. My bedroll lay covered with food. A cooler filled with beef sat against the far wall. The items I stole from the town proved my presence as well. Even if I had time to stash all those things, the embers of my fire still smoldered.

"Hello?" The intruder's voice called out. A man.

I silently breathed through my mouth, hoping I was far enough back in the mine he wouldn't discover me. Maybe the hiker would peek in, see nothing before the first bend, and leave. I lifted the elegant rifle and hid in the shadow of a support beam.

"Hello? Anybody in here?" The man entered my living space. He poked around through my things. "Well, what do we have here?" he said to himself.

I watched his long dark fingers rifle through my belongings. If he even glanced my way he would discover me. It would either be me or the intruder. Adrenaline flooded my brain and helped me to focus. My heart pumped on rapid fire. I pictured slamming a rock into the intruder's skull—the crack of shattered bone, the warmth of the blood as it oozed out from the fractures. My fingers rubbed together with the image of slick, copper-scented gore gliding between them.

I felt around for a stone large enough to fulfill this dark fantasy but my grasp turned up empty.

"Hey, is someone back there?" The intruder pointed a bright flashlight into the shadows of the mine.

Sweat drenched my forehead and I squinted against the salty drips, fiercely intent on my target. I raised the rifle and took aim at the shadowy figure behind the beam, and squeezed the trigger. The sound of the report rang in my head. It was foolish to fire a weapon inside an old mine shaft. The shot could ricochet or cause a cave in, but I had no choice. It didn't matter though, the bullet found its target, center mass.

After the ringing in my ears stilled, I perched next to my victim and stroked his face. Blood blurred his features making the dead man unrecognizable in the dim light. After an intense surge of what felt like divine power, my heart slowed back to its normal pace. I had to get rid of the body.

I pulled the dead man out of the tunnel by his arms. He was heavier than he looked and I tugged harder, slipping on the loose dirt of the mine When I made it to the entrance, daylight streamed in and shined on the blood smeared across the lifeless dark brown skin. I'd never been this close to a black man before. His coarse hair sprang back from my touch. The old man's skin was soft and smooth. A smile lifted the edges of my mouth as I ran a finger down a long smile line on his cheek. Jed would say, "One less mud, one more blessing." I was proud to accomplish a holy work.

What used to be a camera hung by a strap around the still neck. The gunshot shattered the lens and the plastic casing pierced inward, into the bullet wound. Bullseye. Uncle Jed would be proud when I called him later. Our compound leader always preached Aryan supremacy along with his anti-government sentiment.

I left the dead man in a heap and ran to get the stolen car hidden under layers of branches and brush. Even though I backed up to the body, I struggled to lift the heavy man into the trunk. Dead weight was a real thing, and blood made his clothes slick. Finally, I managed to stuff him all the way in, then I slammed the trunk and stalked back into the mine to get some rope and the packet of baby wipes I still had in my pack.

I drove my hunting trophy down the road several miles before I turned into a clearing in the woods. I plowed as far as I could into the space without hitting any trees or small boulders. It was a bumpy ride in a car not meant for off-roading.

I opened the trunk and yanked the body part way out. With the rope, I made a noose and slipped it around the man's neck, tightening it. After tossing the other end of the rope over a high branch, I pulled, using my own body as a counterweight. I yanked the dead man up out of the car until the body hung several feet off the ground. Then I tied the rope off, leaving him to swing.

I rested my hands on my hips and tilted my chin up. My chest swelled as tears of pride filled my eyes. The stranger deserved to die simply for being born, but even more so for trespassing inside my mine. Hanging was a suitable end. I leaned forward and spit on the body before I got into the car and drove into a denser part of the forest. There was no way I could clean all the blood out of the trunk, but I wiped down everything that might have my fingerprints, and I covered the car with branches and scrub the best I could.

The sun watched from high in the sky. It was mid-afternoon, and I had a long hike back to my hideout. I'd have to pack up my gear and find a new place to go. It wasn't safe to hang around this little town anymore. But first I'd allow myself a nice calf-steak victory dinner. Tomorrow would be soon enough to break camp.

29

Thursday, the first day of vaccinating, Cade drove over to help Trent and Randy. The work began two hours before sunup. After they finished at Stone Ranch, the men would go to Wolf Run, and start the process all over again with Cade's cows. Trent and Randy rode out to push the first set of cows into the holding pen. Trent trotted off along the north eastern fence-line, herding the cattle as he rode. Randy drove the opposite way.

As Trent rode along, he scanned the forest where he'd spotted the smoke a couple of days ago. The sky was clear today. He wondered if Jack left town without saying good-bye. His chest was heavy. He blew it the other night with his little brother. None of the arguments in the past mattered anymore, so why did they have the power to make him so mad?

The sun stretched its golden fingers up from the east and set the western foothills afire in a warm pink glow. Trent pulled out his thermos and took a sip of dark brewed coffee. He replaced the cap and glimpsed a large black lump near the fence about fifty-yards away.

He pushed his hat down tight on his head and pressed his horse into a lope. Trent approached the shape, and it slowly registered he was looking at a calf, but its legs splayed in four different directions. His brain tried to make sense of what he saw, but his gut won the race. Trent's stomach clenched tight, and he squeezed King into a full gallop.

He slid to a stop at the lump of black fur. It was sticky and resting at unnatural angles. The baby cow's eyes were open and rolled back. Its tongue lolled out of its mouth. Trent jumped from the saddle and ran to the calf. Blood and intestines spread on the dried grass of the pasture.

A cold sweat broke out across Trent's forehead and he knelt down next to the mutilated body of the baby cow. He stared at the mess. The calf had been field dressed. The meat was gone and the bones, guts, hide, and head were left in the open. Flies buzzed over the remains.

A hot furious bubble rose from Trent's gut. This was blatant cattle rustling and would bring predators down from the hills, give them a taste for beef, and ultimately lead them right to a pasture full of it. Trent pulled out his phone and took photos from all angles. Someone had cut the fence. Whoever did this, escaped with the meat into the woods.

When he was satisfied he had photographed all the angles, Trent called the Sheriff. "Tom, someone has slaughtered one of my calves and left the carcass to rot."

"Slow down, Trent. Are you sure it wasn't a wolf or mountain lion attack?"

"Tom, you know damn well I could tell the difference between this and an animal attack. I'll text you some pictures. The meat is gone, and the carcass is all that's left. Someone shot my heifer calf through the skull. There are no claw or teeth marks, only a bullet hole and straight cuts from a sharp knife." Trent flipped through his photos. "Levi Barrett did this."

"Trent…"

"Did you know my brother Jack is back in town? Did you know he is FBI, and he's tracking a fugitive?" When Tom didn't answer Trent realized Tom knew all along. Of course, the FBI would contact the local law. The heat reignited and splashed behind Trent's eyes. "You weren't going to tell me Jack was home?"

"We can talk about that when I get there. Stay with the calf. Does Cade know where you're at?"

"Yeah." Trent's voice was low. His throat ached. "I'll wait here."

"Trent… I couldn't tell you. It's a national security issue."

"Right." Trent ended the call.

Thirty minutes later, Cade drove the Sheriff and his deputy out to Trent on the Gator. They took official crime photos and Tom asked Trent several more questions for his report.

"Look, Tom. I want formal charges brought up against Levi Barrett."

"We'll bring him in for questioning."

"My bet is he's the guy Jack is hunting down. It's all coming together."

Cade nodded. "It is looking that way. No other new folks have been around and he matches the description of Jack's man."

Tom closed his report pad. "It's complicated, fellas. I'll call the Sheriff in Sula, but I can't do anything until I talk to Jack. If it is him, and he's the man Jack is looking for… well, that's above my pay grade. It'll be Jack's decision and I think they want to track the guy, not catch him."

Trent hopped into his saddle. "You do what you gotta do, Tom. I'm going to find Jack." He took off at a full gallop towards the barn.

"I'm coming with you." Cade put the Gator in gear leaving Tom and Wayne to scramble in if they wanted a ride.

Cade opened Trent's passenger door as he turned the engine over and revved it. "Aren't you going to put your horse up? You can't ride him hard and then just leave him tied like that."

Trent glared at his brother. "No kidding. I didn't know," Trent snapped with thick sarcasm. "Get in if you're coming."

Cade glanced at Trent's lathered horse but pulled himself up into the cab of the truck.

"Randy's gonna cool him out for me—I do actually know what I'm doing."

"I know, it's just you're pretty upset. Want me to drive?"

Trent floored the truck in response and they lurched forward, fishtailing on the gravel drive.

Cade buckled his belt. "You think Jack's at the cabin?"

"We'll look there first."

It took almost an hour to drive from the ranch up to the hunting cabin. Trent slowed only to go through town and when he was forced to by the rough road at the end. He honked his horn several times as they flew into the open area in front of the property.

"Doesn't look like he's here," Cade said as he opened his door. "I'll go see."

Trent tapped an impatient beat with stiffened fingers on his steering wheel while he waited for Cade. His brother tried the latch. It was locked, so Cade reached into a hole in the chink and pulled out the spare key. He swung the door open and looked in. Cade turned back to Trent and shook his head.

Trent slammed his fist into the steering wheel. "Damn it! Come on, Cade. Let's go back to Tom's office."

Cade jogged to the truck, and they took off once again on the gut-scrambling ride back to town.

When the road smoothed, Trent asked, "Was Jack's gear still there or did he leave?"

"Looks like he's still staying there."

A flush of relief washed over Trent and cooled some of the heat of his anger. "I'm so pissed at him, you know? But it was damn good to see him too."

"Right?"

30

______

Tonya blew the last curl into her client's hairdo with the dryer. She fluffed the style and sprayed the woman's whole head with hairspray. "There we go. What do you think?" Tonya gave the woman a hand mirror and turned the swivel chair so she could see the back. She spun her to face forward again and unsnapped the plastic cape.

Tonya glanced at her own reflection and patted her platinum finger-waves. Today's outfit was 1930s themed. It was Thursday. One more day until she saw Levi again. She briefly wondered where he would take her. She waited for the small tingle she should feel, but it never came. In fact, she wasn't sure she wanted to date him anymore at all.

After the woman scheduled her next appointment, paid, and left, Tonya swept hair clippings from the floor and tidied her station. She didn't have another appointment until one o'clock. Pushing the pink curtain aside, Tonya went into the kitchenette and pulled her lunch salad from the refrigerator. The bell above the front door tinkled, and she peeked out the curtain. Tom entered, glancing around like he was in a strange, alien world.

"Hey, Tonya."

She came out. "Hi Tom, what's up?"

"I need to get some information from you about Levi Barrett." Tom leaned on the reception counter.

Tonya stepped toward him. "Why? What happened?"

Tom looked down at his hands and then squinted up at her. "Trent was out riding the fences when he found a slaughtered calf. Someone killed the calf, took the meat, and left the carcass to rot. Of course, that will draw in predators who smell the blood and end up threatening his whole herd. Levi's lucky Trent doesn't know where he is. That cowboy is spitting mad."

"But why does Trent think Levi did it? Why on earth would he kill one of Trent's calves?"

Tom shrugged. "He's the only stranger in town."

Tonya's heart dropped, and she twisted her hands together. "Tom, do you think it's Levi?"

"I don't know, but there is enough reason to bring him in for questioning." He pulled out his pad and a pen. "Do you know the name of the ranch where he told you he works?"

"No, I just know it's near Sula." Her eyes drifted up and to the left as she worked to recall. She didn't want to give any information on Levi, but her heart broke for Trent. "I think he said it was southwest of there." Her stomach turned. Losing a calf was a big financial loss on its own, but Trent always took such pride in caring for each animal in his herd.

Tom pulled his phone from his shirt pocket and dialed the Sula Sheriff's Department. He turned away from Tonya when he spoke. She strained to hear what he said, but only caught a few stray words.

"They're calling out to the surrounding ranches." Tom

gestured for Tonya to sit in one of the waiting-room chairs. He sat next to her. "I want you to tell me everything you know about Barrett. Starting with when and where you first saw him."

Tonya told the story with as much detail as she could recall and Tom took notes. After about forty-five minutes of question and answer, his phone rang in his pocket.

"Yeah, Sheriff Dietrich here." Tom nodded and scribbled, then nodded again. "Thanks." He pressed end. "None of the ranches in the Sula area has ever hired a hand named Levi Barrett."

Tonya's vision faded for half a second and a cold perspiration flashed across her fair skin. "What?" She forced her eyes to focus on Tom. "That can't be. He told me he had a job." Tonya blinked several times.

"Did he ever mention the name of the ranch? Or any people he worked with?"

Tonya closed her eyes and let them roll behind her lids. She never asked him. "No, but he just got the job. He probably hasn't made many friends yet."

The look on Tom's face made her feel foolish. Still she couldn't imagine Levi stealing chickens or cars, let alone killing a calf and butchering it in a field.

Tom stood. "Let me get you a glass of water." He disappeared behind the curtain and returned with ice water and held it out for her.

"Thank you."

"Will you call me if you hear from Barrett or if you think of anything else that might be important?"

"Yes." Tonya stood and walked Tom to the door.

"I'll call around to some of the other towns in the area and see if anyone has heard of him."

"Thanks, Tom. I'm sure this is all a big misunderstanding."

When Tom left, she found her phone and called the number she had for Levi. The call went straight to the message. "Levi, please call me as soon as you get this." She wanted to ask him straight out what was going on, but not over the phone. She needed to look him in the eye. Only then would she know for certain if he was a criminal or not. Tonya didn't believe he was guilty. Levi was a wandering soul, but that wasn't illegal.

Tonya walked to the back and grabbed a large canvas bag. She packed her phone charger and tucked in a sweater. She put her salad back in the refrigerator and made herself a sandwich instead. She packed it and some potato chips to eat on the road. Tonya topped the bag off with a couple of sodas and some oatmeal-raisin cookies. Tonya would look for Levi herself.

TRENT TURNED onto Main Street on his way back to the Sheriff's Office. As he neared the beauty salon, Tonya walked out of her shop. She carried a large tote bag. *Where is she going? Is that an overnight bag?*

Trent braked hard, his truck squealed to a stop in the middle of the street. His stomach turned in on itself as though someone punched him. *Is she going to him? To Barrett?* The thought that Tonya would choose another man over him, another man who was likely a felon, was hard to handle. Nausea and a cold chill caused him to grip his arms.

"What the hell, Trent?" Cade's patience with Trent's erratic driving was clearly waning.

Trent ignored his brother and watched Tonya load her bag into the passenger side of her car. She walked around her VW Thing and slid into the driver's seat. She took three tries before her engine turned over and she pulled out. Trent threw his truck into park, opened his door, and jumped down to the street. He waved at Tonya to stop her.

Tonya braked and wound her window down three inches. "Trent, I'm so sorry about your calf. I know you must feel sick about it."

"Where are you going?" He struggled to tone down the panic rising in his throat.

"I'm going to find Levi. Tom can't find him, but maybe I can."

Trent tried to open her door, but she locked it. "Tonya, you can't go to him."

"Trent." Her tone dropped, and she continued in almost a whisper, "Stop telling me what to do." She gripped the window crank and wound it up.

"Tonya!" Trent yelled as she drove away. He walked back and slammed his hand against the side of his truck. She signaled left at the end of Main Street and turned onto the highway. He was torn between following her and finding Jack.

Trent got back into the cab and sat for a minute in the middle of the street. He ground his molars together and shifted into drive. He'd blown it. Tonya was gone. She would never be his again. Bewildered, he gripped his steering wheel.

As long as his memory served, they had fought and got back together, over and again. It was their way. He wasn't prepared for the crushing heartbreak he had now she that refused to come back to him. He'd crossed the line. He wanted to go back in time, to change what he said—change the way he treated her. But it was too late. Bile crept up his throat.

In a quiet, calm voice, Cade asked, "Do you think you should you get out of the middle of the street and park?"

Trent swiped at his eyes, against the sudden blur and

cleared his throat. He reversed his truck into a parking spot in front of the Sheriff's Office. Once parked, he sat staring out the front window.

Cade gave him a gentle shove in the shoulder. "Come on. Let's figure out what the hell is going on around here."

31

Trent and Cade walked through the door of the Sheriff's Office. Tom looked up from his desk as he put the two-way radio speaker back in its cradle. "That was Jack."

"Where the hell is he?" Trent narrowed his eyes, his frustration tight in his jaw.

"Said he'd been tryin' to pick up the fugitive's trail all morning. Jack thinks the guy must be holing up somewhere and not moving. He's headed to the cabin now."

"We were just up there." Trent slapped his cowboy hat against his thigh.

Cade grabbed his arm and pulled. "And now we're going back. We still have some shit to settle between the three of us."

Tom reached for the radio. "Want me to let him know you're coming?"

"No, we'll surprise him." Trent opened the door and followed Cade out to the truck.

Trent eased his foot off the gas and switched his truck into 4W High. With the increased torque, the tires bit into the bumps and ridges of the old mountain road. It was a rough ride, but he knew the road well and navigated the rocks and divots with ease. He approached the fork and veered right, to the family hunting cabin.

Without warning, a man jumped out from the trees waving his arms in wild gestures. Trent slammed on the brakes. *What the hell?*

"Stop! Please Stop!" The man ran to the driver's side window.

Trent lowered the glass. "What's wrong?"

The man gestured up the hill into the woods. Trent looked up, but there were only trees. Then a woman stepped out from behind one of the big pines. The couple was dressed in khaki shorts with light t-shirts. They wore hiking boots and carried backpacks. Land's End would be happy to have them posing on the pages of their latest catalogue.

Trent asked again, "Are you hurt?" He opened his door and stepped out. A vague sense of suspicion made him glad Cade was there too. The man's incoherent words ran together. He frantically pointed up the hill. The woman covered her face with her hands and wept.

"A body. There's a body!" The man appeared as upset as the woman, but those words were clear.

Trent peered up the hillside again. "What do you mean, a body? Where?"

The hiker pointed into the forest. "Up there, about half a mile. He's hanging from a tree. Hanging by his neck."

A shiver shot down Trent's spine and bolted out through his fingers. He opened his back door to grab his dad's rifle, then cursed when he remembered it was gone. He lifted the backseat up and brought out his hunting rifle. After making eye contact with Cade, he grabbed a handful of bullets from an ammo box, turned to the man, and said, "Show me."

Cade took Trent's pistol out of the glove compartment.

He stuffed it in the back band of his jeans as he strode around the front of the truck.

The hikers looked wide-eyed at the rifle. Trent shook his head. *They must be from Missoula. They sure aren't from around here if the sight of a rifle concerns them.*

The man took a step up the hill but the woman held her head and sobbed louder.

"Look," Trent touched the woman's shoulder. "Why don't you get in the truck. I'll call the Sheriff and we'll wait here with you until he gets here."

The woman sniffled and nodded, then clambered into his truck. The locks clicked. Trent rolled his lower lip between his teeth. His keys were inside the truck with her, but there was a keypad on the door. He wondered if he could release the lock before she could start the engine.

This whole scenario felt off. He hoped they weren't being played. As if he didn't have enough to worry about with Tonya running off after Levi. Trent faced the hiker so he could keep an eye on him, his grip ready on his rifle.

32

———————

Cade pulled out his phone and tapped the screen. He put the device on speaker. When Tom answered he told him about the hikers and their report of a body hanging from a tree.

Tom's voice boomed out of the phone and echoed in the trees. "Did you see it? Are you there?"

"No. We're still with the hikers on the road. We thought it best to wait here for you," Cade answered.

This whole scene was sketchy and Trent could tell by his brother's tone that Cade felt the same way. He was glad they both were armed.

Cade continued, "When you drive up, you'll see Trent's truck. There's a lady inside—one of the hikers. She's scared to death." He looked at the man and lowered his voice. "They both are."

"We're on our way. Be careful."

"Will do." Cade slid his phone into his back pocket and considered the hiker. "You said the body is about half a mile up this hill? Straight up or did you come down at an angle?"

The man glanced up the hill and shrugged thin shoulders. "I guess it was at an angle. I mean, it's pretty steep."

Trent studied the scuffed earth and underbrush. They could follow the tracks with no problem. He glanced at the man. "What's your name?"

The hiker fidgeted and wiped his hands on the legs of his shorts. "Higgins. Mike Higgins." He peered up the hill in the direction they had come. "We've never hiked here before. The map said there was an abandoned sapphire mine around here, but we never found it."

"You took the wrong fork in the road. Where's your car?" Trent asked as he loaded four bullets into his rifle.

"I'm not sure exactly. I'm kind of disoriented. I should probably find it." Higgins searched their surroundings as if trying to get his bearings. He fiddled with the snap on the leg pocket of his shorts.

"Don't worry. We'll stay here with you until the Sheriff and his deputy get here. The last thing you need is to get lost wandering around looking for your car. Besides, the Sheriff will probably see it on his drive up." Trent glanced at the woman. She sat on the passenger's side with her legs pulled up and her head bent to her knees. Her arms hugged tight around her shins.

Before long, tires sounded on the road and the strain of Tom's engine filled the air. Tom and Wayne parked the Bronco behind his truck. They got out, each situating their duty belts more comfortably on their hips as they walked forward.

Wayne stood in front of the Sheriff's car. "Why is it you're always where the trouble is, Stone?"

Trent gave him a hard look but didn't waste time on answering. Instead, he addressed Tom. "This is Mike Higgins. He and the woman in my truck say they saw a dead man hanging."

Tom nodded and took out his report pad. He guided Higgins several steps away and questioned him, writing notes as they spoke. The hiker gestured toward the hill, his voice was elevated and Trent couldn't make sense of his words. Tom placed a calming hand on the man's shoulder, walked him to his Bronco, and gestured for him to sit in the backseat.

He returned to the other men. "Wayne, you stay here and keep an eye on the hikers. I'll question them further back at the office. Trent and Cade, you two come with me. We need to find this body."

Trent gave his friend a curt nod and slung the strap of his rifle over his shoulder. "Let's go."

They stayed to the side of the tracks the hikers left in case there was any evidence they may need for an investigation. It was close to a mile before they found the level clearing. The body hung heavy from a huge birch tree, back-lit by the waning sun.

Trent's limbs turned cold, his frame frozen in place as he took in the macabre sight. "Matthew!"

Tom stood next to him. "Is that Matthew Jefferson?"

Trent shook his head and though he knew it was his friend, he cried out, "It can't be." He rubbed his eyes with his thumb and middle finger. "Matthew never would have killed himself. I spent a long Saturday morning with him—lent him my camera. He had plans—dreams." Trent turned to Tom, hot tears burned in his eyes. "It doesn't make any sense."

There was a moment of silence before Tom responded. "I don't believe he hung himself. Nobody touch anything, this just became a crime scene."

Trent stared at the dead body of his friend. "Do you think the hikers...?" he choked on the words.

"I don't know what to think at this point, but there are tire tracks here and no car." Tom stepped a little closer to

Matthew's body. "There's no way Matthew could have climbed up to that branch without a ladder. I don't see how he possibly could have hung himself."

That's when Trent noticed the blood. Thick beads of dried red drops stained the ends of Matthew's fingers. Trent's mind struggled to make sense out of the sight.

"Someone shot him in the chest." Cade took a step forward, reached up and pulled back the front of Matthew's jacket vest. "Look."

Tom moved to stop him.

Trent eyes followed the stream of blood up Matthew's arm to his chest. His camera was smashed into his friend's ribcage, plastic shards poking out of the wound. Matthew's vest hid some of the damage. Sharp pain coursed through the neural passages in Trent's head and a wave of nausea caused him to back away and cough. Saliva flooded his mouth. He bent over and spit.

Cade approached Trent and took the rifle out of his brother's white-knuckled hands. "You okay?"

Trent nodded. "Yeah. It's horrible… but I'm okay." He turned to his older brother. "Why Matthew?"

Cade laid his arm across Trent's back and gripped the back of Trent's neck. He drew him in tight to his chest.

Tom stared at the trail of blood. "This clearly wasn't a suicide."

Trent pulled away from Cade and approached Matthew's body. "I'm cutting him down." Trent reached for a utility knife in the sheath on his belt.

"No." Tom grabbed his arm, holding him back.

Trent's nostrils flared. He narrowed his eyes at Tom. "Why not?"

"Because this is now a murder investigation." The men stood, side by side in silence, grappling with the fact they were standing in the middle of a crime scene. The murder of a friend.

Trent shuddered and his eyes flew open wide. *Tonya!* His mind screamed in alarm. He snatched his phone. *Tonya drove out to meet Barrett. I've got to stop her.* He punched in the number, but the call transferred to her messages. "Tonya, it's me. Call me as soon as you get this. It's an emergency."

Tom gave him an incredulous look. "Tonya?"

Cade answered Tom's query. "She drove off this afternoon to find Barrett. What if he's the killer?"

"Do you have any reason to suspect him of murder?" Tom looked from Cade to Trent.

"Yes!" Trent yelled. "The same reason I suspect him of all the other crimes, Tom. Nothing bad ever happens in Flint River until strangers show up. The day after Barrett arrived all sorts of shit went missing, my rifle was stolen, my calf was slaughtered, and now we find a murder. Who else should I suspect?"

"We'll need to have evidence to charge him, Trent, but we have enough to bring him in for questioning. I'll put out a state-wide APB"

"Then find some, damn it. Do your job." Trent started back down the hill. "I don't need evidence to worry about Tonya. Come on, Cade—we have to find her."

33

Trent burst out of the trees onto the road. Wayne startled and grabbed the grip of his pistol.

"Damn it, Stone." Wayne glared and a vein in his neck popped, pulsing hard.

Trent grimaced derisively at the nervous deputy as he punched the lock code into the truck door. Addressing the woman sitting inside he said, "Time for you to wait with the deputy, ma'am. We've got to go."

The woman was no longer crying but her eyes were red and swollen. She nodded, slid toward the door, and eased herself down to the ground.

Wayne sauntered over to Trent's truck. "Just where do you think you're going?"

"Get out of my way, Wayne." Trent pressed the unlock button so Cade could climb in on the passenger side.

"You're not going anywhere. You're a witness." Wayne edged his shoulder in between Trent and driver's seat.

Trent pushed him aside, but Wayne clutched the front of Trent's shirt and shoved him back into the door. Heat burst

185

inside Trent's head and adrenalin shot down his arms to his fists.

"Let go of me, you limp-dick, son-of-a-bitch!" Trent took Wayne by his bony shoulders and tossed him off his feet onto the cut edge of the road. He jumped into the cab of his truck and turned the key. His engine roared to life.

Trent threw open the center console and rummaged around in a mess of papers and receipts. He sifted out a business card and thrust it toward Cade. "This is Jack's number. Try calling him, let him know about Matthew and that we're going to find Tonya."

Cade took the card and punched the number into Trent's phone.

"Special Agent Stone." Jack's voice sounded hard and clipped over the truck's speakers.

"Hey, Jack, it's Cade. I'm with Trent. Where are you?"

"Just got back to the cabin. You guys coming up?"

"We were on our way, but something's happened. We came upon a couple of hikers who found a body."

"A body?"

"Yeah." Cade's voice dipped low. "It was Matthew Jefferson. He was murdered."

"Murdered? What happened?" There was a scuffling noise and Jack came back on the line. "I'm on my way. Where are you?"

"Sheriff Dietrich is at the scene. He's about a mile up the hill from the road to the cabin. You'll see the Sheriff's Bronco. Deputy Brown's there waiting with the hikers. He can point you in Tom's direction."

"Cade, where are you and Trent?"

"Trent and I are going to find Tonya. She took off to look for Levi Barrett in Sula." Cade glanced at Trent whose grip was threatening to make permanent indentions in his steering wheel. "We're worried Barrett might be the killer."

"You two stand down. Let me call in backup."

Trent broke in. "You do what you need to do, Jack, but there is no way in hell I'm not going to try to find Tonya."

"Trent—wait for me there. I'll be there in ten minutes." Jack ended the call.

Trent swallowed hard as the image of Matthew's body flashed across his mind. "It doesn't make sense. Why would anyone want to kill Matthew? All he was doing was taking photos to update his website to market his shop." Trent remembered how his camera imploded into Matthew's chest. He blinked away the memory of the bruised and swollen face of his friend. It was obscene to leave him hanging.

"I know, man." Cade gripped Trent's shoulder. "We'll find out who did this."

Tom hiked out of the woods to the group a minute before Jack skidded to a stop next to Trent's truck. The men got out of their vehicles and circled together.

"I took tons of pictures on my phone from every angle." Tom swiped through a bunch and then held the device for Jack to see. "I found tire tracks left in the soft dirt."

Jack swiped his thumbs across the screen and enlarged the image. "Who found him?"

Trent pointed to the Bronco. "Those hikers."

Jack's sharp eyes surveyed all Tom's photos, taking in every detail. "Where did they say they were from?"

"The man said Butte—just out hiking for the day." Tom glanced over his shoulder at the couple Wayne watched over.

"I'll need to be in on their interviews with you, Tom," Jack said.

"Of course." Tom nodded.

"Okay," Jack took the lead. "Deputy, you take the hikers back to the jail and hold them there until we have a chance to talk to them."

Wayne nodded. He told the couple to put their seatbelts on and he closed the back door.

Jack said, "The four of us will hike back up to the crime scene."

Deputy Brown stood next to the Bronco and hooked his thumbs in his belt loops. "Do you want me to start interviewing the suspects? We could start with Trent. I have some questions for him."

"Go to hell, Wayne," Trent barked.

Jack narrowed his eyes at the deputy. Tom stepped between them. "Wayne, now is not the time."

"I'm serious, sir."

Tom turned to him with a look of exasperation. "No, Wayne. Jack and I will talk with everyone later, back at the office."

Wayne rocked forward on his toes. "It's just I've been wondering about the timing, that's all. You knew Mr. Jefferson pretty well, didn't you, Stone? I saw the two of you walking up into the woods a couple of weeks ago. Didn't you say he had your camera around his neck?"

Trent's hands balled into fists and he glared at Wayne. "Yes, you idiot, we were friends. That's why I lent him my camera." All of Trent's muscles bunched, but he resisted the overwhelming urge to slam his fist into the deputy's mouth.

Tom interrupted, "Wayne, go back to town and sit with those folks. And please be comforting—do not question them before we get there."

Wayne's cheeks burned, and he returned Trent's glare.

"Deputy, take those hikers to the jail," Jack commanded.

"He's such an ass, Tom." Trent shook his head. "I don't know how you can stand to work with him."

"He's only an ass to you," Tom answered.

"So you say." Trent grabbed his brother's arm. "Listen, Jack, I'm going to look for Tonya."

Jack's eyes clashed against Trent's. "No, you're not. I have units out looking for her car already. They have a much better chance of finding her than you do. I need you here."

"Why?"

"A medical examiner's team is on the way and you three can help me secure the scene until they get here."

"You just want to keep me on a leash," Trent spat.

"It won't help anyone for you to go off half-cocked, that's true, but I need you here." Jack's dark eyes bore into Trent's. "I'm a good tracker, but I learned all I know about it from you."

Trent stared back at Jack. A fleeting memory of hours spent traipsing through the woods teaching his little brother to track game and predators warmed his chilled blood. Jack gave him a curt nod and turned to hike back up the mountain. A rush of filial love Trent figured was long dead overwhelmed him. He coughed away the catch in his throat and followed his brother's path.

The four men stood before the suspended body of a man they'd known all their lives. Jack gripped Trent's shoulder. "Everyone move back to the edge of the clearing."

Jack started at the spot directly under Matthew. Slowly and methodically he walked, spiraling out, searching for evidence. He stopped often to take photos of the ground.

"Looks like someone dragged Mr. Jefferson's body from a car. There are tire marks under him. If that's the case, this is not the actual scene of the murder."

Tom nodded. "Can you tell what kind of car it was?"

"Looks to me like a smaller vehicle, perhaps a front wheel drive. The front tire tracks are more pronounced. So, not a four-wheel drive or a truck. The tires are too small."

"Could be a smaller four-wheel drive, just not engaged, or an all-wheel drive." Tom murmured to himself but Jack grunted in agreement.

The lawmen studied the crime scene, heads bent together, occasionally pointing or taking notes and photos.

"Guys, there are more tire tracks over here." Trent pointed. The men followed tread imprints leading deeper into the woods.

Cade gestured to a pile of woodland debris stacked high. "Look." He rushed forward and tossed branches and bramble away from the pile. "Hey—I think this is Hilde's car."

Jack made his way over to the discovery. "Hilde's car? You mean Miss Mavers? What does she have to do with any of this."

Tom explained that someone stole her car a couple of weeks ago.

Jack took pictures but didn't touch anything. "There's blood smeared on the trunk."

"Levi." Trent turned around, his arms held akimbo. "This is Levi Barrett's doing. I have to go. Tonya was on her way to find him. She's not safe."

"Trent—stop." Jack raised his chin. "Do you know where Tonya is?"

"No, but I saw her drive out of town and turn south."

Tom held up his hands. "You're staying here."

Trent spun away and kicked the dirt unable to contain his frustration.

Jack braced a hand against Trent's chest. "I already put out an APB on her car. They'll find her." He took a satellite phone from his vest and walked back to the clearing. "I'm calling the FBI office in Missoula to request a crime investigation team."

While they waited for the ME and CSI teams to arrive, Trent paced like a mountain lion. For the fifth time, he dialed Tonya's number and listened. Still no answer. He was helpless to protect her and his stomach churned what seemed like cement. He left another message.

"Tonya, DO NOT go to Levi. Please. I know you care about him, but he's dangerous. We think he may have killed someone. Turn around and come home. I'll come to you as soon as I can." He ended the call, unwilling to tell her on a message it was Matthew who was dead. Trent ran the whole scenario through his mind. "Wait—if the car is here, did the killer leave on foot?"

Jack squatted down to get a closer view of the tire marks. "Not necessarily. He could have had an accomplice."

Trent scowled at his little brother. "Why would anyone want to kill Matthew?" His voice faltered. "It makes no sense."

"We'll figure it out, Trent. I promise."

"Whether or not he was on foot, the killer was on this road, in these hills." Trent resumed his pacing. "He couldn't have gone far. By the look of things, how long do you think Matthew has been dead?." Trent turned slowly around, searching the area while his mind worked. "The only other place up this way, besides our hunting cabin, is the deserted mine."

Trent stopped. His mind zipping over his conversation with Matthew the other day. He strode to Jack and grabbed his shoulders. "Matthew borrowed my camera to take pictures of the old mine for his website. Maybe he was shot because he had photos of the murderer."

"Could be." Jack turned to Tom. "Sheriff, you stay here and wait for the crime teams. I'll take my brothers and investigate the old mine."

Trent dialed Tonya's number once more. "Tonya, I'm with Cade and Jack. We're heading over to see if Levi's hiding out at the abandoned mine. Please, Tonya. Please, turn around and go home. And lock your doors."

The Stone brothers piled into Jack's Explorer and bounced up the rough road toward the mine. Cade's hand gripped the handle above his door. "Before today, the last time I was up here was the night we found Sadie." His voice was low. "The night…"

Trent shivered against the foreboding hovering in his gut.

"When you found Sadie?" Jack glanced at his oldest brother with questions in his eyes.

"It's a story for another time," Cade murmured.

Trent clenched his teeth. "One you would know if you stayed in touch."

Jack's eyes met Trent's in the rearview mirror. Trent expected a defiant glare but instead his brother's gaze was soft—even a little sad.

Jack broke the moment. "We'll stop half a mile below the mine and walk up from there. We don't want to announce our arrival," Jack slid his gun from his side holster. "Are you both armed?"

"I've got Trent's rifle," Cade answered. "But I put his handgun back in his glove box."

Jack parked at the edge of the road. He opened the console between the seats and pressed his finger on the print-pad of a biometric, firearms lock-box inside. The gun safe beeped and after the sound of electronic gears shifting, the box unlocked. "Give Trent the rifle. Are you familiar with the Sig P226?"

Cade shrugged and nodded. "Yeah, the Corps was changing to the Sig P320 before I got out."

"Take this one. It's a back-up. I have another on me."

Trent raised his right eyebrow and took his rifle from Cade. He looked to make sure there was a round in the chamber and he added three more in the breech.

Cade lifted Jack's gun, gauging the weight before he checked the magazine. With a deep breath, he closed his eyes and let the air out slowly.

Jack bent his head down to look into Cade's eyes. Ghosts hovered in the gaze that met him.

Cade nodded once, but didn't speak.

Jack gripped Cade's shoulder, "You good?" They stared at each for a long moment, communicating things Trent could only guess at. He could only imagine the horrors his brothers faced in combat.

Cade cleared his throat. "I'm good. Let's go."

Jack shrugged an FBI jacket on over his tactical vest. "Stay behind me. I have body armor on," he ordered, and led the way through the woods to the abandoned mine.

The brothers moved silently, trained by years of hunting, careful not to snap branches or dislodge stones. They approached the mine but stopped about thirty feet from the entrance. Occasional wisps of smoke floated up out of the small opening at the top. There had been a campfire burning inside, but by the look of the smoke only embers remained.

Trent flipped his rifle's safety off. "Let's go." He marched forward.

"Stop." Jack commanded in a harsh whisper. Trent glared at him. "It's foolish to storm the front entrance. You'd be an easy target."

"I'll walk along the wall. Come on." Trent gestured for his brothers to follow him.

"No." Jack grabbed Trent's arm, his eyes as hard as flint. "Hear me out. I'm trained for this. You're not."

Trent jerked away, but he stopped and bent toward Jack. "Listen to my plan."

"No. Trent, you always think you know best. You've always tried to order me around, but in this case, I'm the expert. You're going to listen to me." Jack's eyes met Trent's with intensity and he did not back down. "You are not going in through the front of that mine. Period." Jack's jacket vibrated and he pulled out his sat-phone. "Tom?" he whispered into the mouthpiece. "We're at the mine. We are not certain anyone is inside, but there was a recent campfire. We'll stake out the entrance until back-up can get here."

Jack listened and nodded.

"Great. That might work. Hurry!"

Trent and Cade asked, "What?" In unison.

"It will be awhile till backup can get here, but Tom said he found some old tear gas canisters in the jail storage closet. He's bringing them up. Until then, we wait."

Jack drew a rough map in the dirt of the clearing before the mine entrance and showed Trent and Cade where he wanted them to position themselves. "If anyone's in there, we'll get him."

Trent cocked his head to the side and regarded Jack. It was strange to see him take charge with such confidence. He'd obviously gained a lifetime of experience since he left home.

"Sounds like a solid plan, Jack."

Jack gripped Trent's shoulder, his eyes piercing. "And if anyone else is in there with him, we'll get them out safely too."

Trent's eyes widened and his mouth fell open. "You think he has a hostage?" He hadn't considered the murderer might have a hostage.

Tonya!

34

————

Tonya turned her music up and rifled in her bag to find the sandwich she packed for dinner. She wasn't sure where to look for Levi, but she figured she'd make the long drive to Sula and ask around for him. Certainly the local bartender would remember him, or maybe some of the other ranch hands.

She bunched the plastic bag away from the bread and took a bite. Tonya couldn't imagine that Levi would lie to her about getting a job. Unless, maybe he was embarrassed about not being hired. She shrugged. No matter what happened, she wanted him to have a chance to explain. Her heart told her he wasn't guilty of stealing Hilde's car or Trent's rifle.

The thought of Trent caused a quick pain that dissolved into a dull ache in her chest. She brushed it away, resolved to move on. Trent was her past.

Up ahead, a man walked along the side of the road. She squinted to see better, but she needed to get closer. Sure enough, it was Levi holding out his thumb as he walked. Relieved to find him, Tonya passed Levi and pulled over to the shoulder in front of him to stop. She watched him through her rearview mirror. Levi hesitated at the rear quarter-panel of the Thing. He adjusted his backpack and approached her window. She cranked it open.

"Hey," he said.

"Hey, yourself." Tonya searched his face. "Where are you headed?"

Levi shrugged. "Wyoming."

Stunned, she gaped. "You were going to leave without saying anything?" Tonya opened her door and stepped out of the Thing. "You weren't even going to say goodbye?" She blinked in confusion. "I thought we had something. Or at least might have had something." They weren't a perfect match, but she had hoped they could work it out.

"I'm sorry." Levi looked over his shoulder at an oncoming car. He watched it pass them by. He returned his attention back to Tonya. "Look, I like you, Tonya, but I have to go where the work is." He stared at the pavement for a few seconds before he met her eyes again. "I didn't get the job at the ranch like I told you."

"I know." Tonya leaned back on her car. "I drove out here to find you because there's a lot of people in Flint River that believe you've stolen some things from them."

Levi responded with a level look. "Like what?"

"Like a car, for one thing. Which you clearly don't have." She crossed her arms. Another car passed them going the other way. "Also a rifle."

"Obviously I don't have that either." He cocked his head and narrowed his eyes. "You drove all the way out here to tell me that? How did you know where to find me?"

"I found you by accident. I was driving to Sula and saw you walking on the road."

Levi shook his head, readjusted his backpack, and shoved his hands in his pockets. "I get blamed for a lot of stuff I don't do. I'm a drifter, it's just the way it is."

"Well, I think you'd better come back to Flint River with me to clear your name. Otherwise, the Sheriff will hunt you down. It looks bad, you leaving town without saying a word."

"I didn't steal anything."

"Then it won't hurt to come back with me and talk to Tom."

Levi sighed. They stood in awkward silence.

"Why are you going to Wyoming?" Tonya asked, and realized the thought of him leaving didn't sting, she was simply curious.

"Heard there were jobs there."

Tonya nodded. "Well, it may take a couple of hours to talk to Sheriff Dietrich, but it could cost you a couple of days if they have to find you and hold you for questioning."

Levi closed his eyes and sighed. "I guess—if you say so." He yanked opened the back door and tossed his pack in, then walked around to the front.

Tonya lifted her phone from the cup holder. She had several messages. "Shoot, I accidentally left my ringer off." She opened her messages. There were a bunch of calls from Trent. She listened to Trent's warnings, but rolled her eyes, obviously Levi wasn't a thief or a killer.

"It's lucky I found you. Sounds like the Sheriff is already looking for you. I'll take you to them and we can clear this whole mess up. You'll be on your way in no time."

Levi gripped the door handle with one hand and rubbed the leg of his jeans with the other. Tonya's brows pulled together at his nervous demeanor, but she turned her car back toward Flint River.

"You know, maybe it's better if I just get myself to Wyoming," Levi said.

Tonya shifted gears. "No, I'm sure it's better to get your name cleared here. This kind of thing will follow you forever if you don't deal with it."

Levi reached in the back for his pack and pulled it onto his lap. Tonya glanced at him and her eyes fell to a smear of dried blood on his forearm. He rushed to unfold his cuff and cover it. A warning chill raised bumps on her skin. Trent believed Levi was dangerous, but he'd been nothing but kind. A little pushy maybe, but kind.

"Is that blood?"

Levi rubbed his sleeve and shrugged. "I had a bloody nose, that's all." He wiped his hands on his jeans and shifted. "You know what Tonya, pull over and let me out." Levi barked. He pulled the door handle even though she was still driving. "Unless you want to drive me toward Wyoming, I want out here."

"Why? What's wrong? You're not guilty of anything, are you?"

Levi bit down and closed his eyes. "Nothing that's any of your damn business."

35

Tom crept up behind Trent and his brothers carrying a backpack. "I found two tear gas canisters. I'm not a hundred percent they'll work."

"They're better than nothing and certainly worth a try. We don't even know for sure our perp is in there, but if it's the guy I'm after, I don't want him killed. I need information," Jack explained. "Either way, if he's holding someone else in there," Jack flashed his gaze at Trent, "the gas won't be fun, but the irritation isn't permanent. This is the best way to save someone's life."

Jack knelt down behind a large tree twenty feet from the mine entrance. He motioned for Cade to take cover to his right. With another hand signal he pointed for Trent to take his position behind a boulder on the opposite side of the opening. Tom stayed next to Jack.

Jack shouted, "FBI—come out slowly, with your hands in the air." Trent strained to hear, but no sound echoed from inside.

Jack repeated his request. "There is no way out. Come out with your hands in the air."

Nothing.

Jack pulled a pin and threw the first tear gas canister through the entrance. The tin container bounced and rolled along the dirt floor and clanged against a rock before the hiss of chemicals sounded. Soon after, a cloud of noxious gas floated out of the opening.

Trent listened for any coughing coming from deep inside the shaft. His eyes burned and his nose ran. He was the closest to the opening of the mine and the veil of tear gas. "It's not working." Trent yelled through the haze.

A car approached. He turned toward the road and leveled his rifle. Tonya's Thing pulled to a stop in the clearing at the mouth of the mine.

"Tonya!" Trent yelled. He rushed out from behind the rock and aimed his rifle at Levi, moving deliberately toward the driver's door.

Levi held his hands up, empty. From his position behind the tree, Jack trained his gun on the man. Keeping an eye on the mine, he maneuvered to pull Levi out of the car.

Tonya opened her door and stepped out. "Trent, what is going on? I got your messages, and I drove Levi up here to prove his innocence. Put down that rifle."

Trent lowered his firearm and ran to Tonya. He pushed her behind him with his free arm. "This is the guy, Jack." Trent was light-headed thinking about Tonya driving alone in the car with Barrett.

"Trent! Behind you!" Cade yelled.

Jack pivoted and crouched low behind the open car door as he levelled his gun at the entrance of the mine.

A man stumbled out of the mine with a shirt wrapped around his head.

Before Trent could register his presence, the man pointed a gun at Tonya. "Don't move. Don't any of you move, or I'll shoot the lady."

Trent, still holding his rifle in one hand, stared at the newcomer. Time slowed, his every sense on crisis alert. His breath sounded loud in his head like he was breathing into a microphone. His blood echoed through his veins. Tonya froze, trapped between him and the shrouded killer.

Cade, stood in what seemed like slow motion and took aim. Jack braced himself behind the protection of the car door, his gun steady. Levi dove behind Tonya's car.

No one else moved. Silence draped over the scene. Jack spoke, "You can't escape. We have two guns trained on you and a rifle that could blow you clean away. Put down your weapon and surrender."

"I'll shoot her. I swear I will, if you don't all put down your guns." The man shouted from under his shroud. He wiped his forearm across his streaming eyes.

"If you shoot her, we'll shoot you. There is no way out of this for you," Jack shouted.

The man's shoulder twitched. Trent didn't wait. He lunged to his side like a panther and knocked Tonya to the ground. He dove in front of her just as the shot rang out. Instantly, two more shots blasted. Stinging ice pierced his shoulder with the force of a charging bull. Heat exploded through his arm and chest immediately following the freeze and his head crashed into something hard. Pain screamed inside his skull. Then nothing, but a ringing silence which hovered in the air tangling with the cloud of gas and all went dark.

Chaos—Smoke—Blood.

The acrid scent of spent gunpowder. Tear gas stung her streaming eyes. Tonya couldn't make any sense of what was happening around her.

Shouting—Commands—Blood.

Something heavy crushed her down onto the earth. Sharp stones dug into her shoulders. There were more voices, but she couldn't understand the words. They sounded like they were underwater. Her mind drifted on a current.

Sometime later, a large weight lifted off of her. She blinked. Hands pulled her up and set her on a soft pad. A man she didn't know spoke to her and flashed a light in her eyes. Tonya drew her arm over her face to guard against the painful beam.

"Ma'am, what is your name?"

She blinked her eyes several times. "Tonya. Tonya Anderson."

"Good. That's good." The young man took her wrist in his hand and studied his watch. "Where do you live?"

Tonya squinted at him, realizing he was a paramedic. "Um—Flint River, on Main Street."

The EMT nodded. "You're going to be all right ma'am, but we need to take you to the hospital for a complete exam to be sure. You fell hard and could have a concussion."

"What?" The dullness of the surrounding sounds cleared and entered her head with loud clarity. Too loud. Her head complained at the noise ricocheting between her ears.

A voice she should recognize shouted. "Life Flight Medical Transport, ETA twenty-five minutes."

"We've packed the gunshot wound." A stranger. "Looks like it traveled clean through the shoulder."

"Still unconscious?"

"Yes. There is profound head trauma."

Tonya blinked her burning eyes and swallowed. As the air around her cleared, so did her memory. "Trent!" she screamed.

Two paramedics flew to her side. "Try to lie still, Ma'am."

Tonya strained to sit up, but they held her down on a stretcher.

Cade's face appeared over hers. His eyes were dark as night. "Everything's going to be okay, Tonya. Try to relax."

"But Trent? What happened to Trent?" Panic bubbled at the back of her throat and she tried again to sit. "Cade?"

He knelt beside her, took her hand, and pressed her shoulder back down. "Trent will be okay."

"Where is he? What happened?" Fear gripped her in a frigid vice.

Cade's jaw rippled like he had marbles under his skin. His eyes were almost black. He closed them and took a deep breath. "Trent was shot in the shoulder," he choked. "He smashed his head into a rock when he dove. He's unconscious." Cade covered his face with his hands and then dropped them into fists at his sides, his breath coming fast.

Tonya sat straight up and regretted the move instantly. Her head throbbed like a bass guitar and she thought for a moment she would throw up. Her mouth filled with saliva and she gulped air.

"You need to lie down." Cade tried to ease her back, but she pushed against him.

"No. I have to go to Trent. Where is he?" Her eyes roamed the scene. "Take me to him."

"Tonya…"

"Cade, take me to him, or I'll find him myself."

The lead paramedic knelt down beside Cade. "Okay, but you need to take it slow. Sit here and breathe until you don't feel dizzy anymore. Then we'll take you to Mr. Stone."

The sound of a large engine echoed through the trees. Rotor blades chopped through the air. The Life Flight Helicopter was landing. Cade covered Tonya's face with his body as he turned his own away from the blowing dirt.

The second the skids hit the ground a medical team

leaped from the chopper and ran to the stretcher that held Trent. Tonya stood with Cade's assistance and took several steps toward them.

"Okay, he's stable enough to transport, let's load him up." The woman who led the team shouted over the motor.

Tonya gripped Cade's arm. "I have to go with him!"

Jack left a group of dark clad, armed men and nodded at Cade and Tonya. He approached the medical team leader and spoke with her.

"Cade, I think you and Tonya should both go up to the hospital in Missoula with Trent. I've cleared it with the team. Tonya can get checked out there." Jack gripped Cade's shoulder. "It wouldn't hurt to have them take a look at you, too."

"I need to talk to Joscelyn." Cade squeezed his eyes shut. "I'm not sure I can get on the helicopter."

"You can do this, Cade. It's okay. We're not in Afghanistan, we're home."

Cade bobbed his head but his eyes remained dark, almost vacant. "What about Gran?"

"As soon as I can leave here, I'll go get her, Joscelyn, and Sadie. We'll be there as soon as we can."

Cade swallowed hard and nodded. "Be careful."

Jack clenched his jaw and gave Cade a terse hug. "You've got this, Cade. Take care of that bull-headed brother of ours. I'll see you soon."

Tonya slipped her arms around Jack and kissed his cheek. "Thanks, Jack." Her throat closed and choked off any more words. She turned and with Cade's help climbed into the helicopter. She sat next to Trent and laced her fingers through his. Willing life to stream from her body into his. She couldn't lose Trent—not in this way.

36

Beep—Beep—Beep. The steady rhythm permeated the silence in the room. Monitors of all types counted, measured, and sounded, tracking Trent's heart rate, blood pressure, respiration, and oxygen saturation. The air smelled of antiseptic, plastic tubing, and something unknowable that stuck in the back of Tonya's throat. Nurses bustled in and out of the ICU room, checking IV levels, pupil dilation, and body temperature. No one had any sure answers—not doctors, not nurses, not the family, not her.

Tonya's back ached from the cold, hard plastic chair she sat in next to Trent's bed. She laid her head next to his sheet-draped leg. Her fingers wrapped around his. She had clung to him since they airlifted him to St. Patrick Hospital in Missoula. The only exceptions were while he was in surgery and when the medical staff insisted she was in their way.

It had been eighteen hours since the shooting. With her eyes closed, Tonya pictured the horror all over again. She remembered her confusion when the strange man stumbled out of the abandoned mine, coughing and sputtering from the tear gas and waving a rifle in all directions. Her mind had worked to make sense out of the scene. She had no idea who the man was or why he threatened to shoot her. Then, out of nowhere, Trent shoved her hard and threw his body between her and the man—between her and the bullet that might take him from them forever. He saved her life and now he was fighting for his own.

A strong hand gripped her shoulder and Tonya lifted her weary head.

"Any change?" Cade asked.

She shook her head and her eyes filled, burning her red lids. Cade reached for a box of tissue and offered it to her. Tonya took one and rubbed her chapped nose.

"How's the concussion?"

"I'll be fine. Where is everyone?"

"In the waiting room."

Tonya nodded. "Mary should come in. Trent needs to hear her voice."

"Yeah," Cade agreed. "And you should step out. Walk a little, maybe get some air?"

She shook her head and gripped Trent's hand tight "I can't leave him. He needs to know I'm here. I have to tell him I'm sorry. Tell him how much I love him." Tears overwhelmed her, and she broke down. "We've wasted so much time."

Cade took her arm and pulled her to her feet. He put his arms around her. "You'll get to tell him. You two will have time to work it all out. I know it." He stepped back and lifted her chin, wiping her damp cheek with his thumb. "He's a stubborn S.O.B., Tonya. If he were going to die, he would have done it already."

She blinked at forming tears and wiped her face with the edge of her sleeve. She opened her hand to salvage the spent tissue twisted tight in her fist and attempted to wipe her sore nose again. "Do you really think so?"

Cade nodded and curled one side of his mouth. "I know so. Come on. You need some air and something to eat. Joscelyn'll go with you. I'll let you know if there is any change."

Tonya nodded and after kissing Trent's forehead, his cheek, and finally the corner of his mouth, she allowed Cade to lead her from the room. Her legs were heavy and didn't want to work. She shuddered with a left-over sob followed by a hiccup. Cade led her into Joscelyn.

Joscelyn reached out for Cade's arm. "How are you holding up?"

His gaze dropped to the floor. "I should have fired sooner." His tortured eyes blinked up at her. "If only…" He glanced at Tonya and didn't finish his thought.

Joscelyn put her hands on either side of his face. "You and Jack both did everything you could. You saved Trent and Tonya's lives. If you weren't there, he would have fired again."

Cade closed his eyes briefly and slid his arms around Joscelyn holding her so tight Tonya wondered if she could breathe. He pulled back, kissed her softly, and whispered "Thanks." Then turned and took Mary to see her unconscious grandson.

JOSCELYN'S VOICE was soft when she spoke to Tonya. "How's Trent doing?"

Tonya swallowed. "There's been no change. The doctor said he should regain consciousness when the swelling in his head goes down." She stopped and searched Joscelyn's eyes. "Why isn't it going down?"

"I don't know, sweetie, but one thing we both know about

Trent is he's strong and determined. If anyone can pull through this, he can."

Tonya walked with Joscelyn's arm around her shoulders, allowing her friend to guide her to the cafeteria.

"When did you last eat?" Joscelyn asked.

"I'm not sure. I'm not hungry."

Joscelyn's gaze was kind. "I know, but you have to keep up your strength. How else are you going to put up with Trent when he wakes up growling and ordering everyone around?" She gave Tonya a reassuring squeeze. "Let's get you some protein."

They took their lunch trays outside to the courtyard. The autumn air was crisp but held the warm scent of dried leaves and grasses. Sunshine wrapped Tonya in a comfortable embrace but failed to chase away the chill in her bones. She stirred the food around on her plate with her fork, but couldn't force herself to eat.

"Do you think Trent wants me here?" Tonya choked on her words. "What if he wakes up and is mad I'm here? I'm not family."

Joscelyn reached for her hand and held it. "Tonya, Trent loves you. He always has. He's just—well, he's just Trent. I know he wants you here."

"I'm not so sure."

"In this case, I'm sure enough for both of us."

The familiar cold stone that took up residence in Tonya's throat swelled and she swallowed against it. She searched Joscelyn's eyes. "He saved my life. Did you know that?"

Joscelyn gave her a sad smile and her eyes moistened. "Cade told me." She reached up and pushed a strand of white-blonde hair behind Tonya's ear and let her fingers rest against her cheek. "If that's not love, I don't know what is."

"He would have saved anyone's life. That's the way he's built." She cast her gaze to the table. "We waited too long.

Wasted too much time. What if…" Her breath caught in her throat.

"You must have faith, Tonya. When Trent wakes up, tell him how you feel."

"I hope that happens. Oh, God, I pray I have that chance." Tonya took a small bite of tuna casserole. "But he doesn't want me anymore, Josce." She took a shuddering breath. "I've tried to move on, I have, but it's too hard when I see him every day. My problem is I will only ever love Trent." Her eyes ached. "If—I mean when—Trent recovers, I'm going to move to Seattle. My sister lives there. I can get a job in one of those fancy salons in the city."

"What?" Joscelyn sat up straight. "Tonya, you can't leave. What about your shop?"

"I can't stay in Flint River. Trent will eventually find someone else and I can't watch that. It would kill me." Tonya slumped under the heavy thought.

"Let's not cross any bridges until we need to. Okay?" Joscelyn took Tonya's hand and held it in both of hers.

37

What the hell is that incessant beeping? Trent tried to move, tried to lift his hand but his muscles wouldn't respond. Something was in his throat, but he couldn't swallow it. So tired. His brain retreated to the shadows, and he drifted.

Stop talking. Be quiet. I'm trying to sleep.

"Any change?"

That voice… so soft—is it coming from me? A part of me?

"No."

Cade? Why's Cade here?

"Have you heard anything from Jack?"

Jack? Jack, I should remember… something about Jack.

"Nothing new. He and his team are still at the hospital in Flint River, interrogating that Eugene Werner bastard. They're pressuring him to give up the location of the terrorist compound. The guy admitted to being a part of the failed bombing in Chicago but the FBI is after the mastermind behind the plot. I think Jack's coming by tonight, though."

Terrorist compound? Bombing?

"It's all so hard to believe."

"I know."

"How bad are Werner's injuries? Didn't you shoot him?"

"Yeah, and so did Jack. I shot his firing arm and Jack took out a leg. They weren't kill-shots—Werner has too much information that's crucial to the FBI investigation. He may not walk again, but he'll live."

Trent focused on opening his eyes, but they wouldn't budge. The voices stopped and there was a scuffing sound, like scraping a chair across the floor. Trent's thoughts sifted back into a dark fog.

"Josce told me you're thinking of moving to Seattle?"

Seattle? Who's Cade talking to?

"Yes. I can't stay in Flint River anymore. It's too hard to see Trent every day and know there's no hope. I tried to move on, but I can't, so the best option for me is to move away."

Tonya? Tonya's moving? Trent tried to focus on the words but they kept fading in and out. He had to open his eyes.

"Tonya, Trent loves you."

Yes! Tell her Cade. Why can't I open my goddamned eyes? Trent concentrated on his hands. *My hands don't work!*

"No, he doesn't. Not anymore. I mean, of course he cares about me. We've known each other forever, but love? No. I wrecked it and he doesn't want me anymore."

Not true! Cade, tell her! Trent strained with all his might. Nothing. Whatever was stuck in his throat hurt like hell. He wanted to cough. His head screamed in pain and so did his shoulder. The pain was new. *Tonya!* He willed the words to come out of his mouth but there was nothing.

"I don't believe that. You two have always been on and off. I'm sure this is one of those times."

"It's not. I never told anyone about Perkins and people Trent loves got hurt. He blames me and he's right. I broke his trust."

"He wasn't right to blame you. The situation upset Trent because it scared him. And you guys can rebuild trust."

"Yes, if he wanted to, but he doesn't."

Footsteps. Trent was aware of pressure on his thigh, then his hand. *Someone's holding my hand. Tonya?* Trent strained against his unresponsive body.

"It's best for everybody if I go. I'll stay with my sister until I can get set up."

No. Tonya, don't go. I've been an idiot, thinking we had all the time in the world. Please, Tonya. Don't go! Trent seemed bound in something that prevented any movement. He flexed with all his might against it.

"Trent?" Tonya's grip tightened on his fingers. "Cade! I think he just moved his fingers."

Encouraged by her awareness of his efforts, Trent concentrated on his eyelids. *Open, damn it.*

Cade's voice was loud in his ear. "Trent? Trent, wake up. Can you hear me?"

His eyes refused to open, but his fingers responded again.

"I think he hears you, Cade. He moved his fingers again."

Tonya. I need to wake up, to see you.

"I'll get the doctor," Cade said.

Trent squeezed his eyelids tight before they would open. They were sticky and difficult to lift. His head throbbed. He tried to say something, but that thing was caught in his throat. He searched for Tonya's face.

"Hi." Her voice was warm honey. "You gave us quite a scare." She squeezed his hand again and tears pooled in her eyes. "Everyone is here."

Trent blinked. *Here? Where is here?*

A doctor rushed up to him, followed by Cade. Gran's face appeared, then Joscelyn's and Sadie's. Trent tried to speak.

"Don't say anything until we get the endotracheal tube out of your throat. Hold on a minute." The doctor said something to a nurse, and they poked and pulled at something on his face before they pulled a long tube out of his mouth. "Okay, Mr. Stone, your throat will be sore for a couple of days. It's best if you don't try to talk."

"Ton…" He rasped and then tried to swallow.

"Can he have some water?" Cade asked.

"One small sip." A nurse said and held a straw to his lips. "Just a little, now."

Trent swallowed the cool balm. His throat was raw, but he craved more. The nurse took the cup away.

"Ton…"

"I'm here. Shh—don't talk. Just rest." She tucked his blanket around him.

Sleep pulled at him. His body yearned to slip backwards into the abyss. *No—I have to tell her.* "Ton, don't." It was so hard to focus. "Don't… I… Only…" That was all. He couldn't fight the pull any longer. Sleep sluiced over him like an ocean wave. *Don't go. I've always loved you, only you, Tonya. Always.*

As long as the meds kept coming, Trent was feeling better. He was able to sit up with his bed inclined. His head ached but not as much as his chest and shoulder. He'd like to beat the bastard who shot him. The bullet entered the top of his shoulder as he dove. It passed through and grazed his head slamming his skull into a rock on the ground. Trent grimaced. He was thankful he was the one who took the bullet and not Tonya. Tonya. He smiled.

"Good morning." Mary trooped in followed by Sadie. "How's the patient?"

"Hey, Gran." Trent winked at his niece. "I'm gonna live, like it or not."

"That's not funny, Trenton. You scared me to death and back." She straightened the furniture and threw away two empty cups from his tray table.

"Uncle Trent, what does it feel like to get shot?" Sadie plopped down on the side of his bed.

A groan escaped his throat against his efforts.

Sadie sprang up, eyes wide. "I'm so sorry, Trent."

Trent nodded. His pulse shot up, and the nurse rushed in to check on him. He waited for the pain to recede before he spoke. "It isn't a lot of fun. I don't recommend it. Where's Tonya?"

Mary didn't answer right away. She rummaged in her purse and then rearranged some flowers in one of the many vases.

"Gran?"

Mary breathed in and looked him in the eye. "She's been packing. She might come in to see you before she leaves."

"Leaves?" Trent adjusted his position. "Leaves for where?"

"She's moving, Trent." Mary took his hand. "To Seattle, to live with her sister."

Trent's heart kicked. He tried to push himself up. "You've got to stop her, Gran."

"I've tried to talk to her, but she's afraid of being rejected again. Trent, I'm sorry to say it, but you pushed that girl away one too many times."

The truth in her words made it hard for him to breathe. "I know, Gran, you're right, but I have to see her. Make her come here before she leaves."

"I don't know if I can. Now she knows you're going to live, she doesn't want to risk seeing you."

Trent shifted and swung his legs over the edge of the bed.

"What are you doing, foolish boy? You can't get out of bed."

A wave of dizzy nausea forced him to sit still for a minute.

"If she won't come here, I'll go to her."

"Get back in bed, this minute." Gran reached to push the nurse's call button. When the medical staff hurried in, there was no fight left in him. He'd never been so weak in all his life. They helped him lay back down and checked all the monitor connections. Then raised the bedrails, snapping them into place with a vicious finality.

"Gran…"

"Right now, you need to concentrate on healing." She tucked his covers around him. "When you are strong again, you can decide what to do."

38

Tonya struggled to close the hatch door at the back of her Thing. She shoved hard against all her world's possessions packed inside. Tonya resisted the gush of sorrow that threatened to defeat her. She couldn't chicken out now. She needed this. Heeding the life lessons she'd learned the hard way, she had to go off on her own and start over. It was the only way.

Choosing the key from her ring of many, Tonya closed and locked the front door of her shop. She stood facing her pre-dawn reflection in the glass. "You can do this. You must do this," she said to the girl with the sad blue eyes looking back at her.

Tonya inhaled a deep breath that accentuated the ache in her chest and walked away. She got into her Thing, started the engine, and with a gulp, drove down Main Street. She turned toward Missoula and ultimately, Seattle.

Her sister insisted she stay with her, at least until she found a job. That was a relief, because at this point, Brandy was the only one she could turn to. Seattle was so big and frightening. She wondered if she would ever get used to living there—if the city could ever come to feel like home.

She stayed on the highway to bypass Missoula, but she stared hard at the exit she took when she drove up to visit Trent. Relieved that he was conscious and would be okay eventually, Tonya left Flint River before Trent got out of the hospital. If she saw him again, she didn't think she'd have the strength and resolve to move. Even thinking about him now left her with a heavy sort of wretchedness. But she had to go. Tonya needed to learn to rely on herself. She wanted to know she was enough on her own before she ever tried again to be a part of a couple.

The ache in her throat increased until she reached the far outskirts of Missoula. As she drove north, the pressure eased, and she felt freer than she had in years. This was the right decision—she almost believed it. Breathing came easier and Tonya turned her music up. She let Louis Armstrong and Ella Fitzgerald's Summertime slip deep inside her soul. The music swept her up, and she sang along in her best jazz impression as the miles sailed by.

It was dark by the time Seattle loomed across the horizon. Tonya called Brandy and told her she'd be there soon.

Her sister's apartment building was gray with white trim and looked like a thousand other apartment buildings on the outskirts of the city. She drove through the maze of parking lots until she found the right address and then searched for a place to park.

Tonya slipped her overnight bag onto her shoulder and lugged it up three flights of stairs to her sister's place. She raised her hand to knock but before her knuckles rapped the wood, the door flew open and Brandy threw her arms around Tonya, almost knocking her down. Tonya's sister welcomed her with plenty of love and sympathy, bustling her inside from the doorstep.

"Baby Ton Ton! It's been far too long." Brandy backed up a couple of steps and looked Tonya up and down before she embraced her again. "You are as beautiful as ever!"

"Hi, Bran. Thanks for having me." Tonya said into her sister's hair. She was tempted to dissolve into Brandy's strength and weep but she stood firm. This was a new start. No looking back.

"I'm thrilled. It will be so much fun to have you living up here now. I can't wait to show you the city."

Tonya laughed, "Okay, but can I put my bag down first?"

"Yes, of course. Sorry." Her sister clapped her hand over her mouth. "Come in, come in." Brandy led the way into the small apartment.

The kitchen was to the left of the door, along the wall. A free-standing breakfast bar separated the cooking area from the rest of the great room. Beyond the main living space were Brandy and her roommate's cramped bedrooms.

Her sister gestured to a sofa that had seen a long life. "You can sleep here until you find a place."

"Thanks again, Brandy." Tonya set her bag down next to the couch and considered the small apartment. The only other furniture in the modest room was an old trunk repurposed as a coffee table and a card table used as a desk. A local news broadcaster yelled out from the huge TV mounted on the wall.

Tonya bit her lower lip. Living out of her bag and waiting to go to bed until after her sister and her roommate retired to their rooms would get old fast. She had hoped to save up for a couple of months before finding a place of her own, but it was clear that renting an apartment needed to move to the top of her to-do list.

"I know it's a little crowded, but it'll be like having an extended slumber-party. It'll be fun."

Brandy poured two large glasses of wine and carried

them to the couch. She bent to pass a glass to Tonya and slopped some cabernet on the sofa. With her hand free, she rubbed the spill into the fabric.

"Oops." Brandy giggled and took a sizable gulp. "So, dish. What happened? You finally got tired of Trent's crap?"

Tonya placed a careful smile across her lips. In the past fifteen minutes, she already noticed a chasm between her older sister and herself. She had always looked up to Brandy, thought she was so grown up and sophisticated. But in those few moments, Tonya glimpsed how much she, herself had grown in the last couple of years. Brandy was right, she was tired of Trent's crap, but she loved him and she didn't want to "dish".

"It's just time for me to try something new. You know— get out of Flint River and see a little more of the world."

Brandy narrowed her eyes at Tonya. "But, you've left Trent. Why?" She crossed her legs and sat sideways, facing Tonya. "I didn't think I'd ever see the day that you left him."

"It was mutual this time." Tonya sipped from her glass. "I mean, not at first, but I came to see the wisdom of being apart." She set her glass down on the trunk and tucked her knees underneath herself. "I need to figure a few things out for myself right now. That's why I'm here."

Brandy studied her so close she shifted under the scrutiny.

"What?"

"It's just not like you, that's all." Brandy leaned back on the throw pillows.

"What isn't?"

"Being spontaneous. Figuring things out for yourself. Not chasing after Trent Stone. All of it." The doorbell rang and saved Tonya from having to respond. "I ordered pizza— figured you'd be hungry after your long drive."

"Great." Tonya's answer sounded loud and overly bright. She cleared her throat and stood. "I'll set the table."

"Nah, there are paper plates over the microwave. Let's eat on the couch."

Tonya smiled and swallowed her grimace. *How many and what kinds of spills am I going to be sleeping on?* She sat back down on the cushion and a whoosh of displaced air rose up around her. *Oh my god. What is that stale, salty, stench?*

It was difficult to keep Brandy off the topic of Trent, but Tonya steered the conversation to possible job opportunities. Brandy didn't know of any salon jobs but offered Tonya the use of her computer. The ancient desktop monitor perched on top of the card-table-turned-desk in the corner.

"What are you going to do with your shop in Flint River?" Brandy asked.

The pizza turned to a cold lump in Tonya's stomach. "I don't know. Sell it, I guess."

"To who?" Brandy looked at her like she just said she was flying to Mars.

"I don't know. Something will come up."

"You really didn't think this thing through, did you?" Brandy pursed her lips. "Makes me wonder about Trent."

A spark of anger ignited deep inside. Tonya didn't need second guessing, not from Brandy. "The two have nothing to do with each other."

"Yes, they do. You would have never left your cute little shop if you weren't brokenhearted over Trent. You're letting him chase you out of your home."

"I am not." Tonya stood and walked to the bar. "The truth is, Trent wanted me to stay. I chose to leave. It was my decision to move." Even her sister saw her through the lens of her relationship with Trent. It was time to find out who she was without him.

· · ·

EVEN THOUGH SHE WAS EXHAUSTED, sleep was a challenge. If it wasn't the mystery scents seeping out of the cushions, it was their stiff lumps. Tonya woke to the sound of kitchen cupboards, the coffee machine, and Brandy's roommate leaving through the front-door. She wiped pale bangs out of her eyes and sat up.

"There's a Great Clips just down the street that might be hiring." Brandy offered her with a cup of coffee.

Tonya licked her lips and blew on her drink to hide her grin. She would not be starting out at a Great Clips. They sat together at the desk and clicked the power button of the computer on. A whirring sound signaled the device waking up. Tonya sipped her coffee while she waited. Her job search began with upscale salons in down-town Seattle. By ten o'clock, Tonya had scheduled three interviews for Friday.

Next, Tonya turned her search toward finding an apartment. She typed her location, size, and style requirements into the search feature. Several photos popped up on the screen along with rent prices that made her veins run with ice water. She'd never be able to afford the luxury apartment she'd been dreaming of. So much for the glamourous city life.

Brandy cocked one side of her mouth back. "Yep. That's why I live way out here in the suburbs and still need a roommate." She turned a chair around backwards and straddled it. "Hey—maybe we could all three find a cool place together that's closer to Seattle. Our lease is up in two months."

Tonya raised her eyebrows and turned back to the screen. She started a new search for three bedrooms, quashing a shudder at the idea of sleeping on that dirty lump-couch for two months.

"I'd have to rent a storage space for all the stuff in my car until then."

Trent called every day and left messages on her phone.

She couldn't risk answering or even listening to his voice on the recording. He was like a crack addiction. She had to quit him, cold turkey.

The day Joscelyn left a message about her wedding, Tonya stayed home sniffling into a Kleenex and watching silly romantic comedies on Netflix all day. She deleted the messages, unable to bring herself to return their phone calls or to attend the wedding. Seeing Trent would destroy her. At the very least, it would ruin her resolve. Joscelyn and Mary could handle the simple wedding with no trouble. After all, that was what Joscelyn wanted any way.

By Friday, Tonya flat out resented living in the middle of her sister's tiny apartment. She should be grateful, and she was. But camping in the midst of two other women's lives was awkward. She lived out of her suitcase which sat at the end of the sofa. Tonya had no privacy. There was no place for her toiletries in the microscopic bathroom. She was an inconvenience and couldn't imagine living like this for two months.

Tonya plumped her hairdo and checked her make-up. Today she hoped to get a job. At least she could be out of the apartment for a majority of the day if she had a job to go to.

Her first interview was at a salon on top of Queen Anne Hill. Tonya drove up to an older house that someone converted to a full-service salon. She straightened her skirt and touched the pink stripe in her hair before she opened the door and entered.

"Good afternoon. Do you have an appointment today?"

All business—no dose of friendly. "Yes. Well, not a salon appointment. I have an interview."

The receptionist, outfitted in the grunge style, gave Tonya the once-over and shrugged. "Have a seat." The girl made no move to call anyone. Instead, she lifted an emery board and attacked her already short nails.

Tonya waited ten minutes before she picked up Hairstyle Magazine and read about Hollywood Coiffure to pass the time. Another twenty minutes later, a thin man with dark hair, worn short on the sides with a long sweeping bang that hung over one eye, approached her.

"Hey. Are you Tonya?"

Tonya set the magazine aside as stood. "Yes." She held out her hand. "And you must be Stephen?"

Stephen nodded and as an afterthought glanced at Tonya's outstretched hand and shook it without enthusiasm. He shrugged and tossed his bangs back.

"Follow me."

Tonya walked behind him through the salon. The main room was dim and in great need of a sweep. She stepped over a pile of hair clippings. Stephen led her to his station in the rear corner.

"Sit." He spun the seat of his barber chair toward her.

Tonya scrunched her brows together. "Are we having my interview in your chair?"

"In a manner of speaking."

Hesitating, she sat down and held her purse on her lap, unsure what to think. This interview was headed south. Tonya glanced at her watch, she didn't want to be late for her next appointment.

Stephen spun her to face the large mirror. "Do you know much about grunge fashion?" He folded up his red and black flannel sleeves and pushed his fingers into Tonya's up-do.

Tonya pulled away from his hands. "Not really." This guy gave her the creeps. She slid to the edge of the chair creating more space between them.

"I didn't think so. You've got a blonde bombshell thing going on here." He picked out a section of her hair and inspected the color. "Do you do your own hair?"

"Yes."

"Hm."

Tonya quashed the irritation building behind her breast-bone. Stephen was an ass, but she needed a job.

"I'm not sure your personal style fits in here." He looped the pink strip around his finger and let it fall. "What do you call this hairstyle?"

"I call it ruined." She'd had enough of his snotty conde-scension. No amount of money could make her work for this jerk. Tonya reached up and took the pins out of her spoiled hairdo. Fluffed the waves and stood. "I don't believe we're a good match." Without another word Tonya left the elitist grunge salon. Back in her car, she sat for a minute regaining her resolve.

Her next interview was at an ultra-modern salon. She didn't fit in there either, but at least they offered her a glass of cucumber water. Her third option was at a place called Chez Ciseaux which ended up being a dressed-up version of Great Clips with a pretentious French name. The day was a bust, so Tonya stopped by a wine bar to treat herself before driving home.

The venue was small, only one room, but cozy. Her heels clicked across the polished wood floor before she slid onto a leather barstool. Candlelight glowed from lanterns hung on the rough plastered walls and smaller matching lamps perched sporadically across the bar top giving it a warm feel. She ordered a cabernet from a handsome, young sommelier. Sniffing inside the glass, she smiled at the scent of blackcur-rant and sweet wood. She sipped the wine slowly while she relaxed to classic piano and considered her situation.

The server interrupted her musing. "You remind me of an old-fashioned movie star from the forties."

She smiled. "Are you an old movie buff?"

"My mother was." He offered her a second pour. She nodded, and he continued. "I grew up watching old movies."

"I did too. I love the era. I wish I lived back then."

"I don't know. There was that pesky war going on."

Tonya laughed. "Yeah, well in my fantasy there was either no war or at least a terribly tragic, wartime romance."

"Sounds good." He served another customer before bringing Tonya a bowl of mixed nuts. "Do you work around here?"

Tonya grimaced. "I'm trying to. I had several horrible interviews today." She held up her glass. "Which is why I needed this."

"What kind of work are you looking for?"

"I'm a hair-stylist."

"I might have guessed. Creative types have all the interesting style." He winked and went to attend to a newly seated table of four.

A woman in a sharp modern dress entered and sat down near Tonya. She addressed the sommelier as a friend. He set out a glass for the woman and poured from the same bottle Tonya was sampling.

She held the glass to the light and gave the wine a swirl. The man leaned on the bar and watched her. "So, Aunt Giselle, how's the hair chopping business?" He raised his eyebrows at Tonya and tilted his head toward the elegant woman he spoke to.

"Ha!" The woman set her glass down. "How's the grape stomping business?" She turned and casually included Tonya in their banter. "Pay no attention to him. My salon is the most elegant in town."

"As is my wine bar."

Tonya laughed along with their friendly playfulness. After introducing themselves their conversation naturally moved on to fashion and hair. Tonya shared anecdotes from her day of interviews.

"You know, Tonya," Giselle grew serious. "I adore your

sense of style. It suits you. How long did you say you've been doing hair?"

Tonya's heart bumped. "I attended cosmetology school right after high school and have been working since—a little over ten years. I ran my own shop for most of that time in a small town in Montana."

"Really? What brings you to Seattle?"

Tonya weighed her answer. "It was high time I struck out on my own. I want to see what life is away from… away from the town I grew up in."

"An adventure!"

"I guess so." Tonya raised her glass. "To new beginnings."

Giselle touched her glass to Tonya's. "I'd like to be a part of this new step. Why don't you come to my salon in the morning? I'd like to see your work. How does that sound?"

Tonya forced herself to stay seated and appear calm while inside she did cartwheels and hula-hooped. "I'd love to. Thank you." Her voice sounded so confident and rational. As soon as she was alone, she would let loose a gale-force scream. Seattle might work out after all.

39

The saddest thing about betrayal is that it never comes from your enemies. Sometimes the person you'd take a bullet for is standing behind the trigger...

My hand hurt worse than my leg, and it was fucking killing me. They didn't give me as much pain medication as they should. It was their way of punishing me. Damn government men. They interrogated me for days, but they'll never get what I don't want to give them. Suckers.

Once my public defender arrived, they had to let me make my phone call. Jed was gonna be angry that I got caught, but I focused on how proud he'd be of me for killing that coon. One less impurity. I settled my mind on our dream for the future. One pure race and no outsiders telling us how to live our lives.

An officer unlocked my cell door. He entered and wheeled me out. The medic propped my leg up to keep the wound elevated, but the cops shackled my ankle to the wheelchair. They cuffed my left hand to a chain around my waist because my right arm was in a cast from being blasted all to hell. They told me I would have limited use of both my hand and leg from then on. If I got stuck in jail, I'd sue the crap out of the assholes who shot me. If I got set free, I'd kill them in their sleep.

The cop wheeled me to the edge of a metal desk and picked up the phone.

"Time for your phone call. Number?" he asked me.

"I'm not giving you the fucking number. Give me the phone and back off. I want my privacy."

The cop shrugged and shoved the receiver toward me. He moved about twenty feet away but stared at me while he rested his hand on the grip of his service weapon. I shielded the handset from his view and dialed the number.

"Yup?"

I dialed my code series and Uncle Jed's raspy voice answered.

"What the hell is going on?"

"I've been arrested. But don't worry, Uncle Jed. You know they'll never get me to tell them anything."

"How'd you get caught? I thought I told you to lie low?" Jed growled across the miles.

"I know. You did, but some sneaky, thieving mud started snooping around my camp. I had to... take care of the problem. I did it the way you taught, like he deserved, too. You'd have been mighty proud of me, if you saw him." I laughed expecting Jed to laugh with me. "One down, several thousand more to go. Right?"

Silence crackled in my ear.

"Jed? Did you hear me?" My gut sloshed.

"You stupid bastard." Jed's voice was low and acidic. "Are you telling me you were hiding from the Feds and did something so stupid? Then advertised it, displayed it like a trophy?"

Uncertainty washed through my intestines. "How you taught me. Remember?"

"And then you hung around? Did you think you wouldn't get caught? How stupid are you, exactly?" It sounded like Jed covered the phone with his hand. I heard him shouting, but I couldn't make out any of the words.

"Uncle Jed?"

He came back on the line. "I'm no uncle of yours. You are out. We can't afford your stupidity."

"But Jed. I'm on the inside now. I can let you know what the cops are doing."

"You idiot. We have to move now. You've blown everything we dreamed of because of your blood lust."

"But—"

"Don't call me again. This line is dead." Jed hung up on me. I glanced at the officer watching me and chanced redialing the coded sequence. It didn't even ring. Jed cut me off. He abandoned me.

All my muscles bunched and clenched tight as my bowels loosened. "Guard, I need the toilet right away."

40

"She won't answer my calls." Trent grumbled and stuffed his phone in his back pocket. He glared at the fire blazing in the farmhouse fireplace. He was finally home but now the sitting around was driving him crazy.

Mary knitted two and purled one before she said, "Why don't you give her some space?"

"I've given her too much space already, Gran. That's the problem." His tone was irritable and bordered on disrespect. Trent dropped his chin to his chest. "I'm sorry. I shouldn't take it out on you."

A soft chuckle rose from his grandmother. "I can tell you're getting better because you're terrible grouchy. It's a good sign."

Trent's teeth ground together. "It's taking far too long to get back on my feet. Things are falling apart on the ranch. I have work to do."

"Randy is handling everything just fine and when he needs help, Cade always comes. Even Jack has pitched in on his free time."

Trent's ire softened when he thought of his brothers. He was more than grateful that he and Jack made amends. It wasn't like Jack was going to move home and take on his third of the ranch, but at least he would visit now. They were friends again after so many years of not speaking. If only he could fix it with Tonya.

"They've all been great. I'm just itching to get back to it. That's all."

Mary smiled fondly at him. "I know you are, and you're getting there. Try to be patient with yourself."

"Did Jack ever get any information out of Werner?"

"He refuses to name the leader of their hateful militia, but I think they've been gathering clues to their location. Jack thinks it's somewhere in the wild part of northern Idaho."

After finishing her row, Mary set her knitting down. "Would you like anything? Are you hungry?"

"All I want is for Tonya to answer my damn calls." Trent sat up and worked his shoulder through some of his PT exercises. "What ever happened to Levi Barrett? Is she still seeing him?"

"No, no. Tom ran a check on him and apparently he was hiding from an arrest warrant in Nebraska. So, they sent him back there."

"What'd he do? Was he dangerous?" Trent grimaced against the pain he pushed into.

"No. You should ask Tom, but I think he stole a car or something like that. The Nebraska State Police took him to Omaha to face the stolen car charge."

Pleased to hear Barrett was no longer in the picture, Trent eased back into his chair. "I knew he was a dirt-bag. What's going on with Cade and Joscelyn's wedding?"

"With Tonya in Seattle, I think Joscelyn will end up with the simple wedding of her dreams." Mary's soft laugh soothed his irritation. Trent's mouth curled up on one side. Tonya had a flair for the dramatic, that was for sure.

Gravel crunched on the drive outside. Trent peered through the window. "My drill sergeant is here."

They scheduled an in-home physical therapist three days a week for the first two weeks after Trent's release from the hospital. The simple exercises were grueling. His shoulder burned like liquid fire shooting through his veins. It frustrated him to be so weak, unable to do the simplest tasks without help. Only three more sessions at home and then he would have to go in to the office for continued therapy. Or not.

Mary interrupted his thoughts. "Cade and Joscelyn are coming over for lunch and to talk about the ceremony. You'll be done with your therapy by then."

"Sounds good—being done, I mean."

During lunch, Trent leaned close to Joscelyn. "Hey, would you try to call Tonya? Maybe she'll answer someone else's calls."

The sympathy in Joscelyn's eyes made him feel like a chump. "I'll try Trent, but she hasn't answered my calls either. I've left several messages. I've told her about the wedding and gave her the date and time. Maybe she'll show up."

Cade leaned his elbows on the table. "That's a good sign. If you can leave her messages, then she still has her same phone number."

Startled, Trent said, "I didn't think about her changing her number. What if she does? I won't be able to reach her at all."

"I guess you'd have to accept that." Cade looked at him, his gray eyes warm. Trent dropped his gaze so no one could see the hurt in his eyes. *I've been a damn idiot. Tonya's been in my life as long as I remember. Matthew was right—I assumed she always would be. I can only hope she'll come to the wedding.*

TRENT TUGGED at the collar of his white dress shirt. He hadn't worn his suit since college and it was tight in the shoulders and across his chest. A soft breeze decorated Wolf Run, the site of Cade and Joscelyn's ceremony, with a shower of colorful autumn leaves. It was a beautiful day. The weather held up nicely for October. Trent stood with Cade before the handful of guests as Jack escorted their grandmother to her seat.

She didn't sit, though. Instead, she approached Trent and took hold of his elbow. Mary tilted her head up and motioned for him to lean down so he could hear. "I have something for you. Something I hope you'll need today."

Trent lifted his brows in question and Mary reached into the pocket of her sweater. She pulled out a small velvet box. "Matthew had this in his safe. His daughter, Laiken, brought it over this morning." She placed the box in Trent's open hand. "Your grandpa gave me this ring on the day of our wedding. I haven't worn it since my knuckles got thick with arthritis." She flexed the fingers on her left hand. "Cade is giving Joscelyn your mother's ring, and now you have mine with a new setting. Give it to Tonya when the time is right."

Pure love filled Trent's whole body in that moment. Love for his parents, for his grandparents, and for Tonya. He bent down and kissed Mary on the cheek. "Thanks, Gran." He swallowed hard. "I hope she comes. I hope she'll have me."

Guitar music started up and Mary took her seat. Trent glanced at Cade whose dark eyes were misty as they searched for his bride. Joscelyn appeared in a simple ivory dress. She walked proudly toward her future husband. Trent remembered his crush on Joscelyn when she first arrived in Flint River. She knew though—knew he was never serious about anyone besides Tonya.

Tonya wasn't among the small congregation. Trent's heart was heavy even though he was happy for Cade. He bit down on his disappointment and gave his attention to the best day in his brother's life. The pastor presided over the ceremony. Cade turned to Trent for the wedding ring.

Mary served a lunch of roast chicken, rosemary potatoes, and green beans at tables set up on the porch of Cade's log cabin home. Trent stood to toast the happy couple. He spoke of love and commitment, of family and abiding friendship, all the while his soul yearned for these things in his own life. Sadie, who was Joscelyn's only bridesmaid, was next to give a toast with her sparkling cider. Still no Tonya. How could she miss Joscelyn and Cade's wedding? Trent willed himself to be angry rather than crushed. He should never have let himself give in to the blind hope that she'd come.

When Cade and Joscelyn stood to cut their cake, the sound of a car came from the gravel drive. Trent stood and craned his neck to see if Tonya's Thing was finally arriving, his heart rising on a tide of hope.

"Damn it," he muttered when he realized the sound was the limousine Cade hired to drive them to the airport for their Hawaiian honeymoon. Trent's heart plummeted, shattering when it hit bottom. *She isn't coming. She must truly hate me if she missed Joscelyn's big day to avoid me.*

They used the large porch as a dance floor. Cade stood and held his hand out to his beautiful bride. The light in Joscelyn's eyes when she joined him told the story of their love. Trent closed his eyes. It was hard to watch their happiness, knowing he lost his. He couldn't wait for the duration of his obligatory presence to be over and he could go off somewhere by himself. Until then, he would smile and participate as expected.

Cade danced with Sadie next and Trent took Mary for a few halting spins. He had hoped to be dancing with Tonya, hoped beyond reason that she would forgive him and come home. At the end of the song, Mary reached up and touched his cheek. All her love radiated from her kind face and Trent knew she wanted to comfort him, but it only made him feel worse. He flashed her his crooked smile, but there was no joy or tease behind it.

When he returned to his table, Tom and Wayne joined him. Tom leaned toward Trent. "Tonya's a no show?"

Trent gave him a curt nod. "Looks that way."

"No big surprise, the way you treated her," Wayne piped in.

"Wayne, for once, can you keep your thoughts in your head?" Tom grimaced and rolled his eyes for Trent's benefit.

Trent shook his head. Normally, Wayne was merely a nuisance, but this time his words cut razor sharp with their truth. "Nah, it's okay, Wayne. I screwed up. No denyin' it. I've been an ass."

Wayne grunted. "That's putting it mildly."

Tom glared at his deputy, but Trent's eyes rested on the smaller man without malice. "You're right, Wayne, and I haven't always been much of a friend to you either. I'm a changed man now though, after gettin' shot. Makes a man consider his life, ya know?"

"I'll believe it when I see it."

Trent nodded. "Fair enough."

As soon as the newlyweds left for their trip, Trent made his excuses and escaped into the cabin's guest room to change. He couldn't get out of the stiff suit soon enough. He threw the dressy clothes on a chair and pulled on his jeans. When he reached for his shirt, there was a knock on the door.

"Yeah? It's open."

The door swung in and Jack stepped through. "Couldn't wait to get back into your jeans?"

Trent gave him a rueful grin. "I hate that straight jacket." He eased on his shirt and sat to pull on his boots. "Wanna go for a ride?"

"I'd like that, but they've called me in. The interrogation team had a breakthrough. Werner is finally willing to talk. I've got to go."

Trent's heart missed a beat. He wanted more time with Jack. It seemed like most of the people he loved were leaving. "When do you think you'll be back through?" His voice was rough.

"Can't be sure. Depends on what we find and how long it takes to break it down."

"You'll still be home for Christmas though, right?" It was hard for Trent to speak through the swelling lump in his throat. "It would break Gran's heart if you weren't."

Jack gave him a knowing look and curled the corners of his mouth up. "It would break my heart too, big brother." He held out his hand.

Trent grasped the offered hand and drew Jack in for a hug. "It's been good having you home. You'd better keep yourself safe out there."

"That's the plan." Jack patted Trent's shoulder before he let go. Trent grimaced but welcomed the physical pain in his shoulder that flamed through with the brotherly affection. It distracted him from the ache in his heart. "Hey, now the ceremony is over, I have something to tell you. I wanted it to come from me."

"What's the matter?" Fingers of ice stirred in Trent's gut.

Jack shrugged. "Nothing to worry about. The crime scene investigators found a ton of evidence inside the old mine—chicken bones and Hilde's axe. Werner had also been collecting the ingredients he needed to build another home-made bomb."

"Shit."

"Yeah, that's the evidence that made the bastard nervous. He made his phone call and after that he was ready to do some talking." Jack ran a hand through his black hair.

"That's good news though, right?" Trent wondered at the tension in his brother's movements.

"Yeah, it is. But they also found Dad's old rifle."

"Yeah? Well, that's good too." Trent studied the expression on Jack's face. "Isn't it?"

"Yes… but because it belongs to you, it casts you as a potential suspect."

Trent cocked his head and drew his brows together.

Jack flattened his lips into a thin line. "So, of course Wayne wants you arrested."

Trent's head snapped up. "What?"

"It's just procedure. We all know nothing will come of it, but Tom has to take you in for questioning."

"You've got to be kidding?"

"Unfortunately, I'm not. Brown is being a stickler for procedure. Says he wants all the loose ends tied up." Jack checked the clock on his phone. "It won't take long, but if Tom doesn't go through the motions, it could look bad for him. And Wayne's not wrong. We don't want to give a defense attorney any foothold."

Trent dropped his shoulders and shook his head. "What-ever. I have nothing better to do. I guess this explains why Tom and Wayne were at the wedding."

"Tom didn't say anything because I wanted to wait till after the ceremony and talk to you myself." Jack leveled his gaze on Trent. "I'm sorry Tonya didn't show."

Trent nodded, he didn't trust his voice. He picked up his hat and led the way downstairs to find Tom.

41

"So are you going to handcuff me?" Trent held his wrists together out toward Tom.

Tom looked up at Trent from his seat on the living-room sofa, but didn't quite meet his eyes. His face was ruddy, and he set his mouth in a grim line. "Of course not. You know I don't want to do this, Trent. It's ridiculous. But Wayne has threatened to go above my head—and Jack's too, if we don't investigate all the leads. He's a fanatic about procedure."

"It's okay, I was just jokin'. I have nothing to hide. Let's go."

Tom tilted his head to the side and gave Trent a long look. "Don't be cocky in there Trent. There is real evidence, both hard and circumstantial that could point to you."

Trent narrowed his eyes at his friend.

"I mean, no one thinks you killed Matthew, not even Wayne. But we have to account for all the facts."

Trent shook his head. When he woke up this morning, he hoped this day might be one of happy celebration, for both Cade and himself. He wanted to be dancing with Tonya right now, not promenading to the Sheriff's Office with Tom, Wayne, and the frickin' FBI.

"Let's get this over with." Trent led the way out the door and got into the back of the Sheriff's Bronco. "Come on Trent. You don't need to sit in the backseat like a common criminal."

"This is where suspects sit, isn't it?"

When Trent didn't move, Tom shrugged. "Suit yourself." He got behind the wheel and they drove back to town in silence.

Trent sat at a scarred wooden table across from Tom and Wayne. An anonymous FBI agent stood in a black suit next to the closed door of the interrogation room. He crossed his arms over his chest.

"This is just a formality, Trent. We need to account for all the details of this story before we prosecute the man we have in custody. We all know he's the killer."

Wayne sat forward. "There are some things that must be cleared up, though."

Trent's shoulder's sagged, his injury ached. "Like what?" All he wanted was to take some Percocet, go to bed, and sleep for a week. The hope he held all morning was costing him emotional dollars now.

Wayne stared hard at him in what Trent supposed was an attempt at intimidation. "Like... Can you explain the fact it was your rifle that killed Matthew Jefferson?"

"What?" Stunned, Trent's gaze flashed to Tom. He hadn't heard about this. His chest tightened, crushing his lungs. He shook his head.

Tom nodded. "That's what the ballistic report shows."

Trent pressed his temples and held his head between his hands. "No. No! That son-of-a-bitch." He abruptly shoved away from the table and stood.

"So, how do you explain that?" Wayne's myopic eyes

bulged toward Trent.

"I can't be a hundred percent sure, Wayne," Trent's answer dripped with sarcasm and fury. "But I'd guess the man who shot Matthew is the same guy who broke into my truck and stole my rifle."

"We have to consider the possibility that it was you who broke the window and claimed someone stole your rifle. Maybe you were setting someone else up for a murder you were planning?"

The skin between Trent's eyes creased and he held back a sick laugh. "Are you kiddin' me, Wayne? Hell, if I was gonna shoot someone, I wouldn't use my daddy's antique rifle that's easy to trace. I'd shoot him with one of my many rifles you know nothin' about."

"Trent…" Tom's warning tone was met with a scoffing sound from Trent's throat.

"You need to register all your weapons with the state, sir." The FBI agent intoned without moving.

"Yeah, yeah." Trent pierced Wayne with an icy stare. "Is that it, Wayne? That all you got?"

"All? Let's see…"

Tom stared at his deputy. "Come on Wayne. Ask your questions, but let's keep this civil and quick, all right? We all know Trent is innocent."

Wayne snapped his papers, obviously enjoying the upper hand if even for a few short minutes. "I have a man killed with your gun that has your fingerprints all over it. That is enough to put you in jail right there."

"That's ridiculous. Of course my rifle has my fingerprints on it—not to mention, I was shot by that rifle myself." Trent struggled to keep his temper. Physical and emotional exhaustion conspired against him. "Does it have Werner's fingerprints on it too?"

Wayne ignored Trent's question. "When was the last time

you saw Matthew alive?"

Trent closed his eyes and pictured his friend on the hiking trail. "It was a Saturday, I think about two weeks before he was found."

"Yes, you were seen going into the woods with Matthew that Saturday morning and a witness said it looked like you two were having an angry conversation."

"Angry?" Trent burst out. "We weren't angry. Matthew was telling me what he thought of my situation with Tonya. That's all." Trent thought back over their talk and then rubbed a hand over his face. "I guess it might have looked angry from far away, but I was more… exasperated." Trent sat back down and in an undertone to himself he added, "Mostly because Matthew was right."

"So, you were angry… or as you say, exasperated, in the woods with Matthew?

Trent sat forward. "Stop twisting the truth, Wayne. You know goddamn good and well I had nothing to do with Matthew's death." He turned his piercing gaze to Tom. "Do I need to call a lawyer?"

Tom sighed. "It is within your rights to do so, but I don't think you need to. Do you, Deputy?" He glared at Wayne. "Aren't we here just to clear up a few things?"

"We have to follow every lead." Wayne leaned back in his chair. "In fact, another witness reported seeing you shouting at Matthew the previous Friday afternoon of the same week, when you were coming out of the Gem Emporium." Wayne flipped through some pages on his notepad. "Says here you told him to, quote 'mind your own business, old man.'"

Trent opened his mouth to defend himself but he couldn't deny the statement. He shook his head, a sick, helpless feeling closed in on him.

"Is that an accurate statement?" Wayne peered over the top of the pages at him.

"It's completely out of context, Wayne."

"Hm." The deputy scribbled a note on the side of the page.

Tom leaned forward, his forearms on the edge of the table. "Trent, can you account for your whereabouts on that Wednesday? The day before we found Matthew? The ME determined he was killed about 24-36 hours before the hikers discovered his body that Thursday."

"I can tell you I was out on the ranch, but are you asking if I can prove it?" Trent pushed away from the table again. "I can't. I mean Gran and Randy saw me that morning, but later I was there on my own." He stood and paced the two steps to the wall and back. "Don't you have a confession from the guy who shot me? Don't you have evidence he was in Hilde's car? That he hung Matthew's body?"

"He hasn't confessed to the murder. He claims he never knew Matthew, which I suspect is true, and that he had no motive. The only thing he's copping to is the evidence of the explosive device he was trying to build that we found in the mine, and now finally, hoping to make a deal with the court, he's bartering to giving up the location of the compound the FBI has been searching for."

"What about the fact that he had my rifle in his hands when Cade and Jack shot him?"

"He says he found it hidden there when he holed up inside."

Trent let out his frustration on the chair he'd been sitting in, knocking it over sideways onto the floor. "Damn it. Why is he innocent till proven guilty but you're treating me like I'm guilty unless I can prove myself innocent?" Trent's icy glare shifted from Tom to Wayne and settled on the silent FBI man.

"It's not like that," Tom consoled. "We're asking questions, that's all. We have to gather all the information before we can build a case." Tom got up and walked around the table to pick up the chair and set it right. "Sit down. I will give you a pad of paper and I want you to write out a statement. Start with the Friday afternoon when you visited Matthew at his shop. Include the morning you met Matthew for breakfast and tell us about that, then explain what you did the day of Matthew's murder, the day before we found his body. Include anyone who might have seen you at the ranch."

Trent slumped back into the chair. "Fine. Got a pen?"

When he finished writing his statement, Trent tossed the pen onto the table. "That's it. Can I go now?"

Tom stood. "Yeah, I'll run you home."

"You can walk me over to the pub."

Tom offered Trent a weak smile. "First round's on me."

The FBI agent finally moved, but only to uncross his arms and open the door. Trent walked through followed by Tom and then Wayne.

"Hey, Stone," Wayne stopped in the hallway and Trent glanced back at him. The deputy stuffed his hands into his pockets and looked down. "For what it's worth. I don't really think you had anything to do with Matthew's murder. Just following procedure. We don't want to leave any cracks for Werner to slip through."

"I know you guys have a job to do and no one wants Werner to get off, especially me. But you enjoyed every minute of that interrogation." Trent turned back toward the front door.

"You know—a couple of weeks ago, I would have. But you've changed."

It was true, Trent's perspective on things had changed. Even Wayne Brown could see it. If Tonya were still around, maybe she would see it too and give him another chance. Trent followed Tom out the door and stepped onto the walk. He looked back over his shoulder. "Hey Wayne, you think we can we bury this old hatchet?"

Wayne hesitated and drew his chin back into his neck.

"I'm serious. We've been at this since high school. Don't you think it's time we got over it?"

Wayne's eyes bulged more than usual. "Yeah—I guess so."

"Good. Let's go get a beer."

"Me? You want me to come?" Wayne rolled up on the balls of his feet.

Tom laughed, "Don't make it weird, Wayne."

"That'd be great."

Trent rode shotgun in Tom's Bronco on the long drive back to Stone Ranch. His phone buzzed in his pocket. When he pulled it out, Jack's number appeared on the screen. "Hey, I thought you were off hunting down a domestic terrorist compound."

"I am, but I got a call from our guy who sat in on your questioning."

"Yeah?"

"Listen Trent, you need to find someone who can verify you were out at the ranch when Matthew was killed."

Trent sighed. "There is no evidence that puts me in the mountains above Flint River."

Jack's voice intensified. "No, I'm not talking about proving your innocence. I'm talking about your statement. When it's read alongside Eugene Werner's, it could give a jury reasonable doubt that he is the murderer. We all know he did it, but your account along with the statements of your frustration with Matthew might get him off."

"Shit."

"Yeah."

"I'll think it through again, but Gran was over at Wolf Run, planning the wedding with Joscelyn."

"What about Randy?"

"He saw me ride out in the morning, but he was gone by the time I rode back in. Then I cleaned up and left to pick up Cade."

"Did anyone pass you on the road? You've got to remember something."

"I'll think on it. I sure as hell don't want to be the reason that son-of-a-bitch gets set free."

There was a pause on the line. "Don't worry. He won't get free. We have him on intent to blow up a school. I just want him sent up for murder in a state that has the death penalty."

"I'll let Tom know if I come up with anything. You be safe out there."

"I will."

"And Jack… I'm really glad you came home."

The line was silent. Trent closed his eyes and swallowed.

When Jack responded his voice was low and husky. "Yeah, me too."

Trent patted the top of the Bronco before Tom drove away. He turned and strode straight to the barn to saddle up King. A long moonlit ride was exactly what he needed to process all that was going on. When he led his horse out through the double barn-doors, Mary was waiting for him in the glow of the porch-light at the bottom of the farmhouse steps. "Hey, Gran. I'm going for a ride. I'll be back in a couple of hours."

"Trent, come here a minute." Mary had a strange, nervous expression on her face that caused Trent's stomach to tighten.

"What's wrong, Gran?"

"Nothing's wrong." She ran a hand down his arm. "I really thought Tonya would show up today."

"Me too." He kicked the dirt. "Well, I was hoping, anyway."

"Listen, I have Tonya's sister's phone number. She told me

to use it only in case of an emergency. And I've decided her not showing up today qualifies."

"You've had Brandy's number this whole time?" Trent's heart hammered. "Did you call?"

"No, I'll leave that to you." Mary slipped a piece of paper into Trent's hand. "Go get her, son."

42

———

Tonya leaned in toward the mirror at Cheveux Magnifiques, the elegant salon on First Avenue, where she now worked. She inspected the deep red lipstick staining her full lips and plumped up the side rolls in her hair. Her vintage style always stood out, but in this salon, it made her feel out of place.

Women in Seattle leaned toward a natural, less made-up, earthy look. Tonya supposed the women in Flint River did too, but the people there knew her. Here, her personal style seemed like a costume instead of a genuine part of her personality.

It had been difficult adjusting to city life, and she wondered if she would ever get used to the set-up of this ultra-modern, swanky Seattle salon. There were aspects of Seattle she genuinely loved. The coffee, craft beers, and seafood couldn't be beat. The city had a wonderful energy to it that made life seem exciting.

Lately, she found herself daydreaming about finding a small space to rent and opening her own beauty shop where she would be free to express herself. She would call Tom and find out if anyone had rented her shop in Flint River yet. If not, maybe she could have her shop accoutrements and barber chair shipped to Seattle.

Tonya slipped on her apron and prepped her work station by polishing the black-granite counter, and switching on a black ceramic waxing pot. A pristine, white-leather barber chair faced a wide full-length mirror. The chair looked like it belonged in a Manhattan cocktail lounge and was far too modern to be comfortable. It had an electric hydraulic system that elevated the seat up and down. No awkward pumping on a step with her foot. Tonya sighed, wishing she was already in her own place. She realized she enjoyed being her own boss.

All of her beauty supplies were hidden away in a sleek black cabinet that clicked open when she pressed it. A crystal chandelier illuminated her workspace until a client sat in her chair. The pressure in the seat caused bright lights to emanate from behind the long mirror. The motif of the salon was elegant minimalism—sophisticated and cold.

Tonya's first client arrived ten minutes early, but she was ready. She'd scheduled her whole day with color and cut appointments. The receptionist escorted the woman to Tonya's station.

Tonya pasted a smile on. "Hello, Sylvia. How can we make you even more beautiful today?" She asked her scripted question while trying not to roll her eyes. Tonya thought of her little shop in Flint River, where she knew everyone and enjoyed catching up on all the local gossip. A breeze of wistful melancholy blew through her spirit. Here, at Cheveux Magnifiques, they discouraged the stylists from talking about anything personal. It was a lonely job full of people.

After receiving her beautification orders, she offered her client a magazine and a beverage. Clients almost always asked for mimosas in the morning. Once she occupied the woman with her early cocktail and reading material, Tonya stepped into the back room to mix the color recipe. When she returned, she wheeled a supply caddy along with her that held three pots of color, hair foils, and a set of combs and clips.

This particular client wasn't talkative. She kept her nose in the gossip magazine and sipped her cocktail, so Tonya slipped on her black rubber gloves and started working on the woman's highlights. She began in the back layering the various colors between sheets of foil. Tonya spun the chair to the side and started on the right side of her client's head, foil and hair sticking out at odd angles.

Salon customers both entered and left to the sound of elegant chimes. Soft jazz played in the background and everyone kept their voices low as if they were in a church sanctuary. It was normally a peaceful place, but that morning, mid-color, the chimes clanged together in an unpleasant bash and the voices rose. A charged feminine undercurrent swept through the salon. Tonya peered toward the front to see what had caused the commotion.

Trent.

He stood in the middle of the entryway taking in his surroundings, a cowboy who landed in an alien world. When his eyes landed on Tonya, his features softened, and he strode past the reception station aimed in her direction. The receptionist was on his heels with her notepad and a frantic expression. The entire salon hushed in utter silence. Stylists turned hairdryers off, mouths opened in astonishment, and Tonya dropped her color brush in a splat on the floor.

"What are you doing here?" she whispered.

TRENT STARED at her for a full minute before he replied, his pulse deafening behind his ear drums. "I'm here to get you." She stood out like a sparkling diamond set in the black surroundings of the salon. Trent smiled at her signature pink stripe wound up into her hairdo.

"What do you mean?" Her expression closed, and she stepped back.

Trent took a deep breath, ignoring the jitters inside and the people staring at him. He took three more steps forward until he stood right before Tonya. He took off his cowboy hat and dropped to one knee.

The bowl of color she held slipped to the floor and landed next to the brush. White-blue cream splattered across the gleaming tiles. She took another step back, her eyes as wide as the ends of her Velcro curlers. "Oh, for crying out the window."

A sheen of sweat cooled Trent's hairline and dampened his shirt. His chest ached from the slamming of his heart against his ribs. "Tonya, I've loved you since I was five. And cuz I've known you all my life, I somehow figured you'd always be there waiting until I was done being an idiot. I took you for granted and I'm sorrier for that than you'll ever know." He cleared his throat, reached into his pocket and pulled out a small box. He rubbed his thumb over the top before opened it and held it up to her. "Will you forgive me and become my wife?"

TONYA'S WORDS refused to leave her mouth. Tears blurred her view of the ring Trent offered her. A sob escaped before she could stop it. "Trent... I..." Her hand flew to cover her mouth, and she turned slightly away from him, glancing back at him over her shoulder. Anguish washed into his eyes as he knelt before her on the glistening floor.

His Adam's apple bobbed when he swallowed. "Please, Tonya," he whispered.

"Are you sure?"

"Never more sure of anything in my life." His eyes were moist in his earnest face.

She wiped a tear with her gloved hand and smeared hair color gel on her cheek. "Oh," she gasped and pulled off the dirty gloves. She could only stare open-mouthed at the man on his knee in front of her.

"I want to marry you, Tonya—make you mine and start a life together." He leaned forward and raised the ring higher. "Will you have me?"

Tonya's heart skipped in her chest and her head swam. "If you married me, you would belong to me." She swallowed. "Only me. Forever. Could you do that?"

"I've fooled around long enough. The truth is, I've always, only ever been yours. When you left, I realized what I fool I'd been. Coming as close to death as I did, changes a man's perspective. Life's too short to be so stupid." He wiped perspiration from his forehead on his sleeve.

"I've learned, Tonya and I've changed. I want to see your beautiful face every night before I go to sleep and wake up with you every morning." Trent lowered the box in his hand to his knee. "This was my gran's wedding ring. It's been fitted with the pink sapphire Matthew said you admired. Gran wanted me to give it to you, if you agree to marry me."

"Oh, Trent..." Tonya's eyes flooded, and she threw her arms around his head and held his face to her belly.

He stood and as he did, he scooped her up into his arms. "Is this a yes?" His intense blue eyes burned bright with tears.

"Put me down—your shoulder!"

"Say yes."

Tonya nodded. "Yes!"

Trent kissed her, his mouth devouring hers. She pulled him closer. The salon which had frozen, now broke out in cheers and applause. Tonya held Trent's face between her hands and lost herself in his kiss. He turned on the heel of his boot and carried her toward the door.

"Wait, Trent. I'm in the middle of a hair-color appointment."

He spun back to the crowd of people, customers and stylists. "Sorry ladies, can someone finish up for Tonya? I'm not waiting another minute." He leaned against the exit with his back and strode to his truck parked on the street. He placed her in her cowboy-carriage and jogged around to the driver's side. Tonya looked back at the salon. Her coworkers and several clients watched them out the window. Her boss waved at them from the shop door, bouncing on her toes.

43

———————

"I'd marry you today if it were up to me, but I suspect you'd like to have a fancy to-do." Trent grinned down at her as he pulled Tonya over next to him onto the middle seat of his truck. She snuggled into the crook of his arm and gazed at the ring glistening on her finger.

"I can hardly believe this is happening." She beamed up at him. "Are you really here?"

"Believe it. Believe it every day for the rest of your life." Trent bent his face to hers and kissed her softly with reverence. Her body surged with electricity. "I'm not going anywhere, ever again."

He started the engine of his truck and pulled out into the street. "But before we go to your sister's apartment to pack up your things, can we get something to eat?"

Tonya glanced at the dashboard clock. "Didn't you have breakfast?"

Trent's smile was self-deprecating. "I was too nervous to eat."

Tonya had a hard time picturing Trent as nervous at all, let alone too nervous to eat. "Seriously?"

"Well, you didn't answer my calls. I had to consider the possibility you'd tell me to go jump in Puget Sound."

Tonya's throat ached when she answered. "I'm sorry I didn't respond. I just needed more time, but when I saw you this morning, I realized no amount of time would ever help me get over you."

Trent held her tight and Tonya directed him to her favorite breakfast spot. "Bacco Cafe has the best biscuits and gravy in town."

"You know what I like." Trent grinned and parked his truck on the street, taking up two spots. They stepped inside the tiny cafe and waited for a table. Tonya ordered a Nutella mocha which looked as though an artist had painted leaves on the surface.

"That's the fanciest coffee I've ever seen."

Tonya took a delicate sip. "It tastes as good as it looks, too."

"After breakfast, we can get your things and then come back to the hotel."

Tonya shook her head, finding the events of the morning hard to believe. "How did you find me? Did my sister call you?"

"No. Gran finally coughed up her phone number though. She wanted to keep the promise she made you not to give it to me, but when you didn't show up to Cade and Joscelyn's wedding, she took matters into her own hands."

Tonya's chest expanded with warmth. It was wonderful to know that not only Trent wanted her, but so did his family. Trent kept his arm around her the entire forty-five-minute drive to Renton. It didn't take long to pack the few things she had at her sister's condo before they drove back to Seattle. Trent had a room booked for them at the Fairmont.

Doubt niggled at the edge of Tonya's mind while they waited for the elevator. "Were you so confident I would come with you, you already had a room?" Was she so predictable? Of course—he and everyone else expected her to chase Trent home.

He waited until the doors closed behind them before he turned her to face him, his hands resting on her shoulders. "I wasn't confident at all. I just couldn't bear to think of any alternative. I've been as nervous as a cat coming up here to the city." He pulled her into his chest and held her tight until the elevator opened on their floor.

Tonya remained quiet until they got into the room. She had never stayed anywhere so elegant. Trent set her bags in the closet. She drew a deep breath. "What would you say if I told you I want to live in Seattle?" she asked, testing him.

Trent stared at her. He blinked and cast his gaze to the floor. After a minute he walked to the window and looked out.

Tonya waited for his answer. The more things change, the more they stay the same.

Finally, he cleared his throat. "I admit it never occurred to me you might want to live somewhere other than Flint River." He turned to face her and searched her eyes. "I've never wanted to live anywhere but Stone Ranch. Always thought I'd raise my own kids there one day." He bit down and his jaw flexed.

"But, if movin' here's the only way you'll marry me, I guess I'll have to move." He swallowed and looked miserable before he angled back to the window. "Maybe Jack would come home and take his part of the ranch. I hate to think of Gran being all alone, but she has Sadie and Joscelyn now too."

Warm tears chilled on Tonya's face and she rushed to Trent. She pressed her cheek against his back and slid her arms around his chest. "I don't need to live in Seattle, Trent. I thought about opening a shop here, but honestly, I don't feel at home here at all. I just had to know."

He turned and cupped her face in his big hands, wiping the moisture from her cheeks. "I'd live anywhere as long as we're together, Tonya. I know you're used to me taking you for granted, but now you'll have to get used to that being different." Trent kissed her hair, then her temple, and her mouth. He lifted her and set her reverently on the bed. His eyes darkened and held all his love and longing.

"I'm trying to change, too. I've resolved to being direct and up-front, but I just did it again."

"What?"

"Instead of trusting that you love me, I tested you by telling you I wanted to live in Seattle." Shame choked her. This kind of behavior almost cost her relationship with Trent before. "I'm sorry. Old habits really do die hard."

"At least you recognize it and anyway, I haven't given you a lot of reason to trust me either. Maybe we can work on this together?"

He knelt on the bed next to her and held her face in his hands. Trent's eyes roamed over her features in awe, as though he'd never seen her before. His thumb smoothed over her bottom lip. He stretched up to kiss her and pressed her back on the bedspread. His kisses reached into her soul and she clung tight to him, never wanting to let go.

His hands were at once familiar and new as he swept her clothes away. Tonya closed her eyes and concentrated on the sensations playing throughout her body. Tendrils of electrified heat wound through her and found their targets. Her body pressed into his. She wanted him—more and more of him. She was insatiable.

He lifted her further up on the bed and kicked off his boots. They landed with a thud on the floor. His hands never left her skin. His kisses wandered where they would, intertwined with gruff murmurs of adoration. His touch resounded through her nervous system like a concerto demanding a crescendo. Her body complied, tight as the strings of a violin in fortissimo before she drifted back down.

She lay, exhausted and content, with her head on his chest. Trent drifted to sleep, and she listened to his steady breathing. Tonya laughed when his stomach growled and he stirred, pulling her on top of him. He blinked open his sleepy blue eyes.

Tonya traced her fingertip along the purple scar on his shoulder left from his gunshot wound. She kissed his chin. "Hungry?"

He laughed. "Starving."

TRENT WALKED with Tonya to Pike Place Fish Market. The place was jam-packed with people. They got there too late to see the fish mongers throwing fish to their customers, but it was still an amazing place to visit.

Trent pointed to a lobster tail as thick as his calf sitting on ice. "That could feed four people," he laughed.

They walked arm in arm down through the market, purely happy to be together browsing through lingonberry jams and honeys that lined shelves next to hand-crafted jewelry. It jarred his senses to smell chowder and fresh fish in one breath, and flowers, cinnamon, and garlic the next. Trent stopped at the flower stand and bought Tonya a luscious bouquet of pink and white dahlias. His chest swelled when she pressed her face into the blooms and breathed in.

On one of the lower floors of the multi-level market, they found a magic shop and took silly pictures in a photo booth. Trent couldn't remember when they last simply had fun together. He made himself a promise they would take time to play more often.

"Let's stop for a beer. There are some amazing local brewers in Seattle. You have to try some new IPAs." Tonya tugged Trent's arm, and they found a table in a restaurant overlooking the water.

"No arguments here." He patted his belly.

"Afterward, I thought we could get some chowder for lunch and then maybe take the ferry to Bainbridge Island for the afternoon?"

"Sure." Trent grinned, "You're the tour guide. I'll follow wherever you lead."

The autumn leaves were brilliant with color on Bainbridge, but the air hinted at winter. Trent and Tonya strolled down Main Street, stopping in many of the trinket shops along the way. They walked down to the docks to admire the boats and drank mochas at a quaint little coffee shop covered in ivy that had gone from a summer green to a fiery red. After a lazy and romantic afternoon, the couple stopped by Mora's for ice-cream cones and licked them on their trek back to the ferry, dreaming together about their future

"This island would be a great place to come for a weekend getaway. Maybe an anniversary?"

Tonya smiled and stood on her toes to kiss Trent's cheek. "Thinking ahead?"

He laughed. "Yep. I figure you'll want a break from all our kids every once in a while."

"All our kids? How many kids are you thinking about, Trenton Stone?" Tonya pretended outrage.

"At least five." He made a solemn face to cover his mischief. "But I'd rather shoot for eight."

"Eight?" Tonya sputtered and laughed. "You better be planning on carrying at least four of them yourself."

Trent pulled her close. "Seriously though, can you imagine us having a family?" His chest was buoyant.

Tonya pressed into him. "Yes. I love the idea of having children with you. In fact, I've imagined it since I was a little girl. You're all I've ever wanted, Trent. Well, you and several mini versions of you at your heels."

After a fancy dinner of fresh salmon and halibut, Trent and Tonya walked hand in hand an uphill mile to the Space Needle. The night lights of the Seattle skyline were breathtaking.

Trent stood behind Tonya with his arms around her. "I feel like we could see Stone Ranch from here if it were daytime."

Tonya's hands rubbed his arms. "I can't wait to get home."

Home. Trent smiled and holding her tight, kissed the top of her head.

44

———

A thrill swelled though Tonya's belly when they drove under the sign for Stone Ranch. She'd seen that sign countless times in her life, but this time the sign spelled "Home". Trent must have felt it too because he reached over and clasped her hand.

"How soon can you get this wedding fandango planned? I don't want to have to wait long to make you Mrs. Trent Stone."

Tonya laughed. "You'll have to wait as long as it takes. I only plan on doing this one time in my life and I want it to be perfect."

"You'll move in right away though, right?"

"No. Actually, I don't want to move in until we're married." Trent looked at her sideways and she giggled. "I'm serious. It will do you some good to wait for something for once."

"But—"

"No buts. This is non-negotiable. I want to have my space to plan and prepare. I promise I won't take too long. I've been planning this day in my head since we were five. I already know what I want."

He parked his truck, stepped out and drew her across the driver's seat, into his arms. He carried her like a bride and kissed her long and lusciously. "So do I."

"Mmm," she murmured.

Trent set her on her feet and when they noticed Tom's Bronco was there. Tom opened the door and stepped out onto the front porch. Mary followed him.

"THERE YOU ARE. I've been waiting all day for you two to get home." Mary raised her arms and motioned with her hands for the couple to come to her. "Come on in. I want to hear all about it." Mary squeezed Tonya tight to her ample bosom, and turned back toward the screen door. Trent followed. The scent of something baking swirled together with joy and spread throughout his system.

"Tell me all about the proposal." Mary said as she herded Tonya into the house. "You boys coming?"

"Tom." Trent shook his friend's hand and noted his serious demeanor. "You ladies go on in." Tonya looked back over her shoulder as she passed through the door. Her eyes held concern, so he sent her a reassuring smile.

"Sorry to disrupt your homecoming. You two finally got things worked out, huh?"

"Yeah." Trent couldn't stop the silly grin from spreading across his face. "Wedding plans are afoot."

Tom nodded, but he didn't offer congratulations. "I hate to do this, Trent. But I have to take you in for a few more questions."

"What?" Trent's chest heaved like it was hit with a wrecking ball. "Is this a joke?"

Tom looked down, not meeting Trent's eye. "I wish it were."

"You know I had nothing to do with Matthew's death."

"I know that, but we're still hoping to prove you were somewhere—anywhere but in the mountains that day."

"Has the FBI released Eugene Werner?"

"No, they still have him on charges for the car bomb in Chicago and for the murder of his partners and two police-men. Unfortunately, that all happened in Chicago, so if he is convicted, he'll spend the rest of his life on Illinois' dime. Illinois doesn't have the death penalty. It's why we want to get him convicted of murder here in Montana, where we do."

"I can't believe this." A cold hard lump settled in Trent's gut right underneath the hot fury that accompanied the injustice of the situation.

"Let me talk to Tonya and Gran." Trent turned to go in the house.

TONYA TURNED at the sound of the screen door. The light in Trent's eyes had gone out. Alarm sent spikes of apprehension across the back of her neck and down her arms. "What's wrong?"

Trent's mouth formed a smile but there was no warmth in it. "Nothing to worry about. Tom needs me to come in to the jail with him."

"Now? What for?" Tonya's gaze moved to question Tom.

"I'm sorry, Tonya. We have some more questions for Trent."

Both women stood. "What?" they asked in unison.

A shudder coursed from Tonya's head to her feet as Tom escorted Trent out to his Bronco. "Wait!" She ran after them. "Trent, what should I do?"

"It'll be okay, Ton. I didn't do anything wrong." Trent bent to kiss her one last time before he got into Tom's car. "Call Cade."

CADE PROMISED to come out to Stone Ranch right away and figure out what was going on. When Tonya tried Jack's phone, she was sent straight to the message service, so she called the FBI office in Salt Lake City. They told her they would get a message to Jack as soon as possible.

"Gran, what can I do?" Cade asked when he arrived.

"Will you go out and feed the horses in the barn while I start dinner? Then we'll sit together and think this through."

"Sure." Cade strode out the front door.

Fifteen minutes later Cade burst through the front door, followed by Randy who ran in behind him holding a blue heeler puppy.

"We're going to the jail. We'll be back as soon as we can!" Cade shouted.

Tonya stood. "Why, what's happening?" She reached for the puppy and took him out of Randy's arms. "And where did this little guy come from?"

Cade lifted his chin toward Randy who took up the story. "I brought a pup out for Trent to take to Miss Hilde. Cade came out to the barn and told me what happened with Trent and I think I have some good news." All eyes stared at Randy. "I was still here that Wednesday when Trent rode in. I saw him lead King back to his stall and then he went into the house. It must have been about four o'clock. Later, he came back out, eating a sandwich. Then he drove off without feeding, so I fed the horses before I left around five."

"Trent never saw you?" Tonya asked.

"I guess not. I waved when he left, but he didn't wave back. He must not have seen me."

Cade pushed Randy's shoulder, directing him to the door. "Tonya, call Tom right away. Tell him I'm on my way in with Randy—with evidence that Trent was at Stone Ranch on the Wednesday afternoon Matthew was killed. This will seal the tomb on Eugene Werner's case."

LATER, Tonya sat with the Stone family around Mary's farm table and enjoyed baked ham and scalloped potatoes. She sat back, contentment and relief engulfing her. This comfortable scene would soon be a daily experience. Before too long, there might be new little faces joining them at the table. Tears sprang to her eyes and Tonya reached for Trent's hand.

Trent leaned toward her and wiped an escaped tear with his thumb. His voice low and intimate, he said, "What's wrong, darlin'? Everything is going to be okay now."

"I know. I'm not sad. These are happy, hopeful tears. I was picturing our future children's little faces around this table."

Trent's laugh rumbled from deep inside his chest and was low and comforting. "I want to fill all the rooms, and if we need to, we can build on." He grinned. "I told Tonya I'd settle for eight."

Cade laughed outright and Joscelyn's jaw dropped open.

"I can babysit!" Sadie piped in.

Tonya's body flooded with warmth and she gave Trent a sidelong look. "I suppose we ought to start with one."

Trent kissed her softly. "I can't wait."

Mary beamed at them with moist eyes. "It brings joy to this old heart to see you two finally getting married. I knew all along you would, but you sure took your time to figure it out for yourselves." She stood and set her napkin on her plate. Her wrinkled face grew solemn. "How much time do I have to pack up before there's a wedding?"

Trent cocked his head. "Pack what up? I figured Tonya

and I would take Mom and Dad's room, but there are only a few boxes in there. I can move those tonight, if you want."

Mary shook her head and her voice was low. "No, I mean how long will I have to get my things packed up? I've looked into it, and Alice said she would rent me the apartment over her garage."

"Rent it to you for what?" Trent's brows drew together.

Cade glanced at Joscelyn and she nodded. He said, "Gran, we have lots of room out at Wolf Run. You are not renting a room from Alice."

Tonya's heart squeezed at what Mary was saying. "There is no way you are moving off of this ranch, Miss Mary. Not only is this your home, but there is plenty of room." Tonya reached for Mary's hand. "I have no idea how to run a ranch household. If you left, who would teach me? Plus, Trent wants a hundred kids. I'll be counting on you every day."

Trent stood and put his arms around his grandmother. "Gran, this place wouldn't be home if you weren't here. You're stayin' and that's final." He kissed her forehead.

Tears tracked the creases on Mary's old cheeks. "Bless you —all of you." She pecked Trent on the cheek and then busily pushed him away. "I have to admit that is the second-best news of the day." She stacked all the plates and winked at Tonya. "You sit and enjoy your coffee tonight. It won't be long before you'll be taking over this kitchen."

"No ma'am. I'll help you all you want, but I have too much learning to do to take over. If you left the kitchen to me, we'd all starve by Christmas."

Mary laughed, her rounded cheeks a cheery pink. "Joscelyn and I will clear, Sadie, you and your dad can wash, dry and put away. Trent, you go on and take Tonya back to her place. You've both had a long day and we all have an early morning with all the wedding planning." She stacked the plates. "Has anyone heard back from Jack? He needs to be caught up on all the news."

Blank expressions met across the table indicating no one had. "I'll try him again." Cade said.

That fast, Mary was back in charge of the farmhouse and her growing family.

45

"**A** man that flies from his fear may find that he has only taken a short cut to meet it." — J.R.R. Tolkien

I GAVE my public defender the call code and asked him to try calling Jed, but he never answered the line. He kept his word about the line being dead. He never responded again. After all I did for him. After all he meant to me and what I thought I meant to him. He discarded me like dirty trash.

It took about a week for me to accept that Jed had used me. From the beginning, when I met him at that cafe. All this time I thought he cared. I believed he thought of me as a son. But he never did. He took me and trained me up to do his dirty work. To take in his brand of hate and spread it around the country. And all it took for me to trust him was half a damn diner sandwich.

Guilt blended with anguish and mixed up a dangerous cocktail inside my heart. I killed five people for Jedediah Hotchkiss and he needed to be held accountable. I wasn't the traitor in the compound before, but I sure as hell would be now.

"Officer." I called out from my cell.

The guard on duty peered through the bars at me. "What do you want?"

"I need to talk to my lawyer."

"You can see him at your next scheduled appointment." The cop started to walk away.

"I want to talk to the FBI. Call my lawyer."

MY ATTORNEY TOLD me we had no case. We would go to trial, but all the evidence in the murder of Matthew Jefferson pointed to me. Well, I can't say that surprised me. I was going to prison for sure and was going to face the death penalty. I touched my neck, sensing the noose tightening, and I pictured Jed in the front row of my execution, smiling.

The one card I had left to play was my knowledge of the location of Jedediah's compound and the inner-workings of its clan. So I'd better play it smart.

Two special agents sat across from me at a metal table. They looked like bookends except one was black and the other was blond. I wouldn't get any sympathy from either of them.

"My client has information he would like to exchange information for a plea deal," my lawyer said. He passed them each a copy of my formal request.

The blond agent narrowed his eyes at me. "You have an exact location?"

I nodded.

"Can you provide specific directions to the camp?"

"Not only can I do that, I'll also tell you about the defensive security measures they have in place, how many men you'll face in an attack, and the type of fire-power they have. I'll draw a map of their escape routes. Whatever you need."

The agents stared at me for a long time. "Why would you give us all that?"

I thought about my answer. It was more than avoiding the death penalty. I wouldn't live long in prison, anyway. Jed had connections everywhere. The Aryan Brotherhood gang on the inside would make quick work of me.

"Jedediah Hotchkiss is the leader of the compound. He has ordered the death of many men and he was the master-mind of the school bombing and bank robbery plan. His problem is he thinks he's so much smarter than me. But, he was stupid to abandon me before I went to prison. Now I have nothing left to lose."

46

———

Trent and Tonya held their rehearsal dinner at the Silver Spurs Chop House. The restaurant filled up fast with friends and neighbors. A photographer they hired out of Missoula ran about taking pictures. His partner kept busy interviewing the guests on video.

Trent stood at the back of the room leaning against the polished wood of the bar. The four men who would stand up with him at his wedding tomorrow stood with him now. They each held a beer and observed the crowd. Trent took a sip and leaned toward Cade. "You think she invited the whole town to this wedding?" He raised his glass to Hilde who brought her new furry companion with her to the party. He couldn't tell who was walking whom.

Cade chuckled. "Knowing Tonya? Absolutely."

Cade, of course, was Trent's best man. Tom, Randy, and Dalton were the other three. Jack would have made five but he couldn't be there. He was still in Idaho hunting down the renegade militia.

Hilde tugged on Trent's sleeve so he would lean down. "I don't mind keeping this dog as a favor to your friend, Tren-

271

ton, but he needs a yard to play in." Her milky eyes sparkled with mischief.

Trent laughed. "Yes, ma'am. Randy and I will be over when I get back from my honeymoon to put up a fence."

"If you insist." The old woman kissed him on his cheek and patted his arm. "I'm glad you came to your senses, young man. You're in good hands with Tonya."

Trent lifted her weathered hand and kissed it. "I believe you're right, Miss Hilde."

Trent mulled over thoughts of his little brother. He was gratified they had reconciled, and he wished Jack could be here with him now, but capturing terrorists willing to kill children and old men had to come first. A wave of grief over Matthew's death washed through him. A sigh slid over the lump in his throat and Trent sent up a quick prayer that his kid brother was safe.

Tom handed Trent a new beer. "Just heard Werner agreed to plead guilty, and he's turned state's evidence. He's coughing up all sorts of details about the terrorist group. Werner will most likely go to the federal prison in Cañon City. They'll keep him isolated and thereby alive until after he testifies.

"I hope the information he gives helps Jack." Trent took a swallow of beer. "I'll be glad when the whole thing is over. I don't mind admitting, being questioned about a murder is scary as hell."

Mary tapped her champagne glass with her spoon and the guests quieted. "I have a gift I'd like to give Tonya." Mary made her way past round banquet tables filled with friends and neighbors, to the front of the room. She scanned the crowd. "Tonya, will you come up here?"

Tonya, wearing an ivory suit dress with shoulder pads and a peplum, moved to stand next to her future grandmother-in-law. Trent grinned at his glamourous bride when her eyes sought his across the room.

Mary held a long narrow jewelry box as she smiled at Tonya and addressed the dinner guests. "Trent and Tonya met twenty-three years ago, when they were both in kindergarten. They fell, almost immediately, into puppy-love and were inseparable throughout elementary school. In junior high, they started noticing their differences."

The guests laughed. Tom nudged Trent with his elbow and whispered, "Yeah, when the girls got curvy and emotional."

Trent grinned and nodded.

Mary continued, "They were awkward with each other for a few years until high-school when they became a serious item. Those of us who've lived in this town for all these years have seen my grandson and this sweet girl fall in and out of love so many times it became an expected course of events."

Laughter rose from the crowd and Mary waited until the room quieted. "But we all knew they'd eventually be here together one day, celebrating their wedding." The guests applauded and several men whistled. Mary opened the thin box she held and picked up a silver chain. A sterling-silver, heart-shaped locket dangled at the end. "This locket holds those precious memories."

Tonya touched her smiling lips before she reached for the silver heart. "It's beautiful, Mary."

"Open it." Mary draped the chain across Tonya's outstretched hand and folded the younger woman's fingers over the heart. Tonya smiled and unclasped the locket. Her eyes glittered.

She looked first at Mary and blinked away happy tears before she sent Trent a broad smile. "There are two pictures, one of Trent and one of me. If I'm not mistaken, they are from our kindergarten class photo." Tonya's laugh bubbled like the champagne and Trent's chest expanded with warmth and love.

Mary clasped the chain around Tonya's neck. "I knew, even back then. You two belonged together." Mary turned to their guests. "My husband gave me this locket when he courted me some fifty-odd years ago. I want Tonya to have in now. Both the necklace and the photos can be her *something old.*"

"Are you sure, Mary?" Joy radiated from Tonya and Trent wondered again, why it had taken him so long to propose to her.

"I've been planning on giving this to you for years."

Their friends and neighbors laughed and cheered as the women embraced.

Trent clinked his beer glass against Cade's before he collected his fiancée. He slipped his arm around her and pulled her close. Kissing her, he asked, "Want to dance?"

She looked up at him with bright eyes. "Every day for the rest of my life."

TRUCKS HAD BEEN DRIVING into town to deliver boxes to the salon, and twice as many things were delivered to the ranch. Trent woke the morning of his wedding to a semi-truck ambling onto the property followed by two catering vans. He let the curtain fall back over the window and went to take a shower. Cade was coming soon to pick him up. The groomsmen gathered to dress at Cade's place and the ladies took over the whole house at Stone Ranch.

Trent didn't know what to expect exactly, but was sure the event would be no-holds-barred. That was the way of his bride. He smiled to himself. Personally, he didn't care if they got married in a shack, but he wanted Tonya to have the day of her dreams.

Cade's old truck crunched the gravel in front of the house. Trent finished buttoning his shirt and tucked it into his jeans. He grabbed his tux and Dopp kit and hurried downstairs to meet his brother.

Cade walked through the front door. "Breakfast at Alice's on the way back to my place, if that works for you. Gran's too busy to feed you." Cade shook Trent's hand. "You ready for all this?" He grinned.

"Hell, I should've done this a long time ago."

"No argument here." Cade held the door open.

Trent loaded his things into Cade's truck and climbed in. "Any word from Jack?"

"Nope. I've left several messages, but I haven't heard back." They waved at Mary who was in the yard supervising the unloading of rented tables, chairs, and the event tent.

Tonya finished bathing and saturating her skin with silky moisturizers. She rolled her platinum hair in giant Velcro rollers and covered her head with a soft pink scarf. Joscelyn and Sadie would be there any minute to pick her up.

The bells rang downstairs on the front door of the salon. "Tonya?" Joscelyn called out. "We're here. Are you ready?"

"Be right down." She glanced one last time at her mirrored reflection and smiled.

Joscelyn held up a handful of envelopes and loose papers. "I brought in your mail. Looks like you got some cards."

"Thanks." Tonya reached for the stack and sorted it, tossing the junk mail in the bin. With a pink shellacked fingernail she opened three card envelopes and propped two of the congratulations cards up on the counter. The third one she lingered over, rolling her lips between her teeth and biting down as she read it.

"Who's that from?" Sadie asked.

Tonya glanced up. "It's from Levi. He sent congratulations to me and Trent, saying he saw this coming all along and that he is happy for us." She read further. "He even apologizes for not being honest with me." Her eyes moved over the note. "Levi explains he lied about the job in Sula because he was embarrassed to be compared to a guy who owned his own ranch, but that he had then found a job on a ranch in Darby. He was leaving Montana because he heard the Ravalli County Sheriff was in Darby asking around about him." Tonya ran her finger down the words. "He says he'll be in jail for a year, maybe less with good behavior and asks me to send him a wedding photo."

Slipping the card back into its envelope she pursed her lips and gave a small shrug. "I'm glad he wrote."

"Closure is a good thing." Joscelyn placed her hand on Tonya's shoulder. "Are you okay?"

Tonya nodded. "I'm sorry for him. I think underneath it all he's a good guy. Hopefully he'll use this time to figure out his life."

THE LADIES ARRIVED at Stone Ranch and almost didn't recognize the place. The rental company constructed a large white tent over tables covered in white linen that surrounded a wooden dance floor. A band was setting up their big-band style music stands. White swags of tulle, accented with delicate pink ribbons, draped everything. Pink roses hovered in water, suspended under floating candles in glass jar centerpieces.

The caterers organized their outdoor kitchen and serving tents. Sound experts wired speakers, microphones, and lights into huge generators. It was a crisp autumn day, and the weather was starting to turn. So just in case, they strategically placed large patio heaters around the tent. Tonya, Joscelyn, and Sadie picked their way across the cords to the front porch.

"Wow, Tonya. Everything looks amazing." Sadie gawked at the event set-up. "You did all this? It's like a fairytale."

Tonya slid an arm over Sadie's shoulder. "Honey, I've been planning this wedding since I was five.

Joscelyn laughed. "Come on. Let's eat."

Tonya's gown and all the bridal paraphernalia were already waiting for her at Stone Ranch when the ladies arrived for brunch. Mary put out quiche, asparagus spears, fresh fruit and scones. Everything was beautiful, but Tonya's stomach churned with anticipation and she could hardly eat anything. After the meal, they helped each other with their hair and makeup before they dressed Tonya in her gown.

Tonya's gown was floor length white satin with an off-the-shoulder neckline and sash waistline. The full A-line skirt had flat pleats in the front and opened to a long train in the back. An abundant tulle petticoat held the skirt into place and gave her the appearance of floating when she walked. The gown was simple, yet elegant—something Jackie Kennedy might have worn. Brandy pinned a birdcage veil to a cluster of white roses nestled at the crown of Tonya's head, between her rolled up-do, and it floated over her face, stopping at her jawline. She fashioned herself after the mid-century movie star, Lana Turner, and hit the mark dead on.

Brandy was Tonya's maid of honor. Joscelyn, Sadie, and Anita were bridesmaids, and all wore vintage, soft-pink satin, tea-length dresses swaying over matching tulle petticoats. Each woman wore pink, pillbox hats perched on their heads. Tonya carried pink roses and her ladies all carried white. In the limo, on their way to the church, the ladies sipped champagne infused with wild hibiscus flowers. Sadie even had a sip or two.

"I can hardly believe this is happening. I feel like Cinderella." Tonya beamed.

Her sister clasped her hand. "If you're going for Disney Princess status, you're more like Belle. It took a ton of love and patience to tame Trent into a man you could marry."

"He's always been a man I could marry. He just needed to realize it." A soft smile touched Tonya's lips and she gazed at her engagement ring. "Besides, I'm the one who needed to change. In the end, it boils down to trusting each other." Tonya's sister squeezed her hand and nodded.

A LONE CELLO played the Bach Cello Wedding Suite and Trent's pulse vibrated with the strings. He walked from the back of the church to his position in front of the altar next to Cade. Cade's reassuring hand rested on his shoulder. Sadie came down the aisle first. When had she become such a beauty? Joscelyn and Brandy marched next, swathed in their 1950s period dresses and walking in time to the music. Trent's legs flexed with impatience. The congregation stood, blocking his view so Trent stepped toward the aisle so he could watch Tonya walk toward him.

And then, she was there. Tonya. A vision in flowing white with pink roses that matched the strand swept up in her elegant hairstyle. His chest threatened to burst. She floated toward him on Bob Tillman's arm. Trent's eyes locked on Tonya's and neither looked away until he took her hand from Bob and slipped it into the crook of his elbow. They turned together to face the pastor.

They spoke their vows and exchanged rings. All along Trent was in a fog. Amazed this day was here. That he and

Tonya would be together forever. He hoped she'd be happy. Hoped he could make her happy.

"You may now kiss the bride." The Pastor's voice broke through his musing and Trent grinned large. He bent to give his new wife the first kiss of their married life and he made it one she would remember all of their days.

Applause escorted them from the church and birdseed rained down on them as they ran from the door and slipped into the limo waiting to take them to their reception. Their dinner, expertly plated and served, was delicious, though Trent would be hard pressed to remember what he ate.

Pink and white fondant roses covered the cake they cut into and served to each other. A golden sun hovered on the indigo horizon as Cade gave his best-man speech. Trent raised his glass, his heart warm and content.. The day could not have been more magical.

A whispering image of Jack crossed his mind. His brother hadn't called to congratulate him, but Trent refused to think the wedding had slipped Jack's mind. He shook his head and took a large sip of champagne.

This day held the first view, the first kiss, and the first dance. At the end of the evening, Trent spirited Tonya up the stairs.. He took her to the room his parents had shared and opened the door to a room draped in white chiffon. Candles burned on every surface, glowing through the sheer fabric. Pink rose petals covered their white chenille bedspread and romantic music from the 40's lilted in the background. This night would also be a first. The first time as man and wife. The first of forever.

EPILOGUE

Trent pulled Tonya into his arms and kissed her closed eyelids. He ran his lips across her cheekbone and found her mouth. A knock sounded on the door. *Are you kidding me?* Trent deepened his kiss.

Tonya's soft laugh brushed against his mouth. "Aren't you going to answer the door?"

His eyes glittered and darkened. "No." He intended to nibble the velvet skin behind her ear that hid her columbine tattoo.

The knock sounded again, louder and stronger. Tonya stepped back. "We have to answer it."

Trent closed his eyes and groaned. He crossed the room and yanked the door open. Cade stood on the other side. "What?"

"Sorry to… well…" Cade made an apologetic grimace toward Tonya.

"What is it Cade? We're a little busy. It's our wedding night, you know."

"I know, but I didn't think you'd want me to wait." Cade's eyes bore into his.

An internal alarm sounded in Trent's head.

"The FBI headquarters in Salt Lake just called. Jack is missing."

*   *   *

Thank you so much for reading Hidden In The Hills. I hope you enjoyed spending time with Trent and Tonya. The next book in the Flint River Series — Danger In The Hills — continues with Jack Stone's story and more thrilling mysteries and adventures.

Order Danger In The Hills now!

If you enjoyed Hidden In The Hills, I would be honored if you would please write a quick review.

Review Hidden In The Hills

Thank you!
*   *   *

Danger In The Hills
Book 3 in the Flint River Series

WHILE SEARCHING the woods of northern Idaho for neo-Nazi fugitives responsible for a bombing in Chicago, along with a mysterious, unidentified woman, Special Agent Jack Stone gets separated from his unit.

A brutal blizzard hits the mountains, and Jack is caught in the storm—wounded and unprepared. Just as Jack loses consciousness he glimpses her—the enigmatic woman. But is she friend or foe?

If you like edgy suspense, and good vs evil with a dash of romance, you'll love

DANGER IN THE HILLS

Buy Now

Note from the Author:
To thank you for reading The Flint River Series, please enjoy
a free Exclusive Sereis Epilogue:

A Flint River Christmas
FREE Exclusive Epilogue - Novella
And

THE FLINT RIVER COOKBOOK
(FOODS FROM THE SERIES)

Click to get your FREE copy!

Become a member of
Jodi's Reader Group

And receive free maps of Flint River and the Flint River
Valley, updates on new releases, freebies, and other fun free
goodies!

Visit my website at Jodi-Burnett.com

SNEAK PEEK OF HIDDEN IN THE HILLS

Deep in the woods of northern Idaho, Special Agent Jack Stone peered through his Steiner M830r binoculars at the neo-Nazi compound situated two hundred and fifty feet below. Winter glided in on a sleigh of frigid, pine-scented wind. Ice and snow already capped the high peaks. The rocky, cold ground pressed its sharp edges into his skin as he surveilled his quarry. His legs ached, and he flexed his feet to relieve the pin-pricking sensation caused by lack of circulation. Jack adjusted his position and squinted against the early morning sun for a better focus on the rogue militia's hidden camp. He observed the encampment at the base of the mountain in silence as the residents began to stir and start their daily routines.

Three days ago, the FBI hostage negotiators contacted the guards at the front gates of the barricaded compound. Their request that the women and children who lived there be sent out went unheeded. Two days ago, in conjunction with ATF and Homeland Security, the FBI shut down all electrical power to the camp. However, because the group of radicals was prepared to live completely off the grid, they simply flipped on their generators and went about their business as usual. Today, two FBI SWAT teams were poised to force the compound leaders into compliance.

The Special Agent in Command briefed all the men at the basecamp located ten miles down the canyon before the two teams took up their mountainside positions. "Everyone remain calm and stay alert. Our goal is to slow things down —to negotiate. Ideally, without any weapons fired. Let's get them talking about their motivations." The SAC tapped his fingers on a map covering the table. His command voice drilled on. "Remember, we're here because this group has taken terrorist action against American citizens. We are *not* here because their ideology differs from ours. There are women and innocent children inside. Do not fire unless your life is in imminent danger. That being said, be safe and consider *everyone* inside a possible threat."

At least they'd been briefed ahead of time about the families. Jack's gut bunched when he thought of breaching a site with kids inside. He scratched at his dark morning stubble. It sickened him, what some adults did to their children. Maybe they'd free them in time for their brainwashing to be reversed.

Agent Stone raised his binoculars again when he noticed a young woman cross the courtyard. Their informant hadn't mentioned any younger women. The females in the encampment were all supposedly 35 years or older, and all of them mothers of young or teenaged kids. This woman looked to be in her early to mid-twenties and moved with an easy grace. His gaze followed her across the grounds to a lean-to shack. She disappeared inside.

Jack's partner, Rick Sanchez, sat leaned back against a rock outcropping twenty-feet behind him and to his left. Jack glanced back at his friend. "Hey, did you see that woman?"

"Yeah, baby. Didn't know these backwoods Nazi girls were so good-looking." Rick smirked.

Jack shook his head and grinned. "Right? I don't remember any briefing on a young woman her age, though."

"For sure. We should have been given a deck of identification cards, like in Afghanistan."

"Shut up, I'm serious. Who do you suppose she is?"

"Hell, I don't know. Guess we'll find out."

Jack nodded and scanned the compound one more time. There was no one he trusted more to watch his six than Rick Sanchez, and he was glad to have him there. They'd become close friends after they met at the FBI Academy. The two competed fiercely to be top-dog in both academics and physical challenges. Their interbranch rivalry gave them even more common ground as they argued about who was better, Rick's Marine Corps or Jack's Army. They started out as rivals and ended up as friends who trusted and respected each other immensely.

The raid commander had ordered the FBI teams to sit tight and observe only, until further notice. Jack waited for the breach order to come down the pike. He expected to hear something around midnight. His team practiced raids like this continually, so with precision timing, surprise, and some luck, they'd be able to capture the men and isolate their families—hopefully without injury. Their foremost objective was to capture Jedediah Hotchkiss, the compound leader, and Roger MacNeil, his second-in-command. Then they would search the compound for irrefutable evidence that linked this terrorist group to the thwarted bombing of an elementary school in Chicago two months ago. Jack shuddered knowing a mere fluke of intelligence had tipped them off and prevented the explosion and subsequent death of hundreds of innocents.

Static from wind blowing across someone's mic sounded

in his earpiece before the voice of Team Two's leader spoke. "The numbers Werner gave us seem to be fairly accurate. We do not have a confirmed number of children, but family and militant numbers are close to what we expected."

"Roger that," Jack agreed. "As soon as I receive orders, we'll move in on my signal." Several voices acknowledged his command. Jack held up his binoculars and continued to observe. "Remember, there are families down there. The last thing we want is another Waco or Ruby Ridge. As of now, we are EMCON until oh-one-hundred hours."

The encampment occupants went about their daily business. The early winter chill mostly kept everyone indoors, except for a group of kids that ran about playing hide-and-seek after lunchtime. Otherwise, the camp sat quiet. Smoke drifted up from chimneys. It seemed as if no one knew they were surrounded by FBI SWAT teams.

Dusk descended, and with it came lower temperatures and hunger. No matter the circumstances, blazing heat or bitter cold, the body always demanded fuel. Field stakeouts didn't come with music, fast food, and a cup of coffee though, and he hankered for the caffeine. What little activity they witnessed in the camp settled down with the evening, and the inviting scent of dinners baking in ovens drifted up the hill.

Rick tossed a rock at Jack to get his attention. "That food smells so damn good. Are you sure we have to wait to raid?"

Jack chuckled. "You think that smells good? You should smell my gran's lasagna. Man, when we were kids, nothing brought us in from playing as fast as the smell of Italian sausage, tomatoes, and melted cheese. And her garlic bread— oh God." His stomach rolled in on itself and grumbled. He reached into his tactical pack and pulled out an MRE—a Meal-Ready-to-Eat—and a bottle of water. Tonight's selection—reconstituted beef stew.

The aroma wafting up the mountain turned his thoughts to home and to his brothers, Cade and Trent. He had recently reunited with them and his grandma, Mary, after not seeing any of them in almost ten years. He and Trent had fought over the future of the family ranch, and Jack left for West Point without ever making things right between them. They still had some unresolved issues, but he would deal with all of that when this case ended.

Jack had been hoping to make it back home to Flint River in time to stand up with Trent at his wedding. It wasn't likely, though, this situation was dragging out much longer than they expected, and Trent planned to marry his childhood sweetheart in two days. He couldn't contact his family in the middle of a mission and he sure as hell didn't want Trent to take him not showing up to the wedding as another insult. There was already too much pain and misunderstanding to wade through.

Jack glanced at his watch. They had another six hours to sit and wait. He flexed each muscle group in turn, working to stay at the ready. By nightfall, the only movement down below came from two perimeter patrol guards and the lookouts posted on top of four guard towers built at each corner of the fortress.

Jack's radio crackled and the SAC's rough voice came across the line. "Agent Stone, give the order for the raid at oh-one-hundred-hours. Do you copy?"

"Copy that, sir. Out."

At precisely 1:00 a.m., Jack broke radio silence, and in a harsh whisper, ordered his team to advance on the stronghold. He stretched his stiffened muscles and moved in silence down the mountainside toward the compound fence.

The militia had built the barrier wall surrounding the complex out of logs—lashed together and sharpened at their tips, similar to an old western cavalry post. They planned to maneuver close enough to verbally order the guards to drop their weapons. If they did not comply, agents would take them out. Jack's heart pounded with exhilaration. He'd waited over two months for this confrontation and it was finally here, within his grasp. These sick bastards needed to be in prison where they weren't a threat to good people—to children. He ran, crouched low, his vest heavy with grenades and ammunition. The weight of his Colt M4 carbine drawing him forward. All his senses sparked on high alert.

His men approached the perimeter unseen. With hand signals, they communicated the movements of their choreographed attack. Agents called out to the two perimeter guards, but instead of surrendering their weapons, the guards fired at the operatives. *Damn it!* Jack hoped taking this compound would happen without casualties, but that was not going to be the case. The tower guards positioned on the corner platforms joined the action and were consequently sighted in. Six spits tore through the air and six guards fell. Agents launched smoke grenades into the compound to provide cover and prepared to breach the main gate.

The explosives team wired the barricaded entrance, then moved back to take up their offensive positions. To screen their attack, Jack's men popped more smoke grenades over the entrance and simultaneously blew the front security gate off its hinges with C-4 explosives.

"Breach. Breach now!" Jack shouted across the radio to his unit, his blood racing hot. Agents rushed into the fortification, alternating right and left, covering each other as they took up their new positions. A man stationed at the community building door fired at the officers and they blew him off the porch. Following the initial shots, the night exploded into live fire. Shots flew out of every structure on the grounds.

"Flank the main building and secure it. Then light it up."

"What about the kids, sir?" An anonymous voice whispered into his earpiece.

"Use concussion grenades." Jack didn't know where the kids were and it made him uneasy. He presumed they were in their own houses and hoped their parents had them safely tucked away. "As soon as the grenades go off, enter and take the bunker. Secure and search everyone, even kids. I don't want to lose any of our guys tonight. Take nothing for granted."

Jack took cover behind a wooden fence that marked a garden and peered around it, rifle ready. Shots erupted into the night. Air, sharpened by bullets that barely missed him, stung his face. Jack squatted low to the ground and signaled to his partner crouched across from him, asking for cover. Rick nodded once, his dark eyes brimming with adrenaline. Jack sprinted to a position behind a large shipping container that served as a house standing thirty-yards away. Bullets zipped through the air, but his cover held and Jack made it to the new spot unharmed. Jack then laid down a cover of bullets in return for Rick, giving back what he had received seconds ago. The metallic tang of gunpowder burned the back of his throat.

Both men crept around behind the house, making their way toward the large structure. The common area in the center of the compound contained the heat of the battle. The neo-Nazi militants waged their greatest defense from the centralized building, presumably where the leaders, Hotchkiss and MacNeil, were holed up.

As they neared the alleyway that led them to the headquarters, Jack heard growling. The savage snarling and barking of a pack of fierce dogs locked in kennels escalated into a frenzy. Jack was surprised the animals were contained. These people clearly weren't expecting a raid, and he was thankful the dogs were caged in so they wouldn't have to shoot them.

Moonlight flashed off the dogs' glistening fangs and powerful jaws. Jack resisted flinching at the angry and frustrated canines charging their chain-link barrier. He motioned for Rick to cover him and he ran toward the side of the big lodge.

The partners proceeded in their alternating pattern until they were both close enough to the firestorm to launch smoke and concussion grenades inside the main hall. Agents with filtered respirators poured inside after the detonations that temporarily halted the resistance, allowing the operatives to apprehend the shooters.

Militiamen fired from their steel-sided homes, pinning Jack, Rick, and a small group of men to the side of the building. Other agents used the distraction to swing around and approach their targets from behind. They launched concussion grenades into the housing containers and teams followed, taking control of each residence. The FBI subdued militia members, binding their wrists together with zip-ties. After a quick sweep, they confiscated all weapons and marched the captives out to the common area in the village center.

"Where are the children?" Jack shouted to a group of agents who shook their heads and shrugged, unknowing.

"Maybe we got bad intel," an agent suggested.

Jack shook his head. He knew there were kids in the camp. He'd seen them playing. Jack approached one of the bound women standing under guard. "Where are they?"

She stared at him defiantly, but said nothing.

Jack turned to two other operatives. "Find the kids," he yelled.

"There's no one left in the bunker." An agent clad in all black called out.

Jack bounded up the steps to the central building and paced the porch. He stopped and called out. "Check to see if the houses have underground bunkers."

Men dispersed to the steel storage containers converted into homes in search of any secret openings or hidden spaces below. Before long a voice called out, "Found some!" The agent ushered three kids of varying ages outside. "They were hiding down below. We think a series of tunnels connect the bunkers together." The agent handed off the children and turned back inside to help his team.

The smallest child in the trio, maybe five, cried out and ran across the open area to her mother. Her siblings followed, looking sheepish. As teams discovered more kids hidden below, they filtered out from the converted storage containers.

After agents frisked everyone, including the children, and confiscated anything that could be used as a weapon, the kids were allowed to go to their mothers. They escorted families out into the compound yard where bright lights illuminated the clearing. They dragged and shoved the shooters into the open space as well, then took an official count. Ten women and seventeen minors were taken into custody. There were twenty-two militiamen alive and six casualties, but the two leaders the FBI informant told them about were unaccounted for. Jack also noted there was no sign of the young dark-haired woman he observed early yesterday morning. That meant at least three people were missing.

"Where are Jedediah Hotchkiss and Roger MacNeil?" He paced in front of the subdued militiamen who'd been forced to kneel on the ground with their hands on their heads.

Eyes flashed at him or stared down at the dirt, but no one answered.

Jack's neck and shoulders bunched with frustration. He shouted to a contingent of his men, "Run another search through every structure and hiding space. Find them." A small unit separated from the group to locate the missing pair of neo-Nazi terrorist leaders.

An agent approached him. "Sir, we found a building that's been recently used as a stable. No horses or mules in there now, but it looks like there has been within the last couple of days."

"Do you keep horses at this facility?" Jack asked the captives. They continued to watch him without speaking.

Half an hour later, the search team reported back. "We didn't find anyone else, sir. The two leaders are gone. But, we did find a tunnel that leads out from the main building. It goes under the gate and lets out about a half-mile up into the hills."

"Shit! Find them! Apprehending those men is the primary focus of this entire mission." Jack ground his teeth and chewed his lower lip. "I saw a young woman with long dark hair inside the camp yesterday. She's also missing."

A female agent approached Jack with a girl who looked about twelve. "Sir, this is Joy. She told me she helped a woman named Laurel care for a horse, but she doesn't know where either of them are now."

Jack squatted down. "What color is the horse?"

The girl offered a shy smile, her teeth a stark white in her dirt-smudged face. "Wisaka? She's a paint."

He smiled at Joy. "You didn't see Laurel go anywhere with Wisaka?"

Joy's eyes were big and round in her young face. She shook her head.

"When did you last see Wisaka?"

"Couple a days ago."

Jack nodded and patted the girl's shoulder wanting her to feel safe. "Thanks, Joy. Will you let us know if you remember anything else about them?" *How the hell did they sneak a horse out of the compound?*

He stood and turned back to his men. "We are looking for two men in their fifties or sixties who may be with a young dark-haired woman in her twenties. It's possible they have a horse. The sooner we start tracking them the better. There's no time to waste."

ACKNOWLEDGMENTS

First, I thank God for blessing me with work I love, and for the inspiration with which to do it.

I am enormously appreciative for my team. A huge thanks to Chris Burnett, Emily Mueller, Sarah Burnett, Jenn Venereable, Alex Martella, and Barb Lynette, who helped me shape my rough manuscript, and to Emily Bybee, my critique partner who watched over every word. When I think of you I "grin".

I'd like to give a special thanks to Grant Linhart for advising me on police procedure, offering insight on firearms, and on how a small-town sheriff might work with the FBI.

Thank you to all the writers in my critique group. You continue to inspire and teach me much about writing, dedication, and perseverance. I'm grateful for your wisdom, support, and friendship. Another big thanks to my editor, Cate Byer, for her expertise and guidance. Cate, you found all the things, and I'm so glad I found you.

I could not do without the support and encouragement of my family. Writing can be such a solo venture. Thanks for pulling me out of my cave and loving me through the rough spots. I cherish the inside jokes, baseball, horseracing, and they way you all love each other. My cup overflows.

Most of all, I want thank my husband Chris, who patiently listens to my crazy story ideas, my struggles, and fears. He reads all my words and offers honest and practical feedback. When I feel like giving up, he's the one to lift my chin and encourage me to keep going. He loans me his strength when I have no more of my own. I love you, Chris, with all my heart.

ALSO BY JODI BURNETT

Flint River Series

Run For The Hills

Hidden In The Hills

Danger In The Hills

A Flint River Christmas (Free Epilogue)

A Flint River Cookbook (Free Book)

FBI-K9 Thriller Series

Baxter K9 Hero (Free Prequel)

Avenging Adam

Body Count

Concealed Cargo

Mile High Mayhem

Tin Star K9 Series

RENEGADE

MAVERICK

MARSHAL

www.ingramcontent.com/pod-product-compliance
Lightning Source LLC
Chambersburg PA
CBHW061604190726
48288CB00007B/2170